# Facing the Beast Within

## The ANXIETY of CAMERON POOLE

### Book 1 in the Order of the Stones series

## Mark Cheverton

~ ~ Winner: Mom's Choice Gold Award
~ ~ Winner: 2023 International Book Award for Children's Fiction
~ ~ Winner: 2023 NYC Big Book Award for Middle-Grade Fiction
~ ~ Runner-up: 2023 PenCraft Award for Children's Fiction

D1599242

# PRAISE FOR MARK CHEVERTON'S

## *FACING THE BEAST WITHIN*

"Cheverton's middle-grade fantasy series starter shares a timely tale of childhood anxiety about a young camper assisting in a battle to save Earth ... A compelling fantasy adventure with intriguing self-help elements."

— *Kirkus Reviews*

"Kids in my practice have flocked to Mark Cheverton's books for years! This book really helps kids struggling with anxiety to feel understood and empowered."

— Dr. Jennifer Smitkin, Psychologist and Clinical Director Psychology Wellness Practice

"This is an awesome book!! Cameron is down to earth and relatable—a kid with lots of worries, just like me. Facing the Beast Within is a great read for anyone dealing with anxiety and the people who love them too."

— Ania, age 12, *Kids' Book Buzz*

"An excellent book that seamlessly weaves together an exciting adventure story with valuable lessons about coping with anxiety. The book's plot is action-packed, and the mythical monsters are sure to capture kids' imaginations. Cheverton's writing is skillful, and the story's underlying message of resilience and perseverance is inspiring and empowering. A must-read for anyone looking for an entertaining and educational book for kids."

— Abigail L, librarian, 5-star *Netgalley* review

"Facing the Beast Within is a fantastic, emotive, and multi-layered adventure that will satisfy young readers everywhere. I can't wait to see more from this enthralling and socially conscious series."

— K.C. Finn, *Readers' Favorite* Review

"This book takes research-based strategies for youths with anxiety and teaches the reader how to use them, all in a storytelling format that is equally entertaining as it is informing."

— Dr. Zachary Longo, Clinical Supervisor,
Psychological Wellness Practice

"Mark Cheverton paints a landscape of magic, distress, friendship, and strife in *Facing the Beast Within*. As the first of a new series, it's an exciting burst onto a new scene; it kept me on the edge of my seat with uncertainty, and it begs for more installations—soon."
— Audrey Davis, *Independent Book Reviews*

"Middle graders and libraries catering to them who choose *Facing the Beast Within* for its magical realism and fantasy adventure premise will thus find plenty of fodder for group and book club discussion about the roots of anxiety and how it can be addressed, making *Facing the Beast Within* a top recommendation both for its entertainment value and for its educational prowess."
— Diane Donovan, *Midwest Book Reviews*

Flipbook by Ana Mitrovic
Cover by Leah Palmer Preiss
You can see more of Leah's fabulous artwork on her website, here:
http://wordpress.leahpalmerpreiss.com

This is a work of fiction. Names, characters, places, and incidents are either the products of the author's imagination or used in a fictitious manner. Any resemblance to actual persons, living or dead, is purely coincidental.

This book is not intended as a substitute for the advice of mental health professionals. If you struggle with anxiety or other mental health issues, contact a mental health professional for diagnosis and aid.

Don't wait - get help!

# Other Books by Mark

## <u>Order of the Stones series</u>
Facing the Beast Within
Cameron and the Shadow-wraiths (2024)
Cameron and the Gargoyles' Revenge (2025)

## <u>Giants of StoneHold series</u>
Theft of the Giant's Soul
The Giant's Giant
The Giant's Sacrifice (2024)
The Giant's Nightmare (2026)

## Minecraft-inspired Novels

<u>Gameknight999 Series</u>
Invasion of the Overworld
Battle for the Nether
Confronting the Dragon

<u>Birth of Herobrine Series</u>
The Great Zombie Invasion
Attack of the Shadow-crafters
Herobrine's War

<u>Mystery of Herobrine Series</u>
Trouble in Zombie-Town
The Jungle Temple Oracle
Last Stand on the Ocean Shore

<u>Mystery of Entity303 Series</u>
Terrors of the Forest
Monsters in the Mist
Mission to the Moon

<u>Herobrine Reborn Series</u>
Saving Crafter
Destruction of the Overworld
Gameknight999 vs. Herobrine

<u>Rise of the Warlords Series</u>
Zombies Attack!
Bones of Doom
Into the Spiders' Lair

<u>Herobrine's Revenge Series</u>
The Phantom Virus
Overworld in Flames
System Overload

<u>The Wither War Series</u>
The Wither King
The Withers Awaken
The Wither Invasion

For information about all my novels, go here:
https://markcheverton.com/books/

5

# Author's Note

This book was at least 10 years in the making, for it emerged from the struggles my son was forced to endure with anxiety. I decided I wanted to write an exciting action/adventure story that would be fun for kids to read but would also put them (or their parents depending on who's doing the reading) in the head of a child with anxiety. You'll feel what it was like for my son when his anxiety was making it impossible for him to function or go to school. In addition, I worked with multiple psychologists, learning the kinds of coping strategies they teach their patients. Many of these techniques, coupled with what we used with our son, are included in the story. I hope kids with anxiety will see a slice of hope here, maybe a kindred soul in the main character, Cameron. Maybe kids without anxiety will gain an appreciation of what it's like for those who suffer from it and will hopefully offer them some support and understanding.

I am certainly not a psychologist, and you shouldn't use this book to treat your own child, rather, if you or your child are struggling with anxiety, go to a mental health professional, not an author. That being said, I hope you enjoy going on this adventure with Cameron Poole and his friends and gain some insight into what it's like to struggle with anxiety.

Buckle up and get ready for a fun and exciting ride.

# Free Books???

Want some free books? Well . . . okay!!!

I have two FREE Minecraft stories for you, each an exciting action/adventure story set in the digital realms of Minecraft. Buckle up and get ready for some thrilling adventures.

All you need to do is go to my website, www.MarkCheverton.com, and click on I WANT SOME BOOKS. You'll go to a page where you can sign up for my e-Newsletter (with your parent's permission, of course). You can unsubscribe at any time, and you will not be spammed with meaningless dribble. I use the newsletter to tell people about upcoming books, share exclusive graphics, give kids the opportunity to name things in upcoming books, and tell you about contests.

Thousands of people have downloaded these two books, but I'm getting ready to pull them off the Internet and replace them with something different. Sign up and download them, fast, before they disappear.

# Flipbook?

What's a flipbook you ask?

I remember when I was a kid, I would get these tiny books as a prize in a box of cereal, or at a carnival, or in a box of Cracker Jacks (parents, remember those?) . . . and as you flipped through the pages, the character drawn on the page would appear to be animated and move.

I loved those things.

So, I decided it would be fun to put a flipbook in *Facing the Beast Within.* The flipbook in this novel is entitled *The Gargoyle;* you can see the first frame of the animation in the bottom right corner, after a few pages. Flip through the pages and watch the tiny movie, drawn by the fabulous artist, Ana Mitrovic.

I hope you enjoy the flipbook; there will be one in the paperback version of every book in the Order of the Stones series.

Mark Cheverton

# Acknowledgments

As with all my many books, I must thank my wonderful wife and son for their help with this story. It would have never happened without the long, detailed conversations with my son, as well as my wife helping me make this a fun and informative adventure.

I want to also thank Lily Wang, whose constant support and sense of humor never fails to brighten my day.

I'd like to thank my friend, Dr. Jennifer Smitkin, whom I've known for a long time. Her advice about anxiety and the coping strategies she uses with her patients were critical to the book. *Facing the Beast Within* would be a hollow story without her insights and knowledge.

I'd also like to thank the psychologists at Dr. Jen's *Psychology Wellness Practice*. These psychologists were kind enough to read *Facing the Beast Within* and provided input/suggestions as to the anxiety coping strategies I could incorporate into the story. Their knowledge of anxiety and how to help those afflicted with this terrible condition was extremely helpful. I deeply appreciated their help and advice. Here they are:

Psychology Wellness Practice
Dr. Jennifer Smitkin, Clinical Director (Dr. Jen)
Dr. Zachary Longo, Clinical Supervisor
Andrea Kay, Licensed Mental Health Counselor
Griffith Jenkins, Licensed Mental Health Counselor
Shannon Flanigan, Licensed Master Social Worker
Jasmine Sale, Licensed Master Social Worker
Kim Corker, Licensed Master Social Worker
Catherine Gazdik, Graduate Intern
Olivia Burns, Undergraduate Intern
Hailey Novellino, Undergraduate Intern

If you're a parent with a child who struggles with anxiety, here are a few resources Dr. Jen thought might be helpful.

- https://childmind.org/topics/anxiety/
- https://publications.aap.org/aapnews/news/12595
- https://www.aacap.org/aacap/Families_and_Youth/Resource_Cent ers/Anxiety_Disorder_Resource_Center/Home.aspx

# Just a Thought

We all have a Beast – it could be our fear of failure, or fear of people seeing our faults, or maybe you don't know what you fear; you're just afraid. That's okay. Just know that everyone is afraid now and then . . . me too. You're not alone.

*For my wife and son*

# One day before the Super Blood Moon

## Chapter 1 – Camp Pontchartrain

**F**ear nibbled with sharp teeth on the edges of my soul as I scanned Camp Pontchartrain's dining hall, looking for the bully who would surely notice me. Fortunately for me, the bullies targeted the art students, a group of girls silently weeping with their heads lowered. Thankfully, they were leaving the Techies, technology kids like me, alone . . . for now.

I ran my fingers through my brown, curly hair, a self-soothing thing I did when I was nervous, which was a constant state of existence for me. Choosing a corner table, I set my tray down, then checked the seat for the all-too-familiar packets of ketchup or mustard left there to stain the pants of the unwary. Nothing was there this time. I sat and peeled open my grilled ham and cheese, then loaded it with barbeque potato chips, and pressed them into the melted cheese. After a sip of apple juice, I took a bite of the sandwich, the barbeque chips delivering a satisfying crunch as I chewed while scanning the room again.

The walls, adorned in rich, dark wood paneling, and the sturdy hardwood floor stretching from wall to wall gave me the illusion of being nestled within the belly of some gigantic tree monster. A group of bullies laughed and threw French fries at the drama kids, the humiliated victims picking potatoes out of their hair as they kept their heads down, hoping to be spared a second volley. The sea of kids, ages 8 to 18, looked like a patchwork of colors. Each cluster wore their group's t-shirt, the orange and brown lacrosse team sitting between the yellow and black wrestlers and the black and white chess players. A few kids didn't wear their team's jersey and instead wore the dark purple Camp Pontchartrain shirt, a large C and P emblazoned in gold across their chest. They were few in number and quickly learned that the purple shirt made them an easy target. Usually, everyone wore their group's shirt . . . it's what we did at Camp Pontchartrain. Sometimes, I thought it provided a little bit of safety, a herd in which the small and weak could hide, but I think it also kept us separated. Isolated groups and

*The Gargoyle*

cliques had flourished in the camp since my first visit many years ago, dividing the community and creating a fragmented social landscape.

"You know, Cameron, it's only four days until the annual Colossal Water Fight." Bobby sat down next to me and stuffed a massive spoonful of mashed potatoes into his mouth, brown gravy smudging his cheek. "This year, I'm going for a power soaker. I wanna drench people from far away, like the kids from the soccer cabin, before they can get close with their water balloons."

I ate the last bit of my sandwich and shook my head. "You shouldn't do that, Bobby. They'll want revenge if you get them too wet."

"I don't care if I get wet; why should they? It's a water fight, after all."

"I know." I opened a package of cookies, took a few, and then slid them to my friend. "But you need to think carefully." I lowered my voice and scanned the nearby tables, ensuring no bullies could hear. "If you get them during the water fight, they'll torture you afterward. They might throw you into the lake, steal your bed, or try to lock you in one of the gym lockers."

Bobby chuckled, then put both hands on his ample belly and shook it. "Cameron Poole, how long have we been coming to this summer camp together . . . since third grade? After three years, have you ever seen a gym locker that would fit me?" He slapped his stomach and laughed. "They don't make 'em big enough for this."

Wiping his mouth with the sleeve of his Robotics t-shirt, Bobby stood and carried his dishes to the kitchen conveyor belt. "Come on, Cam, we gotta get moving. The ropes course starts in a few minutes, and I don't wanna be at the end of the line."

I gathered up my trash and piled it on the plastic tray, then slung my bookbag over my shoulder, my towel and robotics supplies bouncing about within the bag. Walking next to the wall, I followed Bobby toward the conveyor. I kept my eyes scanning the dining hall for threats. Being the smallest sixth-grader at the camp seemed to make me a favorite target of the bullies.

I placed my tray on the mechanized track pulling the dirty dishes into the kitchen, then turned to the exit and froze. A group of baseball players stood near the doors, each wearing their gray and gold jerseys and harassing kids as they left. A sound, like the faint buzzing of a bee, flickered to life in the back of my mind. Sweat coated the palms of my hands as I stared at the door, my heartbeat pounding in my ears.

14

*No, not again. I don't wanna be afraid.* The thought sent a shuddering wave of fear through me. My pulse raced as goosebumps crawled down the back of my neck. *The anxiety's coming; I know it.* My anxiety amplified the fearful feeling, which produced more anxiety and intensified the fear again. My therapist, Dr. Jen, called it a "thought-loop," but I didn't care what name she had for it. This happened so often to me, it felt like a recurring nightmare.

*The Beast . . . it's coming.* The words reverberated in my head.

I stared at the writing over the door, large, gold letters written on a dark purple square. It was Camp Pontchartrain's Alma Mater, or the camp song. It was the same one written on the wall in the gymnasium, and now and then, the camp director, Mrs. Chakoté, made everyone sing it. In general, it was considered stupid and annoying, but something about it gave me a small bit of comfort. I read the words silently in my head, hoping to distract myself from the anxiety creeping up on me like a stalking lion.

> *The hallowed shores of Pontchartrain.*
> *Will always be our home.*
> *No matter where our paths may lead,*
> *And despite how far we roam.*
> *Your majesty and history,*
> *Are lessons for lifelong.*
> *Alone, we strive to face our tasks,*
> *But together, we are strong.*
> *You taught us that our courage,*
> *Shall shine a golden light.*
> *And cast away the darkness.*
> *For fears that we shall smite.*
> *Camp Pontchartrain*
> *our hearts belong to you.*
> *Your sons and daughters sing your praise.*
> *And to thee remain true.*

My heart slowed a bit as the words tumbled about in my mind.

"We got to get moving, Cam, or we'll be late." Bobby wiped his hands on his shorts and then patted me on the back. "Come on."

Bobby amazed me. The bullies targeted him just as frequently as me. His pimpled

skin, loud mouth, and big belly offered ample ammunition to the bigger kids, their slings and arrows of hurtful comments meant to impale his self-esteem. But Bobby never seemed fazed by it. He never wavered, his confidence and sense of humor seemingly indestructible.

"Bobby, the baseball players are at the door." The buzzing in my head grew louder. I tried to swallow, but my throat felt dry as dust. "We need to wait until they leave."

"Don't be silly." Bobby smiled. "If we're late, we'll have to do push-ups or some other stupid exercise." He turned to me, then glanced at the exit. "Don't worry. I'll get you past them." Bobby chuckled, excitement twinkling in his eyes. "I'll create a diversion, and you can slip by."

"What kind of diversion?" I asked.

He chuckled. "Trust me. You'll know what it is."

And with that, Bobby marched straight for the exit, his full belly bouncing about, me three steps behind, head lowered.

"Hey, look who's coming." It was the team captain, Karl Macarthur. "It's Blobby and his cratered face." The tall sixth-grader laughed, his fellow teammates chuckling with him. "Looking at him is like staring at the moon." Karl laughed again. He glanced at his companions and glared, forcing them to join in on the laughter. "You're so big, Blobby. I'm wondering if you're still in sixth grade, or did you eat your way into seventh?"

The other baseball players roared with laughter.

Bobby kept walking, but when he reached the door, he stopped directly in front of the baseball captain. "Let me ask you something, Karl. Do you think you're hurting me by saying I'm fat? Do you?"

"Well . . . umm . . .?"

"Do you honestly believe I don't know that I'm overweight, and you're revealing some great secret I've been hiding all this time?"

"Well—"

Bobby interrupted Karl before he could speak and took a step closer, pushing the ball player back with his stomach, allowing me to pass behind him and slip through the doorway. "Do you think you're saying something I haven't heard a hundred times? I mean, really, can't you come up with any new material, or is this just the best you can do?"

Karl glared down at Bobby, a hand slowly clenching into a fist.

"When you get some new insults, let me know. I'd love to hear them." Bobby chuckled as he turned and headed out of the dining hall, leaving an uncomfortable silence in his wake.

I waited for Bobby to catch up.

"You take too many chances with those bullies," I said. "One of these times, you're gonna get hurt."

"Maybe . . . but not today."

"Sometimes, I think you're crazy." I smiled as the buzzing in my head slowly faded away. My Beast, that's what I called my anxiety, submerged back into the dark places in my mind, waiting . . . always waiting.

"You okay?" Bobby asked in a low voice.

I nodded.

"Great, let's get down to the lake." Bobby took off running toward the glistening waters of Lake Pontchartrain, robotics parts bouncing about in his bag.

I sighed and tried to devise a way to avoid the ropes course, but I knew it was futile. If I didn't show up, I'd get in trouble. Clenching my teeth, I followed Bobby, knowing failure awaited me on the shores of the lake.

# Chapter 2 – The Beast

**A** **feeling of dread spread through me like a poisonous cloud** as I followed Bobby toward the thing at Camp Pontchartrain that caused me so many nightmares: the ropes course. It was the sixth-graders' turn on the course, and no one wanted to miss the perilous climb to the top except me. I hated this activity. Every time I tried it, fear of falling and getting hurt took over my mind. But how could you get hurt? The whole thing stood over the edge of the lake. I knew fear wasn't necessarily bad; how I reacted to it determined if it was a positive or a negative thing. Like if there's a fire at home, it makes sense to be afraid while evacuating. But for me, I worry about a fire at home all the time for no reason, and that fear turns to panic if I can't calm down, letting my Beast control my mind. For me, fear was *definitely* a negative thing.

My stomach churned . . . the first shot in the war of me vs. my anxiety.

The course consisted of rope swings, rope ladders, seemingly unstable bridges, a zip line . . . all high in the air, ropes, and cables anchored to tall posts. The only thing keeping kids from falling to their deaths were their safety harnesses and the calm waters of Lake Pontchartrain beneath the course.

The worst part about this entire experience for me was giving up. Every time I had attempted the course before, I had to quit and climb back down, my fear just too severe. All the other kids would laugh and make comments when I retreated, my cowardice on full display. I knew I couldn't see into the future, but I had no doubt the same thing was about to happen again.

I slowed to tie my shoe. "Bobby, you keep going. I'm gonna put on my water shoes."

"Water shoes? Just do it barefoot."

"You go ahead. I'll be there in a minute."

Bobby shrugged. "Okay, see you on the ropes."

My friend sped off, running toward the shoreline, sunlight dancing across the calm waters in the distance. The course looked like a giant spiderweb of crisscrossing ropes stretching across the lake. Tall wooden posts stood out of the water, holding the whole thing aloft. Surrounding the ropes course was a fence made of some mesh material that went down to the bottom of the lake. Wooden posts held the fence in place, colorful stones embedded into the supports. They say the fence is supposed to keep out the alligators and snakes, but I never really understood that; the snakes could swim through the holes in the fence. As far as I knew, no one had ever seen a gator or snake near the ropes course, so the fence must be doing something.

I stared at one of the posts holding up the protective barrier, the colorful stones shimmering in the bright sunlight. A clear stone, maybe quartz, seemed to glow as I stared at it. For a moment, I thought I heard a faint whisper in the back of my head. But that made little sense. Likely it was just my imagination, one of the many *what-ifs* that tortured me daily.

Looking back to the ground, I pulled off my sneakers and slipped on water shoes, stuffing the Keds in my bookbag. As I stood, a group of boys, each wearing a purple and white soccer team jersey, formed a line across the trail and harassed anyone brave enough to pass by.

The buzzing returned, this time like a swarm of angry bees—the second shot in the war.

*Am I getting anxious?* The thought instantly triggered a fear response in the worry part of my brain. My heart pounded in my chest as goosebumps prickled my skin, the buzzing growing louder.

*I'm getting afraid.* The thought seemed to amplify my anxiety. My ears pounded with an accelerating pulse, and my body stiffened with tension. *Is the Beast coming?* The anxiety jumped up a level, making the fear even worse. I knew I was trapped in a thought-loop again, the fear and anxiety connected, each making the other stronger as I focused on the problem rather than the solution.

*I gotta get out of this loop.* Clenching my fists, I tried some coping strategies Dr. Jen taught me.

I started with *4 – 7 – 8 breathing,* I took a deep breath as I counted slowly to four, then held my breath for seven counts and exhaled for eight counts. Glancing away from the soccer players, I focused my eyes on the ground and repeated the breathing sequence . . . but the counts were getting faster and faster.

*It's not working!*

I tried *box breathing*, breathing in for five counts, waiting for five counts, exhaling for five counts, then waiting again for five counts before repeating. With my heartbeat as a

counter, I repeated the breathing exercise. For a minute, I just stood there and breathed, hoping my Beast would stay away. Gradually, my heart slowed, and the buzzing in my head grew a little softer, the anxiety lessening, but I knew the Beast was still there, waiting . . . always waiting.

The kids from the soccer cabin were the worst. After winning the Capture the Flag game last night, they acted as if they ruled the camp … and they did. These kids did anything they wanted with their coaches always nearby, ready to get them out of trouble. For some reason, they loved tormenting me, and right now, they stood directly in my path.

*I'll never get past those bullies,* I thought.

The buzzing in my head morphed from a collection of bees to a hive of angry hornets; the Beast grew nearer. My heartbeat felt like a blacksmith's hammer pounding an anvil.

*Please don't see me . . . please . . . please.*

I ran for the boy's bathroom and slipped inside, hoping to hide. Dr. Jen's words resonated in my head, *'Avoiding a stressful situation doesn't help you learn to manage your anxiety. Hiding from the problem doesn't make it go away. Avoiding stressful situations and hiding from the problem just serves to feed your Beast. Facing things and using coping strategies will starve your Beast. You need to apply the coping strategies and make your Beast go hungry, so you can be in control of your thoughts.*

*Be in control of my thoughts?* I thought. *Right now, that seems impossible.*

I ducked into the last stall, slamming the door shut behind me as my breathing turned shallow and ragged. Sitting on the back of the toilet with my feet off the ground, I waited, my body quivering. I tried to slow my pulse, using the breathing exercises again, trying not to concentrate on my fears . . . but I was never very good at that part. The pounding of my heart became a little less frantic, but the exercises didn't help my anxiety.

My skin felt clammy as beads of sweat formed everywhere. It seemed as if the hot breath of some gigantic creature puffed across my body, ready to devour me. Thoughts raced through my mind, each suggesting what *might* happen. The panic intensified, fueling my fear until anxiety consumed my mind, leaving me unable to think.

The last shot in the war between me and my anxiety landed squarely in my brain.

A thunderous pounding filled my ears as my heart raced. Fear blasted through my mind like a hurricane of jagged things from a dark nightmare. My Beast had arrived with a vengeance, its presence overwhelming. The panic felt all-consuming, a maelstrom of terror that threatened to crush me in its dark embrace.

I wanted to escape, but that was impossible. My anxiety filled my mind with worst-case scenarios. I imagined the soccer players humiliating me in front of everyone. Images of them beating and kicking me filled my mind as even worse thoughts of what they *might* do surged through my head. My mind shifted into panic mode. The worry part of my brain was now in complete control.

*Will this fear ever stop? It feels like it's gonna go on forever.*

The door to the bathroom swung open. It banged against the wall with a *SMACK!* The sound echoed off the tile floors and concrete walls like thunder. My whole body shuddered.

"I think I saw a little weasel scurry in here," a deep voice said.

Jackson Viles, the soccer cabin leader, stepped into the bathroom, his sneakers squeaking on the cold floors. The high-pitched sound was like a thousand needles to my spine, the shrill noise so penetrating that it felt like it was scraping the inside of my skull, leaving me a little dizzy. My body shuddered from the anticipation of the torture I knew was coming.

"Where are you, little weasel?" Viles asked.

Jackson was a mean boy with a streak of violence even some of the older kids feared. Making other people suffer seemed to bring him joy. I knew I was in trouble.

"Are you in here, little weasel?"

The door to the first stall slammed open. My body flinched at the sound, almost falling off the toilet. I cupped my hands to my ears, trying to muffle the hornets, but the sound came from inside my skull, anxiety gnawing away at my mind. Arms, legs . . . everything started to shake.

*What do I do . . . what do I do?*

The next door slammed open.

"I know you're here. Just come out, and it'll go easier on you." Jackson chuckled.

The other soccer players laughed.

*BANG.*

The door next to me crashed open. The stall shook, as did I.

The *what-ifs* surged through my mind, my anxiety showing me how Jack *might* punish me for being me. I tried to speak, but my mouth felt like a desert.

"Looks like there's just one stall left."

Viles stepped up to my stall and stood there. The tips of his fluorescent green and black Nikes poked under the door. Fingers curled over the top of the door and shook it. The lock held.

I shuddered, the buzzing like constant thunder. Sometimes, the anticipation of something was worse than the actual event. That's how it feels right now. I knew my fate was sealed, and I'd accepted it; I just wanted the bullies to finish their torment.

"I know you're in there, Poole." Jackson's voice was that of a growling, vicious animal, every word dripping with the threat of pain. "Open the door, or I'll kick it in. Then, we'll really make you suffer."

I sighed as I turned the latch, unlocking the door with a loud click that echoed off the walls. It swung open with a spine-tingling creaking noise like something out of a nightmare. Goosebumps came to life across the back of my neck as a dark chill slithered down my spine. Before me stood the meanest kid in sixth grade. Though we were the same age, Jackson towered over me, as did most kids my age.

"Why do you have to pick on me?" My voice sounded weak, more like a whimper.

"Because I can." Jackson moved back, his Nikes scraping across the floor, squeaking. He motioned for me to step out of the stall. "Because I'm the leader of our cabin." Jackson grabbed me by the shirt and yanked me out. "And because you let me."

I shook with terror, the Beast making it impossible to think.

"And because there are five of you and only one of him," a deep voice said from the doorway.

All eyes turned to the newcomer. Leonard O'Malley, the head of the football cabin and team captain, stared at us from the door. His blue and gold jersey stood out in contrast to the white and purple soccer players' shirts. Leonard was the biggest sixth-grader at Camp Pontchartrain and taller than many of the older kids as well. His broad shoulders, good looks, and kind nature made him popular with everyone.

"I think you need to break up this little party." Leonard's calm, soft voice made his words seem even more threatening. He took a step closer. "That little guy isn't bothering you. It's time to move along; you've had your fun."

"Why should we?" Jackson spat back.

"Because I can have the rest of the football team here in thirty seconds, doing to you what you plan to do to that kid." Leonard took a step closer. "Is that what you want?"

A coach's whistle cut through the air, signifying the opening of the ropes course.

"We better get to the lake." Jackson glanced at his friends.

They all nodded; the excuse to leave was probably a welcome one.

The boys filed out of the bathroom, each glaring at me, some purposely jabbing me with an outstretched elbow or extended shoulder. With my eyes on the ground, I tried to get out of the way, but there wasn't room. The bullies took turns jostling me or stepping on my feet as they filed out.

The buzzing faded in my mind, the Beast going back to sleep, for now. Fatigue washed over me, a parting gift from the anxiety. I thought of it as an echo of the Beast's savage attack. Taking a deep breath, I wiped the sweat from my face, then looked up at my rescuer.

"Thanks for the help, Leonard." I tried to smile, but it came off more like a sneer. "I really appreciate it."

The football player nodded and shrugged. I always found it surprising—Leonard always had such sad eyes. As the most popular kid at the camp, he had everything, yet he seemed the saddest as well.

"So that you know, I didn't do it for you."

"You didn't?" My voice grew quiet. "Why did you—"

"I just wanted to wash my hands after lunch, and all of you were in the way." Leonard spun around, turned on the water, washed his hands, and dried them with paper towels. Crumbling the paper into a ball, he shot it toward the trash can on the other side of the bathroom. It went in, of course.

"Well . . . umm . . . thanks anyway." I wasn't sure what to say, so I just stood there, staring at Leonard, a confused expression on my face. "I was so scared; I couldn't even think."

"Why do you do that? Why do you just stand there and let them pick on you?"

I shrugged. "I don't know—because I don't have a choice."

"There's always a choice. All of us can decide who we want to be and how we want to be seen by others. The trick is having the courage to make that choice."

"You don't understand," I said. "Everything's easy for someone like you."

"Maybe it's you who doesn't understand." Leonard poked me in the chest. "My history teacher at school once told me to look inside myself to see who's hiding in there, waiting to get out. Maybe you should do that too."

Not waiting for an answer, Leonard turned and headed for the door.

I followed him, glad I'd survived the ordeal, but a distant buzzing deep within the dark recesses of my mind told me this wasn't over. Something terrible was going to happen, and somehow, I'd be at the center of it whether I liked it or not. And I was sure I wouldn't.

Slinging my bookbag over my shoulder, I followed the larger boy down to the lake, my eyes searching for the next disaster waiting to devour me.

# Chapter 3 – Monster in the Weeds

**M**y stomach churned as I followed Leonard down toward the lake, the faint buzz of anxiety present in the back of my mind. Doing the ropes course would be another failure for me; I already knew it. The only unknown was – how humiliating it would be.

I reached the line to the ropes course, a step behind Leonard. Off to the side, I set my bag down, then searched the line for any friendly faces. I spotted Bobby swimming to shore in the water, an infectious smile on his face. Apparently, he'd taken his turn and had fallen, as usual. On the rope ladder, Elisa Jarreau, my only other friend at Camp Pontchartrain, climbed up to the zip line. Her long blond hair fell over one shoulder as she ascended, her golden locks swaying about.

"Cameron!" Bobby shouted as he waded out of the lake, waving.

Elisa glanced down, spotted me, and flashed me a smile.

I waved, then moved behind Leonard, hiding from the curious stares of those in line.

"Cameron Poole, why are you always last in line?" It was Mrs. Chakoté, the camp director. "I know you're hoping there won't be enough time for you, but I don't want you to miss out on conquering the ropes course. Come up here." She tapped her cane on the hard-packed ground, the end of the crooked staff making a loud tapping sound. "Come on now, child. Bring your friend, Leonard, with you."

"Cool, we get to cut the line." Leonard grabbed my arm and dragged me to the front.

Many in line grumbled complaints. Mrs. Chakoté tapped her cane on the ground again, the colorful stones embedded in the wood sparkling in the sunlight. She stepped forward, casting her gaze across the kids, her gray hair glittering like a thousand silver threads, the afternoon sun making her locks almost glow. Chakoté thumped her cane on the ground again, this time harder. The kids grew silent as Leonard pushed me to the front of the line.

The buzz of an annoying gnat circled inside my skull, slowly getting louder. I glanced around, hoping maybe an insect

orbited my head, but I knew that wasn't the case. It was the Beast stalking me.

*No, not again,* I pleaded, but my thoughts did little to slow the approaching storm.

I grasped the rope ladder and put a foot on the lowest rung, the lingering fatigue making my legs feel heavy. My heart felt like it was trying to escape the confines of my chest, pounding so fiercely I could feel the blood rushing through my veins. I tried to swallow, but my mouth was as dry as a desert, my throat rough and scratchy, like sandpaper.

"Come on, Cameron. You can do it." Elisa glanced down at me. She'd traversed the zip line without falling and was now climbing the cargo net.

The buzzing grew louder. *What if I fall? What if I get stuck up there? What if . . .*

All the possible ways I could fail flooded my mind, fear growing.

"Come on, Poole. Get moving, ya slow poke. I wanna jump off the high platform before the end of summer." It was Karl Macarthur, the baseball captain and new to Camp Pontchartrain. He pointed at the water where Bobby was wading to shore. "The ropes could support Blobby, so they probably won't break and send you falling to your doom." He laughed, some of the other baseball kids joining in.

"Mr. Macarthur!" Chakoté slammed the tip of her cane on the ground with a thud. All the kids instantly grew silent. "You need to be more respectful."

Karl lowered his eyes to the ground, a smile still on his face.

I scowled at him, then stepped up onto the first rung. Grabbing the rope overhead, I pulled myself up. The gnat transformed into a band of cicadas, the noisy insects amplifying my fear of failure.

*Don't fall in front of everyone . . . it'll be humiliating.*

I climbed a little higher. Fear surged within me as worst-case scenarios played like an endless nightmare through my head.

I looked down at Leonard. His gaze showed a total lack of fear as if doing the ropes course was equivalent to walking down the street. *Maybe if I imagined myself to be him, I could use some of his courage.*

Closing my eyes for a moment, I took a deep breath and thought about what it would be like to have Leonard's confidence and strength.

"Get a move on." Karl reached past Leonard and shook the rope ladder, then laughed.

I squeezed the rope tight, my knuckles turning white. Any thought of being like Leonard evaporated as the rope swung under my grip. The buzzing in my head stabbed at my courage with blades of doubt, thoughts of failure filling my mind. More harassing and teasing comments fell upon my ears; Karl's impatience spread to the others in the line.

"Cameron, I have faith in you." Elisa had reached the top of the cargo net.

*I know I can't do it. Why do I even try?* The buzzing grew even louder, the furious hornets in my head trying to deafen me, almost drowning out my thoughts. *I hate this!*

Beads of sweat trickled down my forehead, the salty moisture finding the corner of my eye, stinging. I reached up, grasped the next rung, and tried to pull myself up. My arms felt like noodles, legs filled with sand.

*I can't do it. I'll never be able to do it.*

Instead of going up, I climbed down the few rungs I'd scaled until I reached the ground, head hung low in shame. I heard Mrs. Chakoté sigh and glanced at her. She tilted her head slightly, smiled reassuringly, and motioned me to step aside.

"Get out of the way, Poole." Karl moved past Leonard and shoved me out of the way, then scaled the rope ladder with ease. "Let me show you how it's done."

Leonard looked at me and shook his head, then followed Karl up the ropes, moving without fear.

I stepped away from the course and moved to a large granite boulder, the massive stone all the camp-goers called the Guardian. It stood maybe six feet tall at its highest point, the top sloping downward, making it easy to climb.

The huge stone felt rough under my fingers as I crawled on top. I turned away from the ropes course as Karl and Leonard climbed higher and higher and stared across the grounds of the camp. A collection of rustic-looking cabins stood amidst gently rolling. Yellow flowers dotted the grass, splashes of color on the swells of an emerald ocean.

One of the camp counselors stood nearby, Mr. Jacobian, the computer programming teacher. It must have been his turn to help with the Ropes. He glanced up at me as I took in the serene view.

27

"You know, they have a fleet of riding mowers to keep the grass in perfect condition."

"Umm . . . what?" I glanced down at the teacher.

"Yep." Jacobian nodded. "They keep all the riders in a barn at the back of the grounds."

I knew that, of course; I'd been coming to Camp Pontchartrain for many years.

The teacher pointed to the far side of the grounds. A tangle of tall grass, prickly weeds, and overgrown shrubs grew behind a waist-high stone wall. On one side of the chaos sat a marble building, the Crypt, while on the other side, a cave opening pierced a tall hill.

"You know the Crypt grounds are off-limits," Mr. Jacobian said.

"Yep, I know that."

"Did you know they buried all the camp directors in the Crypt since this place was founded in 1799?" The teacher looked at me and smiled as if he had imparted a great piece of information known only to him. "You know it's big trouble to go onto the Crypt grounds, right?"

I nodded. "Of course . . . I've been coming to Camp Pontchartrain for a long time."

Mr. Jacobian smiled, then moved to Mrs. Chakoté's side.

Karl shouted something from the course. He was traversing the rope bridge, Leonard directly behind. The two boys synchronized their steps, trying to keep the line on which they walked from swinging out of control, but the obstacle had other ideas. The bridge did not like multiple kids on it at the same time and tended to sway unexpectedly, showing its displeasure.

I stood on the Guardian, vying for a better glimpse of the shrubs and disobedient weeds clinging to the ground around the Crypt. Just then, something colored bright red moved through the tall grass. Stretching my neck, I tried to get a better view. This time I saw it. A creature no bigger than a small child pushed through the weeds, its skin dark red. Tiny wings stuck out from its back, short stubby horns jutting up from its head, and its eyes glowing like two burning embers.

The rope bridge lurched, throwing Leonard and Karl into the air. They fell, each shouting as they splashed into the water.

Their voices barely registered in my mind, my attention focused on the mysterious visitor. Flapping its wings, the tiny red creature tried to take to the air, its long, pointed tail barely clearing the ground before it fell in a heap.

I giggled.

28

Some of the kids in line gasped.

"You find something funny about Leonard and Karl falling, Poole?" Jackson Viles asked, his voice loud enough for everyone to hear.

"Um . . . no, I wasn't laughing at them, I was laughing at . . ." I glanced back toward the Crypt, but the red thing was gone.

"What *were* you laughing at, Poole?" Karl asked as he waded out of the lake, an angry scowl painted across his face.

"I wasn't laughing at you. I was laughing at . . . well . . . something else." I could feel my face getting hot. The buzzing started up again, angry bees in my head with pointed stingers ready to stab at my soul.

Leonard now turned and glared at me. "Not cool, dude."

"Honest, I wasn't laughing at you, I was . . . umm . . ."

"Yeah, whatever." Leonard stepped out of the water and went back into line, an angry stare focused on me.

Karl followed Leonard, his eyes fixed on mine. When he reached the Guardian, Karl stopped and stared up at me, then mouthed, *"You're dead."* Before I could say anything, the baseball player turned and got back in line behind Leonard.

The two athletes whispered to each other, occasionally lobbing angry stares in my direction.

Fear churned through me, electrifying my nerves. A rush of pins and needles prickled the back of my arms and legs. I had angered one of the meanest kids and the most popular boy in the camp; something bad was going to happen; I knew it.

Mrs. Chakoté smacked her cane against one of the thick posts supporting the ropes course, the stick of wood like an extension of the old woman's arm. It made the post ring as if struck by a steel hammer. "Kids, I have an announcement. All of you come down off the ropes. We're done for now."

The kids moaned. Those in line spread out, standing with their cabinmates. The soccer players clustered together, as did the art students, the Techies, and the various athletes. In an instant, the group went from a collection of sixth-graders excited to be on the ropes to a patchwork of cliques and factions, each glaring at the other. Despite the adult's best efforts, an unhealthy competitiveness between cabins had always infected Camp Pontchartrain.

I jumped off the Guardian and moved to Bobby's side, standing near the kids in the robotics cabin, the Techies as we were called, sometimes as an insult.

"As you may have heard," Mrs. Chakoté said in a loud voice, "there's an upcoming lunar eclipse tomorrow night. It should be quite spectacular. Does anyone know anything about it?"

"It's gonna be a special eclipse," one of the techie girls, Lisa Chambers, said. She came to Camp Pontchartrain to study robotics, like me.

"That's right." Mrs. Chakoté nodded. "Do you know what astronomers call the moon during this kind of eclipse?"

"They call it a Super Blood Moon," Lisa said. "The moon will be at its closest distance from Earth, and the light going through our atmosphere during the eclipse will shade the moon to a blood-red color."

"What?" I blurted unintentionally.

"I said the moon will be blood-red," Lisa repeated.

*Blood red, like that little flying devil-thing.*

I stepped back and glanced back at the tall grass. Some blades looked pushed apart as if something had recently walked through them.

"We'll pull the telescopes out for everyone to use. It'll be late, but it should be quite an event." Mrs. Chakoté tapped her cane on the ground.

*Did one of those stones flash with color?* I glanced at Bobby to see if he noticed, but he was busy staring at a bug crawling over his foot.

"It's time for class," Chakoté continued. "Everyone to your classrooms or practice fields."

Leonard led the football kids to the fields where an NFL player waited, ready to teach them some new skills. The Olympic bronze medal winner in archery stood on the archery range. Professional soccer players, tennis players, artists, engineers . . . every group had recognized experts there to teach them.

As I walked toward the robotics building, the buzzing in my head disappeared. I had some new inventions I wanted to test with the NASA engineer teaching our group. As I walked, I glanced toward the overgrown area around the Crypt, hoping to see that red-winged creature. But all I saw were the dense weeds and tall grass swaying gently in the breeze, nothing out of the ordinary in sight.

*Maybe I imagined it. That must be it.* But I saw it for sure, the certainty in me as solid as the Guardian I'd just stood on.

I shuddered, "Something's wrong . . . I know it."

Taking a deep breath, I headed for robotics class, all the while playing back the memory of that monster, its blazing eyes staring directly at me from within my mind.

# Chapter 4 – Revenge

The echo of fear from the Ropes Course still lingered at the back of my mind like tiny teeth nibbling on my soul, but that little red monster had my attention. I walked up the hill, Bobby on one side, Elisa on the other with her bow and quiver of arrows in her hands. The archery range sat near the technology building, so we walked together frequently.

"I think you almost made it up the rope ladder this time." Elisa patted me on the back.

I shook my head. "No, I didn't. I was too . . ." I lowered my voice, "afraid."

"Don't worry, Cam. You'll get it one of these times." Bobby gave me a reassuring smile.

I shrugged, then noticed we were alone. Usually, a whole group of kids would be climbing the hill as we headed for class, but instead, everyone had disappeared.

"What's going on?" I glanced at my friends. "Something's not right. Where is everyone?"

"Who knows, and who cares." Bobby glanced about. "Why do you always assume something is wrong? It's all good, trust me. Let's get to class. I finished my tazer bombs, you know, like your shocker balls. They're ready for testing and I wanna see if they'll work."

With a sigh, I shrugged and followed my friends, my eyes darting about, thoughts of that red creature still tumbling about in the back of my mind. I wanted to tell Bobby and Elisa about what I saw by the Crypt; after all, they were my closest friends at Camp Pontchartrain. No, they're my only friends, and I wanted to tell them, but what if they don't believe me? They'll probably think I'm lying and just making it up. Better to keep it to myself . . . for now.

As we passed the art studio, I noticed a group of students milling about behind us as if waiting for something. Suddenly, Leonard and Karl stepped out of the shadows. With an angry scowl etched on Karl's face, he pushed me against the wall of the art building.

The buzzing sound exploded in my head.

Leonard also stepped forward, standing tall and muscular, his glare fixed upon me.

"Hey, what's going on?" Bobby moved to my side. "We're heading to class, and you two should be going somewhere as well. What's your next class, muscle sculpting, or maybe it's iron bending?"

"Shut up, Blobby," Karl snapped.

Elisa moved in front of Bobby and me, her arms extended. "You don't have to do this."

"Get out of the way, archer." Karl pointed a thick finger in my direction. "That techie sucks. He embarrassed Leonard and me. We need to show everyone what happens if you do that to one of us."

"What do you mean by one of *us*?" I asked. "You mean baseball players?"

Leonard sighed and shook his head.

"I don't mean baseball players, idiot. I mean *us* . . . the cool kids." Karl stepped forward and glared at me. "A bunch of geeks and losers like you can't be seen embarrassing us. You guys are insignificant, like a bugger I pick out of my nose and flick at someone. We run Camp Pontchartrain, the *real* athletes, I mean." He sneered at Elisa. "Your little bow and arrow don't count. That's not a real sport."

Elisa lowered her gaze to the ground, the sadness perpetually orbiting her like a captive moon showing on her face. With posture slumped, she stepped back and stood between Bobby and me. I thought I saw a tear trickling down her cheek, but she turned away when I glanced at her.

"That wasn't very nice." I put a hand on her shoulder.

"No, it wasn't," Leonard said. He moved next to Karl, his huge frame making him seem like a giant compared to the three of us.

The buzzing grew louder. I could feel the panic attack coming. I looked for escape or salvation, but we were alone. This was why the other kids had stayed away. No one wanted to get involved.

Sweat trickled down my forehead. The beads of moisture tasted salty when they found my lips. I tried the *4 – 7 – 8* breathing strategies. I breathed in 1 . . . 2 . . . 3 . . . 4 . . . then held my breath 1 . . . 2 . . . 3 . . . 4 . . 5 . . 6 . . 7 . . and exhaled 1 . . 2 . . 3 . . 4 . 5 . 6 . 7 . 8. But my breathing accelerated. I tried it again, but I couldn't slow down. Gulping in gasps of air faster and faster, I started to hyperventilate.

Karl took a step closer, clenching his fist.

Images of Karl and Leonard pounding me into dust filled my head. The nightmare then changed to a crowd of kids making fun of me because of a black eye and a bloody nose. As my anxiety built, my mind focused on these negative thoughts. Dr. Jen called them *Automatic*

*Negative Thoughts* or *ANTs*. I didn't care what they were called; I hated them.

*Stay in the moment,* I thought. Dr. Jen popped into my head, her words trying to cut through my anxiety, my Beast. '*Ignore the ANTs. They only feed your fears; let them starve. The ANTs are a lie.*' But of course, as soon as I told myself to ignore the *ANTs*, my brain did the opposite.

*Are they going to beat us up? What if I get kicked out of the camp? My parents will kill me. They'll never let me go anywhere ever again. What if . . .* Of course, I knew I couldn't see into the future and know what would happen—Dr. Jen called this *Future Telling*. But it didn't matter; the thoughts felt real to me, sharp nightmares tearing at my soul with cruel, unforgiving claws.

I tried to challenge the *ANTs*; were they realistic? Looking at Karl's clenched fists, I knew he wanted to beat me up.

*This is gonna happen,* I thought as the buzzing grew even louder, a storm of hornets swirling in a chaotic cyclone that threatened to consume my mind. My Beast stirred . . . awakening.

Karl moved closer and raised his arm, fist squeezed tight.

"I'm not sure this is a good idea," Leonard said as he glanced down at me, seeing me shake with fright. "We can't hurt these kids . . . it's not right." He reached out and grabbed Karl's arm. "Let's just go."

Karl yanked his arm free, glared at the football player, and then turned back to me. I could hear Karl's knuckles crack as he clenched his fist harder, ready to strike.

Like something hard tapping the ground, a sound echoed off the buildings. It grew louder and louder, uncertainty flickering in Karl's eyes. And then, Mrs. Chakoté came around the corner, her crooked wooden cane in her hand.

"What's this, what's this?" She pounded her cane on the ground twice.

Karl lowered his fist and backed up, leaving Leonard in front of us.

Mrs. Chakoté turned to my friends and me. "What's going on here, Cameron?"

"Umm, noth . . . nothing." My voice cracked.

"Nice job, Cam. *Very* convincing." Bobby laughed, then looked at the camp director and smiled.

Elisa sniffled and glanced at Mrs. Chakoté, wiping tears from her cheeks.

Karl glared at his intended targets, then unclenched his fists and turned toward the old woman, leaving Leonard still standing in front, tall and motionless.

Without warning, five of the stones embedded into her gnarled cane flared to life, each one emitting a brilliant burst of color that filled the air with a blinding, radiant glow. Green, blue, purple, orange, and white light bathed the area around us as if we were trapped within a supernova. The intensity of the light was almost too much to bear, forcing me to shield my eyes and look away. One of the colors, the shimmering white, penetrated my mind and lit up my soul. The darkest parts of my imagination now stood under a harsh, white glare, driving away the *ANTs* and *what-ifs*. With the dazzling light came soft, harmonious tones that combined to create a calming melody that resonated in my head. For an instant, I was lost in the beauty of it all, caught up in the raw and untamed energy that pulsed through the air like a living thing.

As quickly as the stones burst outward with colorful light, they darkened again. The flash was so short I almost thought I imagined it.

Mrs. Chakoté raised the cane and stared at it for a moment, then turned her gaze to us again, her eyes wide with surprise.

"Interesting. This hasn't happened for a long, long time." Mrs. Chakoté's words seemed to come from somewhere very far away.

"What was that?" I asked, then glanced at Bobby and Elisa. They didn't seem shocked at all. *Was I the only kid who saw that? First, that red creature, and now these flashing stones. Am I going crazy?* I ran my fingers through my hair, the curls grasping at my hand. *What's happening to me?*

Chakoté shook her head as if clearing away an unpleasant memory. "It was nothing, child." She pointed at Karl and Leonard with her cane. "Whatever is going on here, it's done."

"But we didn't do anything," Karl complained. He glanced at Leonard, but the football captain remained silent.

"All of you know fighting is not allowed at Camp Pontchartrain." Mrs. Chakoté focused her steely gaze upon Leonard. "You should know better, Leonard," she turned to me, "as should you, Cameron. I expect better from you two."

I lowered my head in shame.

"But we didn't—" Bobby started to say, but I put a hand on my friend's arm, silencing him.

"It'll be necessary to make an example of you five so the other members of our community know rules apply to everyone." She tapped her cane on the ground, signifying the discussion was over. "All of you will report to the groundskeeper, Mr. Wallace, after your next class. He'll have some work for you to do. Hopefully, it'll keep you out of mischief until I arrive for a little chat."

"But we have an extra practice with our coaches," Karl complained.

Leonard turned to the old woman. "Karl's right. There are special coaches coming today. They won't be happy with this."

"I'll take care of your coaches." Chakoté gave us a grandmotherly smile. "Just do as you're told and head to Mr. Wallace's barn at the end of this next class." She lowered her voice, the kindly smile fading away, leaving behind a deadly serious expression across her face. "Skip this detention at your peril."

Mrs. Chakoté turned and walked away from us, muttering. "So much to read and so little time. Can we be ready, or are we already too late?"

"What are you talking about?" Bobby asked.

Mrs. Chakoté waved a wrinkled hand in the air. "Get to class immediately, or detention will be extended for the rest of the week. No monkey business, no roughing up the smaller kids, Mr. Macarthur, and Mr. O'Malley. Now get to class." She stopped and looked over her shoulder at the five of us.

I glanced at Bobby and Elisa, confused, then turned and headed for the technology building, watching Karl and Leonard out of the corner of my eye. I wanted to mention something about the flashing stones or that little red creature I saw earlier, but they might think I was making it up. They'd probably laugh at me and think I was crazy. I couldn't handle that right now.

Bobby and Elisa followed me until we reached the robotics room. I held the door open for Bobby who walked in without saying goodbye to Elisa, colorful comments already leaking from his smiling face.

"Are you okay?" I asked Elisa.

She nodded.

"You know, Karl didn't mean anything back there."

"Yeah, he did."

"Well, he's wrong." I extended a hand toward her, but she moved back.

"It's okay. I'm used to it." Elisa looked to the ground. "I've heard the same thing a hundred times from my father. I don't think I ever told you, but my dad wanted me to do

35

gymnastics and go to the Olympics. I trained with coaches my dad hired for as long as I can remember, but I was always drawn to archery. There's something peaceful about it."

"Your dad didn't like archery?"

"He only likes what makes him look good. I'll finally gain his respect if I can make it to the Olympics as an archer. But until then, I'm just a girl who gave up on gymnastics and disappointed her father for a bow and arrow." She sighed, then turned and headed for the archery field.

"At least we'll see each other soon," I said.

Elisa waved her hand in the air but didn't look back.

I shook my head. "Sometimes, I really hate this camp. Why can't we all be on the same team, the Camp Pontchartrain team, instead of football cabin, baseball cabin, soccer cabin—"

"Mr. Poole, we need your help programming the robot. Are you coming in?" The technology teacher, an engineer from NASA named Mr. Jameson, asked. "Class has started. We have some mysteries to solve with the bootup sequence on the main robot. Let's get to work."

I stepped into the room and closed the door, shutting out the sweltering New Orleans heat.

"There are mysteries to solve," I whispered to myself, "like those flashing stones and that little red monster." I scanned the room. Everyone stood at workbenches, bent over their robot or little techie invention. "There's much to learn, and for some reason, I feel there's little time to do it," I said to myself, my soft words lost to the clatter of tools and beeping tech.

I put my bookbag on the ground, sat at the nearest computer, and got to work. But instead of working on the robot's software, I searched the Internet for those stones on Mrs. Chakoté's cane. That was the first mystery . . . for now.

# Chapter 5 – Demon Lord of Agartha

The Demon Lord, Malphas, stared down at his pathetic minions, a collection of demons, ghouls, gargoyles, and a hundred other types of monsters all staring up at him. Most had red eyes, signifying they were under Malphas's control. But Malphas saw some eyes that had lost that crimson glow; his hold on them was weakening.

*I'll have to do something about that,* the demon thought.

"I must be certain the monsters of Agartha are my obedient servants," he said to himself.

The Demon Lord glared down at a group of devastators, their huge tusks and gigantic bodies dwarfing most of the other creatures below. Their massive feet and tree trunk-like legs made the ground quake as they moved about, but they were not as fearsome as the mighty annihilators. Those gigantic monsters, as large as a house, were like unstoppable hurricanes of muscle and teeth. They made Malphas smile, but their dark eyes made the demon worry. "I cannot allow them any freedom; they could turn on me. There is still so much to do."

Gathering his powers, Malphas stared down at his army of claws and fangs. As a low, ominous buzzing filled the air, Malphas's eyes blazed with an intense red glow, his demon-magic building to a fever pitch. The power emanating from him made the air shimmer as waves of magic spread out in all directions. Below him, the monsters grew still as they stared up at the Demon Lord, the very essence of their being falling under Malphas's control. Like a wave of fire lit within each creature, the eyes of the monsters now burned bright red, the demon's touch firmly planted into the Agarthans' souls.

Imps, gremlins, and banshees now moved about, each struggling to get closer to the wall on which the mighty demon stood as the larger monsters moved back. Malphas glared down at them, frustrated that he must start with these puny monsters and not the bigger creatures of Agartha: the devastators, annihilators, crushers, or destroyers. But unfortunately, Malphas knew the doorway to Earth would not support those behemoths, not yet. Right now, only his smallest followers could travel to Earth.

Extending his dark wings, Malphas took to the sky, the ever-present soot and ash in the air swirling around his muscular six-foot-tall frame. The small black feathers covering his half-man half-bird body fluttered in the breeze, his long, raven's beak cutting through the air like the tip of a spear.

Gaining altitude, he gazed down at the castle he'd recently captured. Parts of the structure still lay in ruin, scars of the war he'd waged against the Agarthan king. The foolish king was now suffering in his dungeons with what remained of his army. But Malphas's minions were restless and craved more violence. A wry smile spread across the Demon Lord's face; soon, they would get what they wanted.

Agartha had become a wasteland, its rivers and oceans poisoned with pollution, the sky perpetually filled with smoke. The scars of many decades of war were etched deep into the world, evidence of a violent and brutal past that had left Agartha wounded and broken, possibly beyond repair. It would take even more decades before the land healed and could support his greed. But the Demon Lord cared little for repairing the damage he'd caused in the wars. Malphas only wanted to take and consume, not restore. Besides, he had a new target in mind . . . Earth.

Though Agartha and Earth existed in parallel universes, they were slowly approaching realignment again, just like they had over two hundred years ago. Soon, the alignment would be complete, and then Malphas could execute his plan.

As our two planets grew closer together, more of his monsters could use the gateway that led to that pristine world and cause havoc. But right now, the magic that formed the portal could only support the passage of the smallest Agarthans to Earth. Just a few at a time could cross over. To get more of his unwilling servants to Earth, Malphas must open the doorway completely, and to do that, he needed to find all seven of the Skull Keys. The keys resembled human skulls, each carved from a different kind of stone, the magic within them linked to the enchanted gateway.

Centuries ago, sorcerers from Agartha crafted the Skull Keys to keep the doorway open and make passage between worlds easier. But when the monsters of Agartha attacked New Orleans, the Earthers from the Order of the Stones stole the Skull Keys, closing the gateway and separating the worlds. They hid the Skull Keys somewhere near the portal. Because they were formed by the same magic that made up the doorway between worlds, the skulls couldn't be taken far away. They were near that doorway; Malphas knew it. To allow the largest creatures in the Demon Lord's monster army to get to Earth, he needed to fully open that doorway.

"When I find all the keys," Malphas said in a deep, scratchy voice, "the real fun will begin."

A flash of light came from the circle of stone standing near the entrance to his newly acquired castle. Leaping into the air, Malphas glided down on extended wings and landed near the stone circle. The talons at the end of each bird-like toe scratched into the ground, carving deep grooves into the granite. A group of lessor demons rushed to be near, crowding him.

"Get back, you fools!" Malphas swung his arm through the air, the long claws at the end of each finger slicing into their scaly hides. The demons howled in pain and moved back, streaks of moist red marking their chests.

"Never crowd me," Malphas said. "Next time, I won't be so merciful."

The minor demons bowed their heads as they backed away, each clutching their wounds.

Malphas walked toward the stone circle as another flash of light jumped from the shimmering ring. Just then, a small, red creature stepped out of the structure. It stood at the height of a human child, stubby red wings sticking out from its back. The creature's large eyes burned with crimson light as it glanced about, its pointed tail writhing like an agitated snake. The monster turned toward the Demon Lord and bowed.

"What have you seen, imp?" Malphas glared down at the creature. "And what happened to your horn?"

The imp reached up and touched its horns. One was still needle-sharp, but the broken tip on the other horn suggested something had happened. The tiny monster glanced at his master, the imp's eyes glowing red, showing he was still under Malphas's control. "Oh . . . well . . . flying in that world is difficult. I sort of . . . well . . . crashed and broke my horn."

"That was careless." Malphas glared down at the creature. "What is your name?"

"Rylee," the imp answered, his pointed tail twitching nervously, red wings tucked into his back.

"I think I'll call you 'Fool' instead." Malphas raised a hand to strike the tiny demon but held it back for now. "Where did you emerge on Earth, Fool?"

"The doorway took me to a deep cave. I climbed out of it and entered a field of tall grass." Rylee glanced about. Other creatures moved closer to listen. Some of them were imps, like him, but goblins, harpies, and gremlins all stood close, each with glowing red eyes.

"What did you see on Earth, Fool? Tell me what you discovered about our new enemy."

"I found a stone building on the other side of the field of tall grass, maybe a hundred paces from the cave. When I snuck inside, I found coffins of stone; it was a House of the Dead, just as the ancient writings foretold."

"You mean as *I* foretold." Malphas's eyes grew bright with anger.

"Yes, of course, I mean, as *you* foretold." Rylee shuddered.

"Did you find the Skull Keys? Which ones did you see? Where were they? How many did you collect?"

"Well . . . umm . . . actually, I didn't see any of them."

"What?! That was why I sent you to Earth." Malphas stood tall and extended his shadowy wings, a jagged scar across the side of his beak giving the Demon Lord a vicious appearance. "AHHHHH!" His scream echoed across the ruined landscape, monsters all shaking in fear. Malphas clenched his clawed fists and shook them at the gray sky, frustration enveloping his soul.

Rylee collapsed to the ground and shook in terror.

Looking down at the tiny imp, Malphas growled. "Get up, Fool, and continue your report. How many soldiers did you see? What kind of weapons did they wield?"

The imp rose to his feet. "I saw no soldiers, just kids."

"No soldiers? The Skull Keys are unprotected?"

Rylee nodded. "As far as I could tell, they're not protected by soldiers. Maybe the Earthers use magic to protect the Skull Keys?"

Malphas shook his head. "No, magic faded from Earth long ago. All they have now are things of metal to protect themselves." The Demon Lord paced back and forth, hands clasped behind his feathered back. His bird-like feet kicked up small clouds of ash, making it difficult for the imp to breathe. He stopped and turned to Rylee. "Can you at least tell where they keep the Skull Keys?"

"Yes, my Master. I felt their presence; they are somewhere in the House of the Dead." Rylee shuddered as he stared up into the demon's glowing eyes. Those burning orbs blasted away any thought of resisting Malphas's commands. "I searched the room and found none, but I still sensed them in my mind. They could have been in the stone coffins, but I lacked the strength to open them."

"The Earthers would not hide all the Skull Keys in the coffins; that would be foolish. There must be hidden tunnels and catacombs under their House of the Dead." Malphas glanced around and spotted a gremlin. "You, gremlin, come here."

The creature approached, his long arms almost dragging on the ground, gigantic, pointed ears bouncing about with each step. The monster reached up and adjusted the leather straps crisscrossing his chest, knives, and tools attached here and there.

"Yes, my master." The gremlin stared at the demon, his eyes glowing red, just like all the other creatures under the demon's control. The monster smiled at the Demon Lord, his needle-sharp teeth stained and dirty.

"What is your name, gremlin." Malphas leaned forward, the tip of his dark raven's beak in the tiny monster's face.

The gremlin glanced at the jagged scar across the demon's beak, then returned his gaze to Malphas's eyes. "I am called Krak, my lord."

The demon stood tall and glared at the gremlin. "Krak, you are to accompany this imp. He is to search the coffins, then dig through the walls in the House of the Dead and find the hidden tunnels. When you find a Skull Key, place it over the gateway on Earth; it will allow more members of my army to cross over and help with the search. When we have all seven, the gateway will remain open forever, but only if we find all seven before the disappearance of the red moon."

"Red moon?" Krak asked, confused.

"It isn't important for you to understand all the pieces of my plan. Your job is to obey." Malphas pointed at the gremlin with a single claw. "If the imp is unsuccessful, I will make *you* suffer . . . understood?"

Krak nodded his head frantically, then glared at the imp.

"Make sure Fool digs with all his strength," Malphas said as he glared at the gremlin. "*Your* life depends on it."

The creature bowed its head. "I will see it done, master." The gremlin removed every metal tool or blade from his belt and dropped them to the ground, replacing them with stone tools and weapons from his companions; metal cannot travel through the gateway between worlds. Turning, Krak pulled a whip

41

out from beneath his wide, leather belt. With a flick of his wrist, the gremlin snapped the end of the whip next to Rylee's ear. "Let's go, imp."

"My name is Rylee, and—"

The whip cracked again, this time leaving a welt on the tiny monster's arm.

"Ouch!" Rylee quickly bowed, then turned toward the sparkling gateway standing on the ground, colorful glowing stones marking its edge. "I'm going. I'm going."

Malphas stepped to the edge of the doorway and held up a hand, stopping the two creatures. "Remember, get back to Agartha before the moon sets. The ancient books say without the seven Skull Keys in place, Agarthan creatures will perish with the setting moon. So be quick or be dead." His eyes flared bright, two burning embers forever glowing with a thirst for violence.

"Yes, master," the two little monsters said in unison. They turned and stepped into the doorway, disappearing from Agartha.

Malphas glanced at his banshee generals. "Assemble your most trusted and vicious monsters. They must be ready to go through the doorway when those two find the first Skull and put it in its place."

The banshee bowed low, her body floating a foot off the ground in a display of eerie, weightless grace. Her tattered rope swayed gently in the breeze only she could feel. The monster looked up at her master with a pristine white face and lifeless black eyes, her features hauntingly beautiful, though her deathly pale skin told a different story.

Flapping his wings, Malphas rose into the air and landed atop a pile of rubble. With a huge breath, the Demon Lord let out a deafening screech that sliced across the landscape. The features that covered his body sparkled with the raw power of his demon-magic. As he screeched again, sparks burst outwards in all directions, fragments of his magic passing through the nearby monsters. In an instant, the beasts crumpled to the ground, writhing in agony as an overwhelming wave of fear blasted through their minds. Many Agarthan creatures wept as they curled up into tight balls, consumed by terror. Others just stood there, bodies shaking as the force of their fear punished their minds. The explosion of terror was as sudden as it was vicious, a painful reminder of the absolute power the Demon Lord held over his minions. And just as quickly as it had appeared, the wave of fear disappeared, leaving the monsters trembling, a harsh reminder of who was in charge.

Malphas's eyes flashed red like blazing crimson beacons, a faint buzz coming from each, reaffirming his power over those who looked at him. "Let that brief taste of my magic be a reminder of what will happen if any of you fail me." His gaze crept across his minions, daring any to challenge his rule; none did.

"Soon, we will have all seven skulls," Malphas said. "Tomorrow, the planets will align, and we can pass through the doorway. Then we'll remind the Earthers why they fear the night. They chased us from Earth and pushed us back to Agartha centuries ago. They will regret that decision, one way or another."

Malphas laughed a vile laugh as he flapped his wings, soaring higher into the air to survey his kingdom, memories of terrible battles bringing a malicious smile to his face.

# Chapter 6 – Detention

*B*zzzz. **"Ouch." A loud thud filled the air. "That hurt." It was** Bobby, of course.

I shut off the computer and turned. Bobby stood near a workbench, staring down at the ground. Other kids at the same table giggled as they watched Bobby's discomfort. Tools clinked, electric circuits buzzed, and robots whined in every corner of the classroom as future engineers worked on their projects. But, of course, Bobby stood out from the rest of the chaos. He was the only Techie with sparks crawling across his skin. A small metal sphere sat on the ground beside Bobby, shimmering glints of electricity dancing across the device's metallic shell, then jumping to his foot.

"What happened?" I asked.

"Well, I . . . ouch!"

Some of the other kids laughed.

"I built a copy of your shocker-ball thing," Bobby said. "I call mine the Tazer-bomb, but when I turned it on, it zapped me before it could deploy its barbs." He nudged the baseball-sized sphere with his foot. It rolled across the ground, and then four tiny barbs shot out of the sides, thin wire trailing from each. One of the barbs landed in Bobby's sock, the sharp point finding his skin. Sparks of electricity sped across the wire like glistening spiders, the energetic creatures enveloping his foot and seeking tender flesh with electric fangs.

"OUCH! Not again." Bobby jumped up and down, trying to dislodge the barb, but all it did was make the ball flail about, causing more barbs to stick into his sock. Sparks bounced off the edge of his shoes, and tiny puffs of smoke floated into the air like gray spirits coming to life from the burned portions of his Nikes.

I grabbed a rubber glove from a table, put it on, and carefully picked up the device. Turning it over, I flipped the switch on the bottom, deactivating it, and then tossed the device to Bobby.

"What do I always tell you when you're messing around with electricity?" Kneeling, I pulled the barbs from his sock.

"Ahhh . . . I don't remember." Bobby shrugged. "Don't get electrocuted?"

Kids nearby chuckled.

I shook my head, then disconnected the lid and showed him the innards. "Always insulate your tech so you can control where the electricity goes." Moving to a shelf, I grabbed a jar of red rubber paint and handed it to Bobby. "I made this. It's rubber paint. When I built my shocker-ball, I coated the outside of the shell with it so I wouldn't get shocked when I touched it; you should do the same with yours."

Bobby unscrewed the top and looked in, confused.

I sighed. "When it dries, it'll leave a layer of rubber. Electricity can't go through rubber, so you'll be protected when handling your device. Whenever I build electrical gadgets that might shock me, I ensure I have the rubber paint where I need it."

"Good advice," Bobby said. "Note to self: Don't get shocked . . . it hurts."

More laughter from their neighbors.

"You see that?" I pointed to what looked like a shirt made from tiny links of metal hanging from a hook on the wall. Lifting it off, I draped it over my body, the metal rings coated with the bright red rubber paint. Instantly, I felt like a knight getting ready for battle. "I made this during the school year and brought it with me to Camp. I started wearing this insulated chainmail when working with electrical devices that might shock me, just to be safe."

Bobby reached out and touched the rubber-coated chainmail and nodded.

"You did a good job building your Tazer-bomb, Bobby," I said. "Well, except for getting shocked by your own device. Maybe you should rethink that part."

My friend smiled. "It's not as good as the ones you built, but that's not a big surprise. Your tech is always better than everyone else's."

CLANG . . . CLANG . . . CLANG. The ancient bell in the camp's tower rang, echoing across the grounds.

"That's the end of class," Mr. Jameson said. "Everyone, clean up your workstation and put away your tools. Don't forget about the lunar eclipse tomorrow night."

Bobby took the shiny metal ball and put it in his bin next to my collection of shocker-balls and other electric gadgets, then headed for the door with me two steps behind.

Just outside, we found Elisa waiting for us.

"Ready for our prison sentence?" Bobby asked, stopping in the doorway.

Elisa and I both shrugged.

"I guess." I stepped out of the air-conditioned tech building. Instantly, the New Orleans heat slammed me in the face, the humidity like a steamy, suffocating blanket. Sweat trickled down my face until the rivulets of moisture made it down my neck and soaked the edge of my purple robotics shirt.

Overhead, the late afternoon sky showed a crystalline blue tapestry stretching from horizon to horizon. A few puffy, white clouds clung to the sapphire canopy, the constant breeze trying to push them off the edge of the world. The pockmarked face of a full moon was just daring to peek up over the Louisiana landscape. To the west, the sun started its gentle caress of the horizon, making the sky blush with soft shades of orange.

We walked across the neatly cut grass, heading for the rear of the grounds. Here and there, bright yellow dandelion flowers poked their golden heads up out of the rolling sea of green, the threat of a hundred floating white seeds just a few weeks away. Curving around the back of the last building, we went straight toward the bright red barn situated on the edge of the lawn.

One of the enormous barn doors slowly opened as we approached. A tall, skinny man in jeans and a Camp Pontchartrain t-shirt emerged. He flung the door open the rest of the way, then opened the other, mopping sweat from his shiny scalp with a cloth. It was Mr. Wallace, the groundskeeper.

"You must be the rebellious youths," he said. "I thought there were five of you."

"Yep. Five's the number." Bobby held his hand out, each finger extended. "I figured the others would be here already and—"

"Here they come." Mr. Wallace put away his handkerchief and pointed across the lawn. Leonard and Karl walked toward us, neither in a hurry.

I peered inside the barn. A large mirror hung on one of the doors, the wooden frame warped and cracked; it had been there for a long time.

A fleet of eight identical riding lawnmowers sat in a neat line on either side of the interior, a four-wheeler parked nearby. The forest-green machines dripped with water; Mr. Wallace had likely just hosed them down, keeping them clean and sparkling.

"Do you use all these mowers?" I asked.

"We don't use them daily, but workers come in and take the mowers out on grass-cutting day." The groundskeeper wiped at his forehead

46

again. "Each person is assigned part of the grass to cut, and we get it done as fast as possible. We don't want the noise of the mowers to interfere with any of the activities. That's why we have so many. 'Cut the grass quick;' that's our motto."

"That's not a very good slogan," Bobby said. "How about . . . umm . . . we slay the grass with our army of tanks, one blade at a time."

"What?" Mr. Wallace stared at Bobby, confused.

"Ignore him," I said. "Why don't you mow that section?" I pointed to the far end of the field, a section overrun with tall grass and weeds, nature reclaiming the land. On one side of the unkempt area stood the Crypt, rusted metal bars covering the stone entrance. Opposite the marble building, fifty yards through snarled thistles and tall clumps of devil grass sat the entrance to a cave, more decaying bars covering the shadowy opening. Much of the metal fence across both had fallen to the ground years ago, time and rust demanding their price. Between the barn and the Crypt area, gentle hills of grass stretched across the school grounds. They reminded me of smooth mounds of mint ice cream, tiny yellow flowers dotting the green surface like candies; I was a little hungry.

"That's the Crypt grounds. Not even me or my gardeners are allowed over there." Mr. Wallace lowered his voice. "You didn't hear this from me, but whenever I've been near that place, I feel like something's watching me."

"Watching?" Bobby leaned closer. "By whom?"

"Not who . . . but what." Mr. Wallace lowered his voice to barely a whisper. "You've heard the rumors, right? Strange sounds and funny lights floating around." He shook his head. "Sometimes, I wonder if the lights are the Le Feu Follets."

"You mean Cajun Fairies?" Elisa asked.

Mr. Wallace nodded.

I shuddered as my mind created monsters hiding in the tall grass and clumps of weeds. The talk about monsters from Louisiana's folklore made me nervous. *What if the stories are real?* I thought as I tried to push aside my fear. I didn't do a very good job.

"Creole superstitions?" I wiped the sweat from my forehead with the back of my hand as I tried to sound like none of this bothered me.

"Maybe superstitions, or maybe not," Elisa said, her voice serious.

I shuddered again.

"That place over there gives me the creeps." Mr. Wallace pointed to the stone wall and the overground area beyond. "I'm glad we don't have to cut the grass and manage the weeds. It's too spooky."

"BOO!"

My friends and I jumped.

"Ha ha ha, look at all of you, a bunch of scared babies." Karl laughed, a huge smile on his face. "You'd think you all saw a demon or somethin'."

Leonard stepped away from Karl, shaking his head as he moved to my side.

I glanced up at him and felt small, as usual. Even Elisa stood taller than me.

"Don't joke about demons, son." Mr. Wallace glared at Karl. "There've been demons and other nasty creatures of the night skulking around the bayous of New Orleans since long before your great-great-great-granddaddy was born."

"The mirror, it keeps the demons away?" Bobby asked.

Elisa nodded.

"Ahh . . . you know your Creole history, do ya, boy?" Mr. Wallace asked.

Bobby shrugged and flashed the groundskeeper a smile.

"Demons and monsters of the night are extremely vain," Mr. Wallace explained. "If they look into the mirror, they'll get caught admiring themselves and can't look away." He patted the mirror as if it were a beloved family member. "This protects my barn and all my precious mowers from those mischievous gremlins."

"Gremlins?" Karl laughed an angry laugh. "That's ridiculous."

"It's part of the Creole culture," Elisa said in a low voice. "I heard the same stories from my great-grandfather."

"Just a bunch of superstitious nonsense; that's what I think." Karl glared at the young girl, then stared at Bobby and me. "You'd have to be an idiot to believe all that nonsense."

Elisa sunk her head low, her posture slumped.

Now it was Mr. Wallace's turn to glare. "You need to show a little respect for other cultures, Mr. Baseball Player." He stared into Karl's eyes, waiting for him to look away.

Karl stared back for a moment, then lowered his gaze, the old man's stern expression putting the baseball captain in his place.

Mr. Wallace turned to the others. "Now, it's time to work. You'll be pulling dandelions across the lawn. I have tools and gloves in the buckets over there." He pointed to a line of five old, rusty buckets, then turned to Karl. "Make sure you return with a full bucket; slackers will get extra detention. Now, get to work."

We picked up their pales and headed across the grounds, plucking yellow dandelions as we walked. But as I pulled weeds, I had the strange feeling something was watching us, just like Mr. Wallace had said. Those hidden eyes peering at us had evil intent; I could feel it in the back of my mind. Was it that little red creature I'd seen before, or maybe something bigger and meaner?

I shuddered as my imagination created a host of hidden monsters, all watching me from the tall grass near the Crypt. As Dr. Jen had taught me, I told myself those imaginary creatures were a lie, but still, I felt something watching. Whoever, or whatever it was, it scared me.

The buzzing started in my head.

# Chapter 7 – Weeds and Monsters

**W**e spread out into a line and moved across the grounds like the front rank of an invading army, slaying all weeds in our path. The New Orleans heat pounded down upon us with a remorseless fist causing beads of sweat to trickle down my face, stinging my eyes, and leaving me feeling as if I were slowly melting. Each rivulet of moisture trickling down my back felt like a bug crawling across my skin. My imagination ran wild, conjuring up images of vicious fire ants or deadly spiders; *what-ifs* and *worst-case scenarios* filling my mind with dangers never present.

Ahead, on the other side of the grounds, stood the Crypt. An old stone wall, about waist high, kept watch over the overgrown tangle of weeds and bushes, marking the edge of the camp and the beginning of the forbidden territory. Stones of every size and shape formed the barrier, cement trying desperately to hold the wall together, though doing a poor job. Time had caused the cement to flake and crumble, letting many of the stones succumb to gravity's caress and fall to the ground.

At the other end of the wall stood a cave entrance, a dark and ominous passage plunging into the heart of a tall hill. The opening was like the shadowy maw of some toothless beast, a spooky sight that left me feeling uneasy. The darkness beyond the entrance seemed to swallow the light, making it impossible to see what lay within. This only served to make the structure appear even more terrifying.

Students whispered theories about the dark cave, everyone curious of what lay hidden within, but it was instant expulsion to voyage into its shadowy depths. An old, rusted fence stood across the opening, keeping the curious at bay, but time and decay had loosened many a metal bar. Portions of the fence lay on the ground, the iron pieces enveloped by the growth of vines and weeds, leaving large openings for the curious and foolish. Across the top of the cave entrance stood a stone arc, the carved structure cracked and pitted with age. Seven hollowed-out spaces adorned the stone arc, each the same size and equally spaced. Some thought the recessions had, at one time, held something over the dark opening. Maybe a "danger" or "enter at your own risk" sign. But the more imaginative kids thought it had something to do with magic, though I thought that was ridiculous. No one really knew what those seven depressions across the cave entrance meant.

Bobby made funny comments, of course, as he bent over to grab the weeds, trying lighten the mood, but the tension between the athletes and the Techies felt toxic. Karl cast angry glances at me whenever possible, creating a lurking sense of fear that added to the dread I felt from the hidden eyes watching us. The all-too-familiar buzzing echoed in my mind, the rage on the baseball player's face feeding my Beast.

Elisa glanced at me and gave a strained smile. "Look at the Moon. It's kinda weird seeing it like that before the sun fully sets."

It was late, and the western horizon had started its colorful symphony of reds and oranges, the blue sky to the east fading into a dark purple. Only a portion of the moon stood visible over the horizon, its speckled face staring at us as if we were the most important kids in the world.

I knew Elisa was trying to distract me, likely seeing the tension on my face.

"It looks bigger than normal." Leonard glanced at me. "Why is that? Is it just an optical illusion?"

"No, we're approaching a Super Blood Moon." The buzzing in my head started to fade, though the feeling of being watched persisted. "It's because the Earth and Moon are getting closer to each other. Tomorrow, they'll be at their closest, and the Moon will look about fourteen percent bigger. That's why it looks bigger right now."

"Cool." Leonard bent over and grabbed a clump of weeds, and pulled, throwing his victims into his pail.

"Who cares about stupid stuff like the Moon? I should be working on my curveball." Karl dropped his bucket and stretched his back. "We're all here because of you, Techie. And if I were you, I'd—"

Something red flashed through the tall grass around the Crypt.

"Did you see that?" My words came out fast, like bullets from a machine gun. I knelt and lowered my voice. "Everyone, get down. It's back."

"What are you talking about, Cameron." Elisa moved to my side and crouched.

"Everyone, get down and be quiet." I motioned for everyone to get on the ground as I laid on my stomach.

Bobby and Elisa did what I asked, but of course, Karl remained standing.

Leonard moved closer to me and knelt on one knee. "What's this all about?"

A bird screeched from a nearby tree, making me flinch.

"On the ropes course, I didn't laugh at you. I laughed at something I saw in the grass right over there." I pointed at the tall grass near an ancient stone wall. "And it's back."

A splash of red moved through the weeds, its crimson hue rising through the tangle of devil grass and shrubs for a moment, then submerging again, the overgrown plants swaying in its wake.

"I saw it," Elisa whispered. "What was that?"

"I don't know. I thought I was dreaming before, but now I know it's real." I glanced at Leonard, motioning him to get on the ground. The tall boy nodded and laid down on the grass.

"You all look like stupid idiots." Karl glanced back at the barn. Mr. Wallace was nowhere to be seen. "I'm out of here. I'll see you losers back at the barn in an hour." He reached into my bucket, grabbed a handful of weeds, and dropped them into his own.

"Hey. You can't—" Bobby started to say, but I shushed him.

"Shhh . . . be quiet, or we'll scare it away." I waved at Karl as if shooing away a fly. "Whatever, go, I don't care."

Karl laughed, then headed toward a huge Magnolia tree, its fragrant white flowers swaying in the hot breeze, adding a hint of sweetness to the humid air. He sat down, leaning against the thick trunk, and closed his eyes, choosing sleep over helping us.

"What do you think you saw?" Leonard glanced at me, then back to the tall grass.

Just then, a red creature no bigger than a toddler rose into the air. Its crimson wings flapped hard as it gained more height. A long, pointed tail writhed like a snake, helping to keep the creature balanced as it rose higher. Two tiny horns protruded from his hairless head, the red skin covering its body looking scratched and tough. Slowly, it settled to the ground and disappeared into the sea of wild grass. Clumps of weeds bent aside as the creature moved toward the Crypt and vanished into the shadows.

"Did all of you see that?" Bobby's voice rose in volume.

"Shhh . . . keep your voice down," I said.

"Sorry."

A loud crack pierced the air, silencing a squawking bird perched nearby.

"What was that?" I shuddered, the buzzing in my head coming back to life.

"It sounded like the crack of a whip." Leonard rose off his belly and crouched. "Let's get closer."

"You sure that's a good idea?" Elisa asked.

Leonard didn't respond. Instead, he moved toward the stone wall, staying as low as possible. "Come on, everyone, keep up. Let's see what's going on."

With a sense of unease, I moved toward the forbidden area. The air around me seemed to thicken, warning me to turn back before it was too late. I wanted to obey and turn away but knew I couldn't abandon my friends. With clenched teeth, I continued toward the riot of weeds and out-of-control grass.

The buzzing in my head grew louder.

We gathered near the metallic gate built into the stone wall, the metal covered with a reddish layer of rust. Just beyond the wall stood the ominous marble structure housing the bodies of the camp's past directors.

"Why do you think Mr. Wallace doesn't mow the grass here?" Leonard asked.

"I think he's spooked by the spooks in the Crypt, you know, ghosts and stuff." Bobby made a ghostly sound, "oooOOOoo."

"Stop clowning around and—" The cracking of a whip silenced Leonard.

"Dig faster, Fool," a deep, scratchy voice said. "Malphas awaits the completion of our task."

"Yes, sir," a high-pitched voice said, its words quivering with fear. *CRACK.* "Ouch!"

"I said dig," the deep voice said. "We need a larger opening to get more monsters in there to search for the second Skull Key."

"Yes, Krak," the high-pitched voice replied.

A scraping sound, like something hard tearing into stone, floated out of the Crypt.

"What's in there? What's . . . digging?" Elisa glanced at me, her arms shaking. She looked scared.

I shrugged, trying to hide my fear, but my quivering voice gave it away. "I don't know, b-b-but I don't l-l-like the sound of it."

"We need to go see what it is." Leonard stood and moved to the gate.

"Are you kidding?" Elisa shook her head. "We have no idea who's in there."

"Not who . . . what." My voice cracked with fear.

"We all saw that red creature," Leonard said, "but it was far away. We need a closer look." He glanced down at me. "This could be the scientific discovery of the century. We're making history right now." Leonard glanced at the Crypt again, then back at us. "What do you all want to do?"

"I don't know." Elisa shook her head, uncertain.

The buzzing in my head kept me from saying anything. I didn't want to awaken the Beast, so I stared at the ground, feeling like a coward.

"I say we go check it out." Leonard's deep voice sounded assured and brave, the echo of leadership resonating in his words, though his eyes looked sullen and sad. "We gotta take a chance." He knelt and stared straight at me. "There's an old Latin proverb: 'Fortune favors the bold.' You know what it means?"

"Sure." I nodded. "It means no risk, no reward."

"Right. We *need* to do this," Bobby said. "It's easy to make the safe choice, but we'll end up regretting the choices we didn't make because we bowed to our fear." Bobby glanced at me. "Let's do it." Bobby stuck his hand out and spoke in a deep, profound voice. "Together 'till the end." He held his hand there for a moment, glancing from person to person, then slowly lowered it. "We're supposed to put our hands out together, you know, like the 'Three Musketeers.'"

"Together 'till the end? That's the best saying you could come up with?" Leonard shook his head. "It sounds like we're all gonna die."

"Well . . . I guess when you say it out loud, it does sound kinda bad." Bobby chuckled.

"It does." I nodded.

"Yeah, I guess you're right." Bobby smiled. "I'll think of a better saying next time."

"Let's go." Leonard grabbed the metal gate with both hands and pulled it open. The hinges screeched, the layers of rust and decay screaming to the world in a grating chorus, making the many years of neglect known to all.

My Beast stirred in the dark places of my mind, awakening.

The digging within the Crypt stopped.

"What was that?" the deep, scratchy voice said.

"I don't know, maybe it was—"

The deep voice grew louder. "Imp, follow me."

54

"Everyone, duck." Leonard fell to a knee, as did the rest of us.

I crouched behind the stone wall, my head hidden by a large clump of weeds. Peeking just over the rocky barricade, I watched the entrance to the Crypt, then gasped. A small creature with huge, pointed ears and long, muscular arms stepped out of the structure. Its skin was a rusty color, with jagged scars across its hairless chest and shoulders, evidence of the countless battles it had survived. This was obviously a creature of violence.

The buzzing in my head grew even louder.

Elisa gasped. "A gremlin, just like my great grampa described," she whispered.

Fear prickled under my skin like a thousand tiny shards of glass, sending a chill down my spine. The hairs on the back of my neck stood straight up, and my heart pounded in my chest. The atmosphere around me seemed to thicken and constrict as if the air were alive with a sense of danger and evil.

I shuddered.

*That looks like that creature from that Gremlins movie my parents made me watch last year,* I thought. *How is this possible?*

"I don't see anything," the creature said. The deep, scratchy voice seemed out of character for such a small body. Leather straps crisscrossed the monster's chest. In one hand, the gremlin held a vicious-looking whip. In the other, it held a large green stone, its polished surface shaped like a human skull. Behind him, the little red creature stepped out of the Crypt, a tool looking like a clawed stone hand in its grip. Its wings flapped nervously as its red tail thrashed about.

Bobby gasped, then clasped a hand over his mouth, hoping to stifle the sound that had already escaped. But it was too late.

"By the wall," the gremlin said.

The whip cracked through the air, hitting the wall and causing rocky shards to fly into the air. One of the small pieces of stone sliced across my cheek, stinging.

"Let's get out of here." Elisa stood and ran.

The creature brought the whip back and aimed for Elisa.

"No!" I stood, reached into my pocket, and pulled out a small, metallic ball. Flipping the switch on the bottom, I tossed it at the terrifying creatures. It landed in front of the gremlin. A second later, the lid flipped open. Darts shot into the air, a thin strand of silvery wire trailing each. Two of the pointed barbs

hit the terrible monster. Sparks danced along the wires and gave the creature a painful shock, causing it to drop its whip. It shrieked in pain.

"Let's go." Leonard stood and pushed me away from the wall. "Run . . . RUN!"

As we ran, I heard the tiny, winged monster's voice.

"Krak, are you okay?" A crunching sound, then the painful cries of the gremlin ceased.

"Let's go back," one of the monsters said. "We must tell Malphas and . . ."

The creature's voice faded away, lost to the pounding of my heart as I sprinted across the rolling hills.

We headed for the back door of the nearest building—the administrative offices. We ran as fast as our legs would carry us, Leonard making it to our goal first, of course. He stood next to the back door, catching his breath. When Bobby, Elisa, and I finally reached his side, Leonard reached for the door. But before he touched the handle, the door swung open, revealing Mrs. Chakoté, her crooked, wooden cane in her hand.

"In my office, now," Chakoté said in a soft, emotionless voice, the lack of anger making her words seem even more terrifying. She stared at us for a moment longer, then glanced toward the Crypt grounds. With a nod, she turned and headed to her office, her cane tapping the floor with every step.

I glanced at Elisa and swallowed; my throat parched. Nothing good would happen when we reached Mrs. Chakoté's office.

Dr. Jen's voice popped into my head: *What's the worst thing that could happen, and is it realistic?*

*The worst thing,* I thought. *How about getting expelled from Camp Pontchartrain? Then my parents, in their anger, would kick me out of the house. I won't have any place to live.* I knew that wasn't very likely, but my anxiety stayed fixed on it, *worst-case scenarios* playing through my head.

The angry hornets punished me from inside my mind as my thoughts grew darker and darker, the thought-loop feeding itself as it slowly awakened my Beast. Images of those two monsters, mixed with Chakoté's impending reprimand and punishment, surged through my head. The more I focused on it, the worse the scenario became in my mind. I shuddered, knowing I couldn't do anything about this other than suffer.

# Chapter 8 – Order of the Stones

I followed the others into Mrs. Chakoté's office like a condemned prisoner heading for my execution.

*Are we about to get in trouble, all because of me? If I hadn't pointed out that little red monster, we would have never gone to the stone wall to investigate. What if Mrs. Chakoté expels us for being near the Crypt? What if she calls my parents? What if . . .* The *what-ifs* ran wild through my mind, the *ANTs* slowly crushing any remaining hope. I tried box breathing, inhaling for a count of five, waiting for five, then exhaling for a slow five count, and repeated. As I breathed, I focused on my pulse and tried to slow it down, but my heart didn't obey. It pounded in my ears like a huge bass drum, skin prickling with dread as if it itched from the inside.

I shuddered as we crowded into her small office and sat on an old, gray sofa, the material scratchy and rough. The furniture, meant for three, proved to be a tight fit for the four of us, Leonard's muscular bulk and Bobby's size, making it uncomfortable.

Slowly, I brought my gaze from the ground to Mrs. Chakoté, expecting to see an angry scowl, but to my surprise, she didn't look mad. Instead, the old woman seemed . . . scared.

Her worried gaze bored into us, then a questioning eyebrow raised. "Where's Karl?"

"He thought a nap under a tree would be a better use of his time," Bobby said.

"A nap, huh?" She glared at Bobby as if it were his fault. "We'll see about that."

Walking behind her desk, Mrs. Chakoté sat down and reached toward a large bookcase lining one wall. Countless volumes filled the shelves, the books organized by size like schoolchildren waiting for the bus. She slid a dusty, leather-bound book out from between two black tomes. A small cloud of dust puffed out when she dropped it onto her desk with a thud. Across the front, in gold letters, it said *Book of Stones*. Seven circles, each a different color, adorned the cover, their

hues faded with time. As she opened it, the leather binding creaked, complaining of the many years on the shelf.

Mrs. Chakoté brought her steely gaze to us. "Tell me what you saw by the Crypt." She flipped through the book, the binding creaking, and the pages stiff with age.

I glanced at my companions, each looking somewhere in the room other than toward Chakoté or me. Obviously, none of them wanted to speak, nor did I. No one would believe what we saw.

I swallowed, my throat dry and scratchy, like a crusty piece of sandpaper, and started to speak, but Elisa cut me off.

"We saw something impossible, like creatures from a fairy tale," she said. "One looked like a little flying devil, and the other had long, pointed ears and sharp teeth. They shouldn't exist . . . but they did. I've never seen these things before, but I've heard my grandparents and great-grandparents talk about them. I figured those tales were just a Creole thing, you know, like old stories and myths, but—"

"You saw an imp and a gremlin, and they *do* exist," Chakoté said. "And you're right; they're from old stories." Mrs. Chakoté flipped the book around and pushed it toward us. "That's because gremlins have been here for a long time. Here's a picture."

We stood and gathered around the book to see the image. It showed a small creature with long, muscular arms, terrible-looking claws at the end of each finger and toe, needle-like teeth, and large, pointed ears. Its skin looked like the color of dried blood, rough and leathery.

I shuddered.

"Have you ever lost something and searched everywhere for it but couldn't find it?" Chakoté asked.

"Sure," we replied.

"And then you looked in the place you just checked, and suddenly the object was back where you put it?"

"Hey, yeah, that happened to me last week during robotics class," Bobby said.

"Gremlin children think that's funny. They do it all the time." Chakoté frowned. "The smallest Agarthan creatures can come to Earth and cause mischief, then return to their world any time they want. It's like a game to them."

Bobby looked up from the book. "But I didn't see any gremlins in the robotics class."

"That's right, Bobby, you saw nothing." Chakoté stepped out from behind the desk and stood next to Elisa. "When you stare straight at a gremlin or imp or goblin or any of the other creatures of Agartha, you can't see them. But out of the corner of your eye, you can."

"Is that why sometimes I think there's something there, but when I turn, I see nothing?" I asked.

The old woman nodded, then tapped her cane on the floor. "Yes, we can see them with our peripheral vision, you know, at the edge of our sight."

"But Mrs. Chakoté, we stared straight at those monsters near the Crypt, and we all saw them." Leonard turned the page of the book. An image of an imp stared at us from the yellowed parchment, the small devil-looking creature fully equipped with horns and a pointed tail but also with claws and tiny wings.

The color of its skin reminded me of the roses my mom liked so much.

"That's exactly why I'm concerned, Leonard. It can only mean one thing, and that thought terrifies me." She scowled down at the image of the page.

"Why does this terrify you?" I knew the answer wouldn't be good. The hornets grew restless in the back of my mind. "What's so bad about seeing a gremlin and an imp?"

"Kids, sit down. Let me tell you a story." Mrs. Chakoté motioned to the sofa, and we all squeezed back on, me crushed against the arm.

"Long, long ago, many centuries before the French came to this part of Louisiana, Earth was aligned with another world from a parallel universe. That world is called Agartha. Many doorways connected the two worlds, they always existed underground on the Earth side, in a deep cave or tunnel." She flipped through the book's pages until she found an image of many creatures. Holding it up, she showed it to the kids. "Agartha is filled with gremlins and imps, as you know, but also goblins, gnomes, banshees, harpies, faeries, elves . . ."

"All the creatures from fables and fairytales?" Bobby asked.

Mrs. Chakoté nodded her head. "Yes, but you must realize . . . many of those stories are true."

"Like Odysseus fighting a cyclops?" Leonard asked.

"Or Perseus battling with Medusa?" I glanced at Chakoté, fear nibbling at the edge of my senses. *What if, somehow, Medusa was still alive?* The hornets grew louder.

Mrs. Chakoté raised a hand, silencing us. "You see, all these creatures are real, and many centuries ago, when our worlds were

more closely aligned, they could pass back and forth through the doorways. This is why they live in our ancient histories and fables . . . they were here."

"But not anymore, right?" Leonard asked.

"Correct. Only gremlin children can move from world to world, but not anything else. Occasionally, the planets align again, and the doorways open, but only for a short time. The last time this happened was in 1788, and the Agarthans brought nothing but destruction."

"The Great New Orleans Fire." Elisa's words came out soft and tense. "I've heard stories about it."

The old woman nodded. "That's right, Elisa." Chakoté ran her fingers through her long, gray hair. "The Agarthans caused the Great New Orleans Fire and many other tragedies across Earth. There's a group of people who've dedicated their lives to combatting the creatures of Agartha." She reached into her blouse and pulled out a necklace. It featured a silver bar hanging from a delicate silver chain, seven colorful stones mounted into the shiny metal. "We're called the Order of the Stones. We watch, we train our children, and we prepare."

"So, let's call *them*." Bobby stood as if he'd solved the problem. "Let this Order of Rocks take care of it."

"It's the *Order of the Stones,* and we've been expecting something to happen soon. The risk is always the highest during a Blood Moon. The Council expected a gateway to open near Salt Lake City. They sent our warriors there." She put the necklace back under her blouse. "I'm the only one of the Order still here, but I'm old and no longer the warrior I used to be."

"Warrior . . . you?" My voice rose with surprise.

"Yes, me." She scowled, making me lower my gaze.

"Now, listen carefully." Mrs. Chakoté moved closer and lowered her voice. "You've seen an imp and a gremlin, and they've seen you. They have your scent now. Likely, they'll send more creatures through the doorway to find the seven Skull Keys. With these stone skulls, the Agarthans can keep the doorway between worlds open forever. But since they have your scent now, they'll send creatures after you four. The Agarthans will be afraid that you may alert the Order, or maybe the army, or . . . I don't know; Agarthans can be a bit paranoid. They'll see you as a threat that must be eliminated. Whether you want to be part of this or not, you are. The creatures of Agartha don't care about you or me or anyone on Earth. They just want to come here and cause chaos, or worse. You four must help me stop them."

"But we can't do anything." Elisa shook her head. "We aren't warriors; we're just kids."

"We are who we believe we can be," Bobby said, his voice strong and confident.

"Very true, Bobby, very true." The old woman cast Bobby a smile.

"I don't know." I shook my head. "We can't fight those things. We might get in trouble."

"I'm the director of this camp, Cameron. Nothing will happen to you."

"But what if something bad happens?" I glanced at my friends. "We could still get in trouble with the other camp counselors."

Chakoté rolled her eyes. "There are more important things going on here."

"If they're so important, why don't you call the police or the army?" Leonard leaned forward, staring at the old woman.

"You and I both know they'd never believe us." Chakoté shook her head. "No, *we* must deal with it, or many will suffer."

"But why us?" Elisa asked. "You could get some of the older kids to help."

"Because you were chosen." Mrs. Chakoté stepped around her desk and stood in front of us. She grabbed the gnarled handle of her cane and slid it closer, then held the crooked staff in front of Leonard; the purple Amethyst stone embedded in the cane gave off a lavender glow. She then moved the cane to Bobby. The Green Aventurine stone glowed with an emerald hue. Leaning the cane toward Elisa, the Carnelian stone blushed, painting the walls with an orange tint. Finally, Mrs. Chakoté pointed the wooden shaft at me. The quartz stone, clear as glass, burst with bright white light, the glare too intense for my eyes.

The director lowered her cane, the stone dimming until it was just a decorative thing again.

"One thing you must realize about the Order of the Stones: our chief weapon is magic, Earth-magic to be specific." Chakoté paused, waiting for our questions.

"Magic . . . really?" Bobby said. "Come on, that's kinda far-fetched, don't you think?"

Mrs. Chakoté shook her head. "The Order of the Stones comprises many people, each with a specific skill. We're closely linked to the magic that lives within the Earth, and we've learned how to wield that power."

"You mean you can put an enchantment on someone?" Elisa asked, her eyes sparkling with excitement.

The old woman shook her head. "People who can cast spells and enchantments are called Casters. I'm not one of them. I'm a Warrior of the Order, and I can use enchanted weapons."

She held her cane up for a moment, her wrinkled hand gripping it tightly. With a sudden movement, she brought the tip of the cane down to the floor, the sound of the impact exploding through the room. As the crooked wood hit the ground, a burst of energy shot forth from the colorful Chakra stones embedded along its length. The blast of light was so intense, brighter than the sun, that it dazzled my eyes and left me momentarily blinded. The air around us crackled from the raw power of the blast, and I felt the energy coursing through the room like an electrical current. As the light faded and my sight returned, I looked up at Mrs. Chakoté with awe.

Chakoté pulled a lock of gray hair out of her face and tucked it behind an ear. "Earth-magic is almost like a living thing. It must have felt the barrier between Earth and Agartha getting thinner. The magic of the Earth brought you five together for a reason." She moved back around her desk and sat, her cane still in her hand. "The Earth chose the five of you to defend New Orleans against this threat."

"This all sounds ridiculous," Leonard said. "I don't believe in magic. I believe in things I can touch or feel."

"Can you feel the Earth rotating or moving around the sun?" Chakoté asked. "We know it happens, but we can't feel it. It's the same with magic. Just because you can't see or feel something, that doesn't mean it's not there."

Leonard nodded and remained silent.

"You may not know there's Earth-magic in your cells, but it's there, or you wouldn't have been chosen. Someday, you might learn how to use your magic and become Casters for the Order of the Stones. For now, you're our only hope."

"What about Karl?" Elisa asked.

Chakoté nodded. "He has it as well, though I doubt he'll believe it." She took a drink from a bottle of water and continued. "Many centuries ago, the Order sent its strongest Casters to the many gateways across the Earth. Using magic from the gateway, they formed the skull keys, making the Keys forever linked to their specific doorway. These keys would let us close the After the Great New Orleans Fire, the Order hid the Skull Keys here in the catacombs and caverns under the Crypt. They did this for all the gateways across the globe. The Demon Lord has chosen the doorway at Camp Pontchartrain as his target. That terrible monster will surely send his minions into the tunnels searching for them. If he can find all seven Skull Keys, he can keep the doorway between Earth and Agartha open forever."

"Why not just take the Skull Keys to the farthest reaches on Earth?" Bobby asked. "You could put one on top of Mount Everest, maybe throw one in a volcano, dump some in the deepest part of the ocean, and—"

Mrs. Chakoté raised a hand, stopping Bobby. "Because the magic in the Skull Keys came from the doorway, we cannot move the Keys very far away. Casters tried to break the connection between the keys and the doorway, but it proved impossible. Our only choice was to hide them from the monsters of Agartha. We dug the catacombs under the Crypt and hid them as best we could, surrounding the skulls with lethal traps." She took a deep breath and moved her gaze across each of us, a sympathetic expression on her face. "If you can find the Keys and protect them, the doorway will close at the end of the Super Blood Moon tomorrow night, and we'll have stopped the Agarthans. But if we fail, the largest creatures of Agartha will be able to pass through to Earth and stay here forever."

I shuddered. This whole thing terrified me. *What if those monsters attack us? What if the gremlin uses that whip on us, or maybe its claws, or . . .* Every possible and impossible negative thought automatically cycled through my head. The *ANTs* gnawed at my courage until the only thing left was a hollow emptiness within my chest. I felt like a coward before anything had even happened.

*I'm pathetic.*

"You kids can decide what you want to do after dinner. I won't force you to help me." Mrs. Chakoté leaned her cane against the desk, then grabbed the ancient book and slammed it closed.

*BAM*

The sound made us jump with a start.

"If I must battle these creatures alone, then so be it. For now, go rest." She replaced the heavy book to the bookshelf, then grabbed her cane and tapped it lightly on the ground. The colored stones flashed, each splashing a bit of color on the dreary walls of her office.

"After dinner, I need all of you to search for the Skull Keys in the catacombs under the

Crypt, if you're up to this challenge. You must keep these keys from the Agarthans. If they find all seven, they'll keep the doorway between worlds open forever. The Demon Lord of Agartha will order his forces to destroy Camp Pontchartrain, then New Orleans, then . . . who knows how much they'll annihilate." Chakoté pulled strands of gray hair from her face and tucked them behind an ear, her body tense. "I have much to do and little time to do it." She leaned across the desk and stared at us. "Make no mistake, dire times are on our doorstep, and I doubt I can stop the Agarthans all alone. But I'll try if I must." Mrs. Chakoté pointed to the door. "I'll have some supplies that might prove helpful for your search. They'll be waiting for you at the barn, so stop there first before heading for the Crypt. But know this—if the Demon Lord gets hold of a certain item within these supplies, it'll be over, and the Agarthans will win."

"What's so important?" I asked as I ran my fingers through my hair, feeling nervous.

"You'll know when you see it, and you'll realize why it's so important." Mrs. Chakoté leaned forward, her piercing grey eyes boring into me. "Destroy it before letting Malphas have it . . . understood?"

I nodded.

"Good." Chakoté stood and tapped her cane on the ground, signifying the meeting was over. "Now, go get some rest. Dinner will start soon."

We left her office and headed for our cabins, each of us silently processing what we had just learned.

What I'd seen by the Crypt was both exhilarating and terrifying. I had a choice to make: try to stop the monsters from Agartha or hide in the shadows and let them burn New Orleans and Camp Pontchartrain to the ground as they did two hundred and thirty-seven years ago.

Instead of going to my cabin to rest, I headed for the library building. Kids filled the chairs and sofas, many goofing off. The librarians tried desperately to maintain control, but it looked like a losing battle.

With a shudder, I sat in a deserted corner, hopefully out of sight from those who'd pick on me just because they could. Closing my eyes, I brought up the memory of the gremlin and imp. Thoughts of what *might* happen filled me with dread.

But then, I felt an evil presence lingering at the edge of my senses. It was something dark and terrible, a creature of pure evil somehow watching me. An eerie chill crept over me, the biting cold stabbing at me from within.

*Was it another Agarthan? How can it be watching me from its home world if the gateway isn't open yet?*

The thought triggered multiple *ANTs* and *what-ifs*, a storm of growing terror filling my mind. Daggers of fear stabbed at my courage as the buzzing in my ears grew louder. Using the breathing exercises I learned from Dr. Jen, I slowed my heart a little. I tried to ignore the *ANTs* and pretended to be brave, but I knew everyone in the library could probably see my fear, my cowardice. Gradually, my anxiety faded a little, though I still shook with fright. But then, I felt the red eyes of that evil presence turn and focus on me.

"It knows we're here," I whispered to myself, "and it's coming… soon."

# Chapter 9 – Demon Lord's Plan

**M**alphas gave his demon-magic another push as he probed through the gateway and to Earth with his mind. He felt many pathetic minds, none glowing with Earth-magic. A bright stab of pain slashed at him through the portal. He'd found someone with magic, a lot of it.

*It must be one of the Order's greatest Casters,* the demon thought.

Gritting his teeth, Malphas extended his magic toward his enemy, trying to sense his power and skill, but all he felt was confusion and fear . . . strange. And then the words *ANTs* and *what-ifs* drifted through the connection, confusing the Demon Lord even more.

"This isn't a great Caster or Warrior of the Order; it's just an Earther who doesn't know how to use their magic." A smile stretched across his bird-like face as he opened his eyes and released his demon-magic. "Good. I'll destroy him first, just in case."

A flash of light attracted his attention. The Demon Lord spotted Krak and Rylee as they stepped through the gateway and back into Agartha. With a powerful beat of his enormous wings, the demon lifted off his perch high atop the castle wall, his dark form merging with the dull, grey sky. He glided silently through the air, eddies of ash circling the tips of his wings. When he landed, Malphas's eyes fixed on the two monsters before him, a perpetual scowl carved into his raven-like face.

"Why have you returned so soon?" Malphas asked. "The moon hasn't set on Earth yet."

"Humans attacked us, my master." Krak's eyes glowed red, signifying he was still under the demons' influence. But it didn't stop the gremlin from lying; it was something they did. Gremlins can't tell the difference between a lie and the truth.

"Attacked? By how many?" Malphas paced back and forth, his huge bird feet kicking up small clouds of soot and ash.

"At least a dozen, maybe more." Krak glanced at Rylee and shook his whip, warning the imp to stay silent. "We fought them off as we made our way back to the cave, so we could return to Agartha and report to you, my master."

Malphas clenched his hand into a fist and shook it in the air. "They must know my plans and are preparing." The demon turned and glanced at his minions. The smallest inhabitants of Agartha gathered near, for they were the only ones who could pass through the doorway without all the Skull Keys in place. He turned to Rylee. "Did you dig through the wall inside the House of the Dead?"

Rylee bowed. "Yes, master. I found a series of tunnels hidden beneath the structure, just where you predicted."

"Master, we found the first Skull Key." Krak bowed, a hideous, toothy smile creeping across his face.

"What?" Malphas flapped his wings, rising a foot into the air, then settled back on the ground. "Which did you find . . . the Skull of Fear?"

Krak straightened and shook his head. "No, my master, it was the green one, the Skull of Life. It was closest to the entrance of the catacombs, and we found it in perfect condition. The humans may have tried to destroy it, but they were unsuccessful. That's likely why they hid them instead, but I found the first skull's location." The gremlin glanced at Rylee and shook his whip ever so slightly again.

"Good work, gremlin. What did you do with it?"

"I placed it in its location over the cave entrance. It's locked into place, the magic of Agartha holding it there." Krak smiled again, his stained, needle-like teeth reflecting what little sunlight penetrated the gray sky overhead.

"Excellent. Now we can send more creatures through the doorway." Malphas glanced at his followers and smiled, which was challenging to do with a raven's beak for a mouth. "In fact, with the first Skull Key in place, it may be possible for me to cross over as well. With my demon-magic, the doorway should allow me to pass."

"Yes, my Master." Krak bowed.

Malphas flapped his midnight-black wings again and took to the air, a hurricane of ash lifting off the ground and enveloping his army. He gained altitude, then landed atop the remains of a stone wall. Glaring down at his subjects, his eyes flared blood-red, strengthening his control over them. A faint, high-pitched whine came from the demon, a side effect of his enslaving magic.

"We must speed up my plans. I want three imps, three gremlins, and four gargoyles to go through the doorway with me. We'll find more Skull Keys and use them to strengthen the gateway between the worlds, letting more Agarthans transit to Earth."

Krak flicked his wrist into the air, cracking his whip high overhead, then cheered, glaring at the rest of the monsters.

The congregation screeched and shouted their support, many of them glancing nervously at Krak and his whip.

Malphas extended his wings and shook them, demanding silence.

"Soon, my friends, we'll have a new world teeming with life. Agartha is nearly dead, but Earth will support us for centuries." Malphas raised his muscular arms into the air, clawed fingers spread wide. "Nothing is more important than finding the Keys. When you find a Skull Key, you must bring it to the cave entrance and put the skull in its place on the stone arch. I doubt the Earthers have the magical tools to pull the skulls from the gateway and steal the Keys, but we will still guard them. Let nothing deter you from this task."

He stomped his foot on the wall, part of the stone crumbling and falling to the ground under the piercing grip of his talons. "If any human tries to stop you, teach them what it means to suffer. The Earthers must learn who is in charge . . . and that's me!" He clenched his hands into angry fists. "The Super Blood Moon comes in one more day. During that eclipse, the doorway between worlds will open and stay open, but only if we have all the Skull Keys in place. Let no one stand in our way."

Malphas tilted his bird-head back and screeched into the air. Sparkling magic formed on his feathery body, then burst outward, covering his unwilling servants with glistening shards of fear. The Agarthans moaned and wailed as their own personal nightmares came to life within their minds, devouring their ability to think. Many fell to the ground and writhed in terrible agony. And as quickly as the magical wave of terror appeared, it disappeared; a cruel reminder of who was in charge.

As the monsters stood, Malphas swept his gaze across his subjects. "That's the smallest taste of what the Earthers will do to you if we fail. I will protect you against them, but success rides on your shoulders. You must find the keys." His eyes flared bright red again, cementing his control over his army. "No mercy."

"No mercy," his troops repeated.

"NO MERCY!" Malphas shouted.

"NO MERCY!!" his followers screamed, their eyes like glowing coals of hate.

"Go and prepare yourselves. Leave all metal behind and be ready for battle." Malphas leaped into the air and soared high, his mighty wings driving him faster and higher until he reached the summit of his newly captured castle. The Demon Lord settled at the top of the partially shattered marble dome, tucked his wings onto his back, and surveyed his kingdom. He'd destroyed the foolish King of Agartha and taken control of everything, but it wasn't enough. Malphas needed a new home for his army, and he wanted Earth. And as the previous Agarthan king learned, Malphas takes what he wants, and nothing will stop him from taking Earth.

# Chapter 10 – Decisions

**I** **walked from the library to the dining hall, a strange sensation** in the back of my head telling me someone, or something, was watching . . . and waiting. The creatures of Agartha dominated my mind; all those images of mythical creatures in Mrs. Chakoté's *Book of Stones* formed *what-ifs*, ready to ensnare my courage. Overhead, the moon cast a silvery light on the landscape, creating shadows with monster-shaped arms and demon-like outlines. Goosebumps crept down my spine as my imagination brought the shadowy forms to life in my head.

While in the library, I researched Agartha. Multiple websites littered the Internet, all telling the same tale . . . an ancient, mysterious city called Agartha buried deep within Earth's core. But I knew the truth; Agartha did not lie underground. The doorways leading to the mythical world lay hidden in dark tunnels and caves, but Agartha was another world in a parallel universe.

Something moved at the edge of my vision . . . or did it? Stopping, I quickly turned but found nothing.

*Are there gremlins here, or was it just my imagination?*

*What-ifs* surged through my thoughts, amplifying my fears. My Beast stirred. The buzzing had not yet pierced my ears, but I could feel it awakening. It was just a matter of time. The buzzing always came, no matter how much I wished it would disappear.

And the buzzing brought my Beast . . . every time.

I tried to resist the *ANTs*, using the strategies and breathing exercises Dr. Jen taught me over the years, but they never seemed to work. She frequently told me it was about positive and negative thoughts. If I expected the strategies to fail, then they would. I tried some positive self-talk.

*The fear is only temporary, and I can endure it.*

The sound of a mosquito buzzed in my ear. *Was it a real insect, or was the Beast awakening?*

I did a quick *4 – 7 – 8* breathing exercise and imagined my heartbeat slowing.

More positive self-talk went through my head, but the strategy failed; I had nothing positive within me . . . only hopeless negative thoughts. I had accepted, long ago, that my Beast would never let me do things the other kids could do.

*I hate my anxiety and the fact that I'm a failure!* The thought burned into me. The anger and frustration over being unable to deal with my fears made me feel like I was somehow broken. Dr. Jen told me it's okay to be mad at my anxiety when it gets out of control, which seems to be always, but I need to tame my Beast, somehow. *I'm not gonna give in… not this time.*

I stepped into the dining hall, my stomach grumbling, and scanned the crowd, hoping the bullies had some other target to entertain themselves. At that moment, some wrestlers were making fun of the dancers, doing a ridiculous, uncoordinated dance to mock their recent performance. The camp counselors told the wrestlers to stop, ending the abuse, but the damage had been done. Many of the dancers held their heads down, humiliated.

"Hey, Cameron . . . over here," Bobby shouted.

Some of the art students looked my way and glared. The Arties, as they were called, sat clustered together in a defensive formation near the door, their multicolored shirts marking the boundaries of their territory.

I took a plate, spooned macaroni and cheese onto it, and then headed for my friend. Bobby sat in the corner of the dining hall at the table the rest of the students called the *Island of Misfit Toys*, or just *Island* for short. It was our fortress of solitude, where the geeks, nerds, and weirdos sat together—safety in numbers. Strangely enough, no one sat there except for Bobby. Our robotics friends, the Techies, weren't there, nor were the Number-heads (math kids) or Science-geeks. Bobby sat at the Island with his always-present grin, alone, the rest of the table empty.

"Where is everyone?" I scanned the dining hall and found the other Techies and Number-heads on the opposite side of the room. They looked away, pretending not to notice me. "Why are they over there?"

"Word must have gotten out about our detention with Leonard and Karl." Bobby glanced around the room, smiling at all his observers. "I bet they're waiting for the athletes to drop the hammer and punish us with a food attack . . . or worse."

I nodded, then sat and ate a spoonful of mac and cheese. When I looked up, I found Elisa standing there, her tray filled with salad, fruit, and a carton of milk. She sat across from me and lowered her voice.

"The other archers wouldn't let me sit with them. They heard about our detention

71

and didn't want to be seen with me. They're afraid they'll get caught in the crossfire of the food fight they're certain will happen." She popped a handful of grapes into her mouth.

"Who do you think told everyone about the detention?" I took another bite of mac and cheese and saw something from the corner of my eye. I turned quickly, expecting to find a gremlin, but instead, I found Karl Macarthur standing up, wagging a finger in our direction. "Yeah, I know who . . . it was Karl."

The baseball player waved, gave me a malicious grin, and then sat down again.

I glared at the baseball cabin leader and then spotted Leonard coming into the dining hall. The huge sixth-grader grabbed a plate of food and walked toward us. As he approached, the other athletes watched him, their expressions filled with confusion and curiosity. Their murmurs echoed through the hall and grew louder as he made his way to our table. Leonard set his tray down next to Elisa and sat, the dining hall buzzing with confused comments.

I leaned forward and spoke in a quiet voice. "What are you doing?"

"Eating dinner." Leonard speared a cluster of carrots and stuffed them into his mouth.

"This is the Island. You don't have to sit here. You can sit with the athletes. In fact, you can sit anywhere." I glanced at Bobby and Elisa, confused.

"You don't want me here?" Leonard asked.

"It's not that." Bobby took a bite of his burger. "It's just . . . sitting with us isn't gonna help your reputation. People will think you wanna be a geek, like us."

"Who cares what people think." Leonard took a bit of lasagna, some of the thick sauce dripping off his fork, and landed on the table, barely missing his shirt.

"Spoken like someone on the top of the food chain." Bobby patted him on the back. "Welcome to the bottom rung of the social ladder. I hope you enjoy your stay with us."

"Whatever." Leonard shook his head. "We need to talk."

"I agree. Did all of you think about what Mrs. Chakoté told us?" Elisa finished her grapes and started on her salad.

"I don't know . . . I find it all a bit far-fetched," Leonard said. "Order of the Stones, her? Really?"

"I know what you mean," Elisa added. "I find her story about Agartha and all the mythical creatures a little hard to believe. Maybe we didn't *really* see anything near the Crypt. The heat might have been playing tricks on us or something."

"I believe her." Bobby glanced at me, then back to the other two. "We all know what we saw. We just don't want to accept it. Did you see the claws on that imp? I have no desire to meet that little guy inside the Crypt. I'm a Techie, not a warrior." He shook his head, then looked away.

"I did some research in the library," I said. "That fire Mrs. Chakoté mentioned, it was totally real. It happened in 1788, and it burned down ninety percent of New Orleans. People lost everything. Who knows how many died, but I bet it was a lot. Only six thousand people lived in New Orleans back then, but now, we have almost half a million. Many more people will die if we let the Agarthans burn down the city again."

Elisa reached out, put a hand on my arm, and shook her head. "We're just four kids. We can't do anything. Leonard is the only strong one here, and if he gets in trouble, he could get kicked out of the camp. That might affect him making it to the varsity football team when he gets to high school, and then he can kiss a college scholarship goodbye." She took a sip of milk. "If I get expelled from here, my dad will stop paying for all these archery lessons and coaches. That'll shatter his dream of me being in the Olympics. Archery is all I have."

"You have us," I mumbled.

She shrugged.

I shook my head. "I don't know. Ninety percent of New Orleans destroyed . . . do you want that on your conscience?"

Just then, a girl walked up to us and handed each a note, our names written in cursive across the front; it was Mrs. Chakoté's handwriting.

"What's this?" I asked.

The girl shrugged. "She said to give them to you, so I did."

Without waiting for a response, she spun around and walked to Karl, handing him a note as well. Karl took the scrap of paper and approached the Island. He unfolded the letter and read it, then clenched it in his fist.

"What did you say to her?" Karl scowled at me. "You guys are jerks. Did you get me in trouble? I told you earlier; I don't want any part of your stupid little adventure."

I stared down at my note, then unfolded and read it silently.

*In any moment of decision, the best thing you can do is the right thing, the next best thing is the wrong thing, and the worst thing you can do is nothing.*
*-- Theodore Roosevelt*

It was in Mrs. Chakoté's handwriting, and the message wasn't very subtle. She was telling me to do the right thing and help her stop the Agarthans.

"Read your notes," I said.

Each of the others read their messages from the camp director.

"Well?" I asked, glancing at my friends.

Leonard folded his note and stuffed it in a pocket. "Obviously, Mrs. Chakoté is trying to manipulate us into doing what she wants."

I read my note aloud, "In any moment of decision, the best thing you can do is the right thing, the next best thing is the wrong thing, and the worst thing you can do is nothing." I glanced at Leonard. "A quote from Theodore Roosevelt."

"Of course. Teddy Roosevelt was the twenty-sixth President of the United States, and . . ." Leonard's eyes seemed to brighten for just a moment, then he stopped speaking and lowered his gaze as if embarrassed.

"My, my, aren't you a little talking encyclopedia." Karl stared at Leonard and chuckled as he stepped closer, his note still in his fist.

Leonard didn't reply, keeping his eyes on the ground.

I folded my note and put it back into a pocket. "What did your notes say?"

Bobby pulled his out. "Mine said: 'You miss a hundred percent of the shots you don't take,' by someone named Wayne Gretzky, whoever that is."

"He's only the greatest ice hockey player of all time," Elisa said.

I looked at her, surprised.

She shrugged. "My dad loves ice hockey."

"What did yours say, Elisa?" I asked.

She sighed. "It's a Zen saying, 'Leap and a net will appear.' I think Mrs. Chakoté is telling me it's okay to take a risk." She turned to Leonard. "And yours?"

"It says, 'Service to others is the rent you pay for your room here on Earth.' It's from a famous boxer named Mohammed Ali. He was a great boxer, probably one of the best." Leonard lowered his hands to his side.

"Karl, what does your note say?" Elisa asked.

Karl uncrumpled the paper, glanced down at it, then folded it and shoved it into a pocket. "It says *none of your business*. I don't know what Chakoté said to you in her office, but you can count me out."

"But we have to—" Before I could continue, Karl turned his back on us and stormed away.

"We need to decide what we're gonna do." I glanced over my shoulder at Karl, then turned back to my friends. A buzzing sound flickered to life in the back of my head. "I'm going to the Crypt. I can't just stand by and let those creatures destroy everything again, including this camp. Pontchartrain is a second home for me; I know it's like that for all of you, too." I lowered my voice and turned to Bobby and Elisa. "You two are my oldest friends . . . no, my only friends. If the Agarthans destroy this place, I'll never see either of you again. Besides, all we gotta do is find those Skull Key things and keep them safe; that shouldn't be a big deal . . . right?"

No one spoke, the silence amplifying my anxiety a little. My heart pounded, heavy and tense, in my chest. I ran my fingers through my curly hair as the buzzing grew louder. Images of gremlins and imps popped into my head, followed by mythical monsters of every shape and size; the *ANTs* trying to feed my Beast.

I took a deep breath and tried to push the thoughts aside. *I know those fears are a lie, but they feel so real. What if the things I'm imagining really exist? What if they're out there, waiting for me?*

I sighed.

*I hate this. I hate being afraid all the time.* Moving a hand under the table, I clenched my fist, squeezing my hand tight until the knuckles popped. It surprised me, breaking the cycle of frightening images feeding my anxiety which, in turn, created more images.

I looked up at my friends. "Even though I'm scared, I'm not gonna let them take this place away from me, let them take all of you from me." I swallowed nervously. "I doubt I can do this on my own." Turning, I glanced at Bobby, then Elisa and Leonard. "Are any of you coming?"

They all lowered their gaze to the ground, each staying quiet.

I sighed again. "Okay, I get it. But if you change your mind and decide to help. I suggest you gather whatever you think will help fight against the imps and gremlins. I'll be at the barn, waiting, but not for long."

Before any of them could give me another excuse, I left the dining hall and headed for the Robotics class. Hopefully, I'll be able to get into the room and grab some of my electronic gadgets that might help against the monsters. Without my tech, I knew I wouldn't stand a chance against the monsters of Agartha.

As I walked across the school grounds, moonlight cut across the camp, creating sharp shadows. The dark outlines invaded my imagination, creating horrific creatures that stalked my courage like a lion after a gazelle. The *what-ifs* attacked, trying to awaken the terrible monster that hid in the dark recesses of my soul . . . my Beast. I had no doubt I'd be seeing him soon.

# Chapter 11 – Heroes Gather

**A** **hollow loneliness wrapped around me like a second skin**, making the air feel still and lifeless. Chirping birds stared down at me from tall magnolia trees, but the fear stalking my soul muffled their voices. A delicate breeze drifted across the landscape. I knew it should have carried the aroma of wildflowers and freshly cut grass, but everything smelled stale, my anxiety souring the sensation. Everything around me felt empty as I walked toward the barn. Fears and doubts invaded my brain, filling me with dark thoughts. In the distance, the barn looked empty, with no one standing nearby.

I was alone.

I had hoped the others would change their minds, but obviously, I'd been wrong. With my Beast always lurking nearby, it seemed doubtful I could see this through on my own, but I had to try.

The night felt deathly still. The only sound was the *swish-swish* of the thin rope hanging out of my backpack. The line swung back and forth, sparks dancing about the end. I carefully grabbed the line and pulled it from the pack, coiling it into a circle. At the center of the rope sat a small box, its indicator light glowing green.

*I can't believe I left it on; it could have electrocuted me.*

I flipped the switch on my invention, the lightning-rope, turning it off and stuffed it back into my bag with my other techie-gadgets.

Under the silvery light of the full moon, the ordinarily serene grounds around the camp took on a strange, magical appearance. With no clouds in the sky, the stars sparkled and shimmered overhead like jewels sewn into black velvet. On any other night, it would have seemed beautiful, but with the looming threat of a monster invasion from a parallel world, everything seemed a little dim and faded.

I reached the barn and found one of the bright red doors open. A large envelope hung taped to Mr. Wallace's mirror, my name written across the top. I set my backpack on the ground, my tech weapons in the bag clinking together. Reaching into the bag, I adjusted the shocker-balls, spread them out evenly, then pulled out the static-stunners and ensured I turned them off. Scanning the grounds, I hoped to spot one

77

of my friends coming to meet me, but the landscape sat empty; I was alone.

Sighing, I pulled the envelope off the mirror and looked inside. It contained a laminated map, and five necklaces, each with a different colored stone hanging from the end. In addition, a pile of flashlights sat on the ground, their black shapes barely visible in the moonlight.

I glanced down at the pendants and found one with my name scrawled on a small scrap of paper.

"I guess this one is mine." I pulled the paper from the cord and held the stone to my eyes. The clear stone looked like quartz, with one side perfectly smooth and the other decorated with an ornate pattern carved into its face. For a moment, I thought I heard a humming sound leaking from the stone.

"Mrs. Chakoté must have given these to us for a reason." I put the pendant over my head and tucked the stone under my shirt.

"Given *what* to us?" a voice said from behind.

Turning, I found Elisa and Bobby smiling at me.

"Do we get jewelry too?" Elisa set her bow and quiver of arrows on the ground. She glanced at the necklaces and squealed. "Oooo, I like this one." She turned to Bobby. "It even has my name on it." She tore the tiny paper off the leather cord, lowered the orange stone over her head, and then grabbed the green one. "This one's for you." Elisa tossed it to Bobby.

Bobby set his backpack on the ground, a long black tube sticking out of the top. He pulled the little paper from the cord and held the stone to his eyes. It glowed as if lit from within, giving off a splash of soft, emerald light. Bobby put the cord around his neck, letting the green stone dangle outside his shirt.

"Why is my necklace glowing?" Bobby asked.

Elisa shrugged. "I don't know."

"I think I know." I pointed to the cave on the far side of the grounds. A green skull sat above the entrance, glowing the same color as Bobby's pendant. "They already found one of the skull keys and stuck it over the cave." I turned back to my friends. "I guess we know what those recessions are for over that dark entrance. We need to hurry."

"Hurry for what?" a deep voice asked.

"He's here!" Elisa said.

I spun around. Leonard stood just outside the barn, a hockey stick in one hand, football pads in the other, his blue and gold football jersey already sweaty in the sticky evening heat.

"I'm glad you waited for me." He leaned the hockey stick against the barn door and set his pads on the ground.

"Here, this is for you." Elisa picked up the pendant with Leonard's name on it. At the end of the leather cord hung a purple amethyst stone, a triangle surrounded by a many-pointed star painted on one side, the other side mirror smooth.

"Thanks?" Leonard took the pendant and held the stone up to his eyes.

"Any sign of Karl?" I asked.

The football leader shook his head. "No. I tried to convince him, but Karl Macarthur wasn't gonna do anything for anyone other than himself. There's four of us; that needs to be enough 'cause that's what we got." He looked down at his purple stone. "What's the deal with this?"

"They're the Chakra stones Mrs. Chakoté talked about." I pulled mine out from under my shirt to show the others. "She thought it was important we each had one."

"Well, whatever." Leonard tucked his pendant under his shirt. "We should head to the Crypt." He picked up his gear. "Any idea where we go once we're inside?"

"She left us this map." I pulled it from the envelope and held it up. "It looks pretty old, and some of the writing is hard to read, but it shows the locations of the Skull Keys."

"That's what Chakoté was talking about." Leonard glanced over my shoulder and stared at the map. "We can't let the Agarthans get this." He leaned closer, then shook his head. "I can't read it."

"We need light." I handed the map to Bobby, then picked up a flashlight lying on the ground. I turned it on and aimed the light at the map.

It looked like something pulled straight from the pages of a swashbuckling pirate tale. The yellowed paper looked worn and frayed at the edges, with missing corners and deep creases crisscrossing the ancient document. Lines and markings on the map seemed faded with age, but most were still visible. Small X's hidden amongst the caves and tunnels drawn on the map marked the locations of the seven Skull Keys, each X a different color. At some point, someone in the Order of the Stones had laminated the thing to keep the map from crumbling to dust and giving into the ravages of time.

Bobby pointed with his finger. "There's the second skull. X marks the spot . . . like on a treasure map."

"Okay, let's get moving." Leonard slapped Bobby on the back, then bent down and grabbed a light, the others doing the same.

We started toward the Crypt. As we walked, I scanned the grounds, hoping Karl would appear, but he wasn't anywhere in sight.

"I appreciate all of you coming to help." I adjusted my backpack, the contents rattling about, then glanced at Bobby's bag. "What's that thing sticking out of your pack?"

Bobby stopped for a moment and set his bag on the ground. Unzipping it, he pulled something that looked like a paintball gun but with a barrel wider than usual with other modified parts showing as well. Flinging the bag over his shoulder, he held out the weapon for inspection. "This is *my little friend.*"

"Your what?" Elisa asked.

"Get on with the explanation." Leonard pointed at the thick barrel. "How is that thing gonna help us?"

"This is my greatest invention." Bobby mock-fired it like a machine gun, of course adding his own sound effects, "pew pew pew." He smiled at us. "This is my jelly-gun."

"Your what?" Elisa's voice rose with confusion.

"You know, a jelly-gun." Bobby glanced at us, a look of exasperation on his face.

We shook our heads, confused.

He sighed, then reached into his backpack and pulled out a couple of jelly packets from the dining hall. Putting them in the plastic hopper, Bobby switched on the power supply, then fired. Three packets of grape jelly shot out of the barrel and sped through the air, each one breaking open when they hit the ground. "Now, do you get it? It's a jelly-gun... a gun that fires jelly. I don't think I can be clearer than that."

"In what universe will a jelly-gun be useful?" Leonard asked.

"Well . . . you never know." Bobby turned off the gun and put his arm through the strap.

I shook my head ever so slightly. "I don't know, Bobby. It's a brilliant piece of engineering, but I'm not sure how it'll ever be useful."

"You'll see, Cameron." Bobby glanced at the others. "You'll all see. Every dangerous adventure needs a jelly-gun, just in case."

"Whatever, Bobby." Leonard shook his head. "Just keep that thing pointed away from me."

Elisa suddenly stopped and crouched. "Everyone, quiet," she whispered. "I saw something move by the stone wall."

We froze in place, then knelt.

Leonard held his hockey stick at the ready and moved forward, ready for combat. I wanted to go with him, but the buzzing had started, the bees taunting me in my mind. Fear grew within me.

*What if it's that terrible gremlin with the whip?*

Images of gremlins and imps flashed through my mind, each trying to awaken my Beast. The *what-ifs* caused a queasy feeling to churn deep in my stomach, my insides feeling as if they were being shaken like a snow globe.

*Stay in the moment,* I thought.

*'Challenge the ANTs,'* Dr. Jen would say. *'Use your Brain Coach to confront the negative thought.'* But my Brain Coach remained quiet in the fog of fear obscuring my mind.

I swallowed nervously and challenged the *ANTs. That gremlin could be anywhere. I doubt it's right here. It was probably just the wind.*

The challenge did little to soothe my growing panic—my Brain Coach failed, just as I knew it would. I tried other techniques from Dr. Jen, hoping the coping strategies would cut through the anxiety, but the buzzing grew louder. The worry side of my brain took over, locking the logic side in a jail cell made from my doubts and fears.

I took in a deep breath and tried to slow my rapid heart. *Maybe this wasn't such a good idea.*

Elisa notched an arrow to her bowstring and moved forward, the blunt tip of the arrow meant for targets, not flesh. It might not kill a monster, but it would hurt.

Bobby turned on his jelly-gun again and loaded the hopper with more packets. The whir of the power supply's cooling fans filled the air with a whooshing sound.

Leonard glanced over his shoulder. "Turn that stupid thing off; it's too noisy."

With a sigh, Bobby shut it off and slung it over his shoulder. Reaching into his bag, Bobby pulled out a big, high-tech-looking slingshot. Sticking a large marble into the pouch, he pulled back on the rubber straps, aiming at the rocky wall.

Pulling out the lightning-rope, I switched it on, the line shaking in my hands. Buzzing grew louder, filling my mind. The hairs on the back of my neck stood up at attention. Beads

of sweat trickled between the forest of follicles, following the eerie chill creeping down my spine. Thoughts of what might be hiding in the tall grass floated through my brain.

*What if it's something worse than a gremlin? It might be some other mythical creature, maybe a goblin or harpy or . . .* All the mythical creatures I'd seen on the Internet cycled through my mind, each bigger and meaner than the last.

*What was I thinking? I can't do this. I'm not a hero. I'm just a loser, a techie geek that doesn't fit in anywhere.*

But I knew I had to continue. My only friends, Bobby and Elisa, were counting on me. The buzzing grew louder as fear took root deep in my soul. My heart raced faster than a jackhammer, thudding in my chest. Taking a deep breath, I clenched my teeth and continued forward, expecting some terrible monster to leap out and devour us all.

# Chapter 12 – The Crypt

**M**y nerves felt stretched like a string pulled too tight. My arms and legs were spaghetti, weak, and wobbly, and I shook with fear. I clenched my muscles to steady myself and hold back the quivers, but it was like trying to stop a tidal wave with a single hand.

My Beast had awakened.

The urge to run away nearly overwhelmed me. I glanced around, looking for an escape route. Instead, I saw my friends, fear chiseled on their brave faces. *ANTs* surged through my brain, trying to shatter my will and make me flee, but I refused to abandon my friends.

We moved silently across the rolling hills of grass, the light from the full moon painting the Crypt grounds with a mystical glow. A gentle breeze brushed against the tall overgrowth around the Crypt, the tall grasses dancing to an unheard rhythm. I watched the plants, wondering if a monster lurked within the moving weeds, waiting for its prey. I shivered as the angry hornets in my head sang their terrible song.

Glancing at the cave, I stared at the green skull key mounted above the dark entrance. It gave off a faint emerald glow that covered the ground near the dark opening, giving it a menacing appearance.

A clump of tall weeds on the other side of the ancient wall shifted about, moving against the breeze-driven motions of the other plants.

"Something's there," I whispered.

The buzzing in my head intensified.

We stopped and readied for battle. Elisa pulled back on her bowstring, the weapon creaking. Bobby drew back on the thick rubber straps of his slingshot, ready to fire. Leonard adjusted his football pads, then raised his hockey stick, prepared for combat. My sweaty hand gripped the lightning-rope tight. Sparks moved along the end of the device like shimmering spiders waiting to find soft flesh. I held the coils tight, ready to throw the electrified end at a target.

*What if the electricity doesn't hurt the monsters of Agartha?* I thought. *What if it's that gremlin with the whip? What if . . .* The *ANTs* flooded through me, *what-ifs* coming to life in my mind.

We crept forward, the unknown skulking about on the other side of the wall.

The buzzing blared even louder, making it impossible to think. The Beast wrapped its terrifying arms around my soul and started to squeeze. My chest ached as my heart pounded away, going faster and faster. My mouth grew dry as a desert, parched and lacking any moisture. I tried to swallow, but my tongue felt like sandpaper scraping the top of my mouth.

Panic and dread filled my mind.

*What if the panic won't stop? I gotta escape. I should run away. I should hide. I should—*

Again, I imagined myself as Leonard, strong and confident. I tried to stand up tall, like him, and pretend to be unafraid. It helped a little; the hornets filling my head diminished from deafening to just a blaring thunder.

"BOO!" Something jumped out of the weeds, hands held up as if clawed, then laughter filled the air.

The four of us jumped.

"Ha ha ha . . . you look like scared babies." It was Karl.

I wiped the sweat from my brow and turned off the lightning-rope. The buzzing faded from my head, and fatigue, which always followed my Beast, flooded through my body. I wanted to collapse but refused to look weak. Moving to the wall, I leaned against it, letting my body relax a bit.

"I got you guys again." Karl slapped his leg and laughed. He adjusted his gray and gold baseball jersey and smiled. "You should have seen your faces." He pointed at Bobby. "I wonder if anyone peed their pants?" He chuckled again.

"You're such a jerk, Karl. That wasn't funny." Elisa glared at him.

"No, it wasn't." Leonard lowered the hockey stick and picked up his backpack. "If you understood what was going on, you'd be more serious."

"Yeah, like monsters and stuff," Bobby said.

*"Yeah, like monsters and stuff,"* Karl mocked. He reached down and picked up an aluminum baseball bat, resting it on a shoulder. "You don't think I know what's going on? Ha! Chakoté talked to me after dinner and told me her fairy tale. I think this whole thing is stupid, but she made it clear I had to help you losers, or she'd kick me out of Camp Pontchartrain. So, here I am whether I like it or not."

84

Reaching into my pocket, I pulled out the pendant meant for Karl. "Here, this is from Mrs. Chakoté; she wants you to have it." I tossed it to Karl, but the throw came up short.

Stepping forward, Karl caught it deftly in one hand. "You throw like a girl. Next time, try to get it close to me, Techie." He quickly put it on.

"Why do you have to do that?" Bobby asked.

"Do what, Blobby?"

"You see, there you go again, trying to put people down for no reason." Bobby shook his head. "It's like you *want* people to hate you. What's with that?"

Karl glared at him. "Mind your own business, Blobby, or I might decide to stop being so nice to you." He turned and faced the Crypt. "Let's get this party started."

Karl walked toward the marble building while Leonard easily leaped over the wall. The rest of us went through the gate, the hinges screaming their thirst for oil. We all stopped at the spooky stone building's entrance. The metal bars across the doorway lay in a tangle on the ground, many completely rusted through while others seemed as if something bent them aside.

"That looks pretty spooky in there." I glanced at Elisa and ran my fingers through my curly hair. The buzzing started again.

"I don't know if this is a good idea." Elisa turned on her flashlight and moved the spot of light around, shining it on the stone coffins of deceased Directors. "It's so dark."

My rapid heartbeat pounded in my ears, my face feeling tight as if it were about to rip. I glanced about, looking for imps, gremlins, or some other Agarthan creature ready to spring from the darkness and devour me.

Just then, a hand settled on my shoulder. I looked up and found Leonard standing behind me.

"Heroes may not be braver than anyone else. They're just braver five minutes longer." The football captain stared down at me, the sadness in his eyes surprisingly absent. Instead, they almost twinkled. "That's a quote from our 40th president, Ronald Reagan."

"Well, aren't you full of important information, professor." Karl chuckled. "What are we waiting for? That Super Blood Moon is tomorrow, and they already have one skull.
We need to get moving."

"You think you can be brave for five more minutes?" Leonard asked, whispering into my ear.

I looked up at the huge sixth-grader. My chest tightened as the buzzing grew louder. Reaching into my shirt, I pulled out the quartz amulet and clenched the stone in my hand. For a moment, I thought the quartz sang to me, a mystical tune playing faintly in my head. It seemed to muffle the angry hornets a little, the Beast fading a bit. I glanced up at Leonard and took a deep breath, then nodded.

Leonard smiled, then stepped into the Crypt with Karl fast on his heels.

Bobby patted me on the back, then followed, his flashlight probing the darkness.

I peered into the dark opening, and my fear returned, *buzzzzz, buzzzzz, buzzzzz.*

*I don't think this is a good idea,* I thought.

"Come on, Cameron. I'm right at your side." Elisa put a reassuring hand on my shoulder, then lowered her voice to a whisper. "I know you're feeling anxious; I can see it on your face. Try distracting yourself. Count by 8's in your head. Maybe that'll help."

I took a deep breath through my nose and clenched my teeth, then started counting by eights in my head. *8, 16, 24, 32, 40, 48* . . . As I reached the larger numbers, my brain had to work to figure out the next number in the series. The buzzing grew softer, the distraction pulling my mind from the *what-ifs*. Squeezing the flashlight tight, I stepped into the Crypt, knowing the monsters of Agartha hid somewhere in the darkness, waiting for their prey with sharp claws and hungry teeth.

# Chapter 13 – Searching for Skulls

A damp chill clung to my skin as soon as I entered the Crypt. At first, I thought it a welcome relief from the muggy heat constantly gripping New Orleans, but it wasn't. The chill felt unnatural, like the feel of a cold, dead fish left out after too many days or the icy caress of a nightmare. Whatever caused the cool embrace, it put my nerves on edge.

We all stood before the entrance and peered into the darkness. On the far wall stood a gaping hole. Deep gouges in the stone, like jagged wounds, lined the edge of the opening as if something had chewed through the rock, revealing the hidden tunnels.

My arms shook as I pointed the light into the gloom, my entire body begging to flee.

"I feel like we need to say something important to mark this moment," Bobby said. He stood up straight and put his fists on his hips; his superhero pose, as he called it. "I got it . . . As we search for the Skulls, let us keep ours on our shoulders."

"What kind of proclamation is that?" I shook my head. "*Let's keep ours on our shoulders.* Really? What are you thinking?"

Bobby shrugged. "I'm always searching for an epic saying to fit the circumstance."

"I'd say you didn't find it, Techie," Karl said with a sneer.

"So far, you're zero for two." Leonard picked up his hockey stick. "You have the map, Bobby. You lead."

"Okay." Bobby folded the map, making the path to the second skull easily visible. "Follow me." He stepped into the passage, the rest of us following.

The oppressive darkness in the tunnel made me feel as if I was drowning in shadows. Rough-hewn walls and jagged stones lined the edges of the passage, sharp points waiting to snag a bit of clothing or tear at skin. Images of terrible monsters lurked in the darkness, planted there by my imagination, *ANTs* brought to life. The only thing keeping my fear under control was the light from our flashlights. The round splash of illumination from my light represented a small circle of hope, pushing back on the buzzing hornets

hatching within my mind. I kept my eyes focused on the light as I tried to relax my muscles—first my neck, then my shoulders and arms, allowing my awareness to drip down my body, willing my flesh to soften and release the tension. It only helped a little, as I expected.

"When the Order of the Stones dug these passages, they made them like a maze." Bobby pointed his flashlight at the map. "There's an intersection up ahead. We go to the left. If we go to the right, it's a dead end. And if we go straight, it leads to what looks like," he held the map close to his eyes, "yep, it says a 'pit of death' . . . isn't that lovely?"

When Bobby said, 'pit of death,' my body tensed again, stress and fear tightening my muscles.

"Less talking, more walking," Karl said. "I want to finish this little adventure as soon as possible. I planned on destroying everyone in my cabin in Mario Cart later tonight. The less time I spend with all of you, the better."

I glared at Karl's back but said nothing.

We reached the intersection and went to the left, the passage opening a bit. The floor sloped gently downward. A thick layer of dust covered everything. As we walked, our feet kicked up small clouds of dirt and grime, making it difficult to breathe.

We walked for maybe an hour, the path curving this way and that. At times, the tunnel dipped downward, then climbed up again, moving in a complicated, twisting path.

Suddenly, the sound of voices, strange screechy voices, reverberated through the passage.

We stopped and listened.

"Find the Skull Keys," a deep voice said, "or I'll use all of your skulls to hold open the doorway, instead."

"I don't like the sound of that," Elisa whispered.

"Yes, Lord Malphas," a high-pitched voice responded.

"Yes, master."

"Yes, master."

"Yes, Demon Lord."

Countless voices floated from the darkness, affirming the command.

I shone my flashlight into the gloom. "It sounds like this Demon Lord, whoever that is, brought an army of monsters with him."

Just then, a CRACK echoed through the passage.

"Get moving, imps." The crack of a whip pierced the darkness again.

All of us flinched, even Karl.

"I don't like the sound of that," Bobby said as he stared at the map.

"It's no big deal." Karl stared into the dark tunnel behind us.

The whip cracked again. Karl jumped with a start, then stood tall, chest out and chin held high, as if unafraid. When he glanced at me, I saw the fear in his eyes, and he quickly looked away.

"I bet that's the gremlin we saw earlier." Elisa scowled in the sound's direction.

"Let's not wait and find out." Leonard glanced at Bobby. "Lead the way, Bobby. It's time to run."

"Okay, let's go." Bobby pointed his light at the map, then ran, the rest of us following close behind.

We sped through the passage, trying to be as quiet as possible. The sounds of monsters floated out of the darkness, their echoes bouncing off the walls and filling the passage. Each voice felt like a needle in my brain. The buzzing grew louder as terrifying monsters stormed through my imagination, claws and fangs seeking my flesh. My mind created a host of future *what-ifs* that felt so realistic. An eerie chill slithered down my spine as the hairs on my neck stood straight. I knew the monsters were far away; still, I wanted to curl up in a ball and hide but knew that wouldn't help . . . it never does.

*Focus on the positive and what's real. The ANTs are a lie.* I could hear Dr. Jen's voice in my head. I knew the images in my mind weren't real, but that's not how they felt to me. Glancing around at the dark tunnel, the sounds of monsters nibbling on our heels, I searched for something positive but came up empty.

The buzzing increased.

Clouds of dust floated into the air with each footstep, coating my tongue and making my mouth taste like I'd licked the bottom of Mom's vacuum cleaner. Suddenly, Karl sneezed, the sound bouncing off the walls and disappearing into the gloomy passage.

"Did you hear that?" Malphas said, his deep voice like the rumbling of distant thunder. "There must be humans down here. Gargoyles and imps, find them. Let none survive."

"Yes, Lord Malphas," the monsters replied.

"Be quick about it, fools," Malphas said. "Time is short."

Monster footsteps, many of them, pounded the ground.

The buzzing exploded in my head, a storm of hornets pointing their stingers at my soul. My mind became a whirlwind of doubt and *what-ifs*, the *ANTs* amplifying my fear. My Beast focused its gaze upon me.

"It's right up ahead," Bobby said.

My friend's words pushed aside some of my fear for a moment. "Hurry," I moaned.

A high-pitched, piercing wail sliced through the passage. Goosebumps formed on the back of my neck and then crept down my spine. My body reacted to the real danger pursuing us: my heart raced, pumping much-needed oxygen through my body.

*'Fear isn't bad,'* Dr. Jen said in the back of my mind. *'It's how you respond that determines if it's good or bad.'*

I knew what I was feeling wasn't anxiety; it was actual fear, but it still amplified my uncertainties and doubts—the Beast stirred in the darkness of my soul.

"What was that?" Elisa asked.

Leonard looked at her, then shrugged.

A vicious snarl suddenly echoed through the passage. At the same time, the clattering of clawed feet sped up.

"They must have spotted our footsteps in the dust," Elisa whispered.

I shook my head, trying to dislodge the buzzing, but the angry hornets were feasting on my fear and getting louder. My face felt cold and clammy as if all heat had fled from my body, the chill unnatural and frightening; my Beast grew near

"Everyone, run." Leonard put a hand on Bobby's back. "Bobby, get us to the next Skull Key."

With a nod, Bobby ran, watching the map while Leonard and Karl kept their lights on the path ahead.

"I have to distract myself, somehow." I glanced at Elisa as I ran, my eyes begging for help.

"The alphabet," Elisa said. "Think of a food for every letter of the alphabet."

"Food . . ." My mind processed her words. *A – apple,* I thought to myself. *B – banana, C – carrot, D – donut.* The buzzing decreased a little. *E – egg, F – fudge, G – grape, H – ham.* It grew quieter, the buzzing hornets fading with the *what-ifs. I – ice cream . . . J – jelly . . .* the words came slower, *K – kale . . . L – lemon . . . M – . . .*

The buzzing diminished to a whisper, the distraction burying my fears; my Beast went back to sleep, for now. I could think again.

"You okay?" Elisa asked.

I nodded. "Yeah, thanks." I glanced at her, and she smiled back, her eyes filled with worry.

Leonard glanced over his shoulder. "They're getting closer." Even the football captain looked scared.

"Can we hide?" I moved to Bobby's side and grabbed his arm, slowing to a walk. Pointing my light, I stared down at the map. "Look, there's an alcove just up ahead. Maybe we can hide there."

"Good idea." Leonard nodded. "Bobby, get us there, fast."

As Bobby started to run again, Karl moved to his side, snatched the map from his hands, and jogged through the passage, everyone struggling to keep up.

"Hey, what are you doing?" Bobby glared at the bigger boy.

Karl focused on the map, checking their progress. He leaped over a pile of stones without breaking his stride. Of course, I almost tripped over the rocks.

"Really?" Bobby said. "You don't trust me to go the right way, so you have to take over?"

Karl glared at Bobby. "Never trust a Techie to do something right." He burped softly, then smiled. "I'll take care of this."

Bobby shook his head. "Sometimes, I wonder if you've managed to insult everyone in the entire camp. No wonder you always seem to be alone. You push everyone away."

"What did you say?" Karl's words dripped with anger.

"It's okay, Bobby." I reached out and patted my friend on the back. "Let's all relax . . . and focus on finding . . . a place to hide." My strained breathing made it difficult to talk; running was not my best skill.

"No, it's not okay, Cam," Bobby said. "Karl and all the other kids like him think they can do whatever they want because they're bigger and stronger than us." He frowned as he glanced over his shoulder at me. "I'm tired of being called stupid names because I'm different or fat or have pimples. I hate being teased because I'm smart and I like technology." Bobby pulled his jelly-gun off his shoulder, the impractical weapon swaying with every stride. "None of you could ever build something like my jelly-gun, yet no one respects me for it. I get bullied instead."

Karl chuckled. "You built a jelly-gun and thought you should get respect for that?" He laughed a loud, deep laugh as he curved around a large stone in the tunnel. "That is the stupidest thing I've ever seen. You're such a geek."

"At least I have real friends, Karl, not because I'm on the same team, but because they know they can count on me." Bobby

raised his head with pride as he slung the jelly-gun over his shoulder again.

Karl tensed and clenched a hand into a fist, a scowl etched deep into his face.

No one spoke, the tension within the group growing.

"Whatever." Karl handed Bobby the map. "I didn't wanna lead, anyway."

"The alcove is over here." Bobby moved to the left side of the passage as another tunnel split off to the right just ahead. He pointed his flashlight into the area and headed for a large pile of stones near the far wall. "Quick, hide behind all this rubble."

We followed Bobby and hid behind a pile of rocks and gravel. Karl moved behind a large boulder by himself instead.

"Turn off your lights," Leonard whispered.

Suddenly, darkness folded in on us like sheets of thick cloth draped over our eyes. The blackness wrapped its terrifying fingers around my body, the impenetrable gloom amplifying the sense of dread threatening to suffocate me.

"Here they come," Elisa whispered.

A red glow slowly shaded the rocky walls of the passage as the sound of clawed feet grew louder. An imp, its skin the color of blood, emerged from the tunnel and stopped next to the alcove. Like the one we'd seen the night before, the creature was the size of a toddler, with clawed hands and feet, and short stubby wings. Its body lacked any hair, the imp's skin like rough leather. The monster's deep-set eyes blazed a bright red as if aflame. Atop the creature's head, its stubby, pointed horns glowed, painting the walls with an angry, crimson brush.

Behind the imp stood a stone-gray gargoyle, its dark wings tucked across its back. The monster stood about five feet tall, with muscular arms and thick, stout legs. Its large hands looked menacing, with unusually long fingers, each tipped with a midnight-black fingernail. Slender ribbons of smoke rose from the tip of each nail and slithered into the air. The gargoyle's face, almost bat-like in appearance, looked like chiseled stone, the wide-set eyes burning with the same internal fire as the imp's. Something about the creature's hands made me shudder. They seemed more dangerous than its fanged mouth.

"Which way, imp?" the gargoyle asked, its voice scratchy, like stones rubbing together.

"I think it's this way." The imp pointed to the passage splitting off to the right.

The gargoyle swung a fist at the tiny red monster's head, cuffing it on the ear. "You think?" it growled.

"Sorry, Morlon, I mean . . . I know." The imp glanced nervously about the passage. "I can sense the magic in the Skull Key. It must be in that passage up ahead."

The gargoyle dragged three fingernails across the imp's arm, each leaving behind a dark stain, like soot. Instantly, the imp shrieked in pain as its arm went limp and hung uselessly at its side, the appendage somehow numbed by the gargoyle's touch.

"You better be right, imp, or instead of paralyzing your arm, I'll scratch your chest and let you struggle to breathe down here until the moon sets." He extended a single finger and held it near the imp's throat, ribbons of smoke rising into the air like dark serpents taking flight. "Keep searching, or I'll make it worse. Now move!"

The imp and gargoyle took off running, both flapping their wings to push their bodies a little faster.

When the red glow disappeared down the side tunnel, I switched on my flashlight and turned to my companions. "We gotta hurry!"

Bobby held up the map to my light, then moved his face close. "We're almost there. It's just past the next tunnel."

"You mean those two monsters went the wrong way?" Leonard asked.

Bobby nodded. "But they'll learn of their mistake soon enough; that passage is a dead end."

"Let's get moving." Leonard stepped out from behind the pile of rocks, then glanced at Bobby. "Get us to that Skull Key, fast."

Bobby nodded and switched on his flashlight, then took off running, all of us following close behind. As we ran, the scraping of clawed feet against stone echoed through the tunnel, the sound amplifying our fear.

Every scrape and growl from the darkness drew me deeper into my soul-crushing anxiety. The gloom around me felt like a living, breathing entity, the shadows spaces hiding nightmares yet to be dreamt, but I could feel the darkness stoking the flames of panic growing within me. My Beast would overwhelm me soon. It felt hopeless, but I knew I had no choice but to continue and hope we found the Skull Key before the monsters of Agartha found them . . . or worse, found us.

# Chapter 14 – The Second Skull Key

We bolted through the dark tunnel, our feet pounding the rough ground. The sound of vicious snarls and hungry growls echoed off the stone walls, the monstrous voices filling the air around us like a terrifying melody of violence. My heart pounded in my chest like thunder from a hot summer storm. Each beat filled my ear with a frenzied thump. Sweat poured down my forehead in thick, sticky droplets despite the unnatural chill in the catacombs. I tried to wipe the moisture from my face but ended up smearing sweat into my eyes.

Bobby smiled, drawing a scowl from Karl. "We go to the left."

"We need to . . . move faster," I said, my voice cracking with fear.

"Less talking, more running." Karl shoved Bobby forward. "Move, Blobby, before you become a hearty snack for those monsters."

"Karl, be nice for a change." Elisa put a hand on Bobby's shoulder.

"It's okay, Elisa," Bobby said, then turned to Karl. "We can only be the person we believe we can be, and no more. Karl here believes his only choice is to be rude and offensive. It's not his fault. He just doesn't have faith in himself to be more."

"You talk a lot, Techie," Karl growled. "Start running." He pushed Bobby forward again, then glanced over his shoulder. "Are the rest of you ladies coming, or have you all become geeks like him?" Karl tapped his aluminum baseball bat on the ground with a pinging sound.

I scowled at Karl, as did Elisa and Leonard.

We ran through the passage, each listening for claws scratching stone. I glanced over my shoulder and watched for that red glow from the imp's horns. We'd likely see that before we saw our pursuers.

"The map says it should be just ahead," Bobby said, then glanced at Karl, "unless I can't be trusted."

Karl waved his hand as if shooing away a fly, ignoring the comment.

"The location on the map says, *'under the point.'*" Bobby looked closer at the map, then turned it so it was upside down. "But it also says, 'A light step leaves no footprints.' What does that mean?"

"It's a warning, I think." I slowed and pointed my flashlight at the ground. "The hint is footprints; we gotta be careful where we step."

"Right," Leonard said. "Look for something pointed but watch the ground."

We moved cautiously forward, the sounds of monsters still percolating out of the darkness, their angry voices faint but growing. The passage grew wide, the ceiling too high to touch. Here and there, water dripped from the rocky covering, the moisture occasionally falling on our heads and forming puddles on the ground. Over centuries, the dripping water formed shapes on the ceiling and floor. Cone-shaped stalactites stabbed down from overhead like large, stone teeth, each dripping mineral-rich water onto a similar stony structure rising out of the ground. In some places, the stalagmites growing up from the floor met the stalactites hanging from the ceiling, forming a column of stones, water trickling down its side.

"We're here." Bobby folded the map and stuffed it in a pocket.

We scanned the area, aiming flashlights in all directions. Stalagmites and stalactites filled the chamber, creating a stone forest. All of them glistened with moisture, the mineral-rich water that formed them dripping from their rough surfaces. But of all the stalagmites and stalactites in the passage, one seemed curiously dry.

"Anyone see anything?" Bobby whispered.

"Watch your step." I threaded my fingers through my hair.

"I don't see anything pointed on the walls." Leonard moved his light around, searching for the skull.

I stood back from the dry stalagmite and stared up at its companion stalactite hanging from the ceiling. "Notice this is the only dry stalagmite and stalactite pair? Moisture covers the rest of them."

"Why's that such a big deal?" Karl asked.

"It's not normal." I pointed my flashlight at the stony pair. "Mineral water drips down from the stalactite forming the stalagmite on the ground, but there's no water here; it's bone dry." I scanned my light across the rocky structure. "It looks like there's a seam on the stalagmite growing out of the ground." I ran my fingers over the stone, then glanced at Leonard and Karl. "I bet you two can push the top off."

"Under the point . . . of course." Bobby slapped the baseball captain on the back.

Karl turned and glared at the Techie. "Don't do that again!"

"Sorry . . . whatever."

"Let's see if that stone will move." Karl moved closer to the rocky structure.

"Wait . . . the ground . . . it's—" Before I could finish the sentence, Karl stepped

forward. His foot landed on a dust-covered section, and suddenly the ground fell away right beneath him.

I reached out, grabbed the back of Karl's jersey, and yanked. We tumbled backward with arms flailing as a hole opened in the ground. With a sickening thud, Karl's body crashed into mine, knocking the wind out of my lungs. I gasped for breath.

Karl pushed off me, his bulk squishing me like a deflating balloon. He climbed to his feet, but instead of offering a hand to help me up, he just glared at me.

I took a breath, the dusty air calming the fire in my lungs. Slowly, I climbed to my feet, my body aching.

"What are you doing, you idiot!" Karl adjusted his shirt. His eyes narrowed as his anger turned to rage. "I had it under control and—"

"Look!" I pointed to the floor near the dry stalagmite.

A jagged hole opened into darkness right where Karl had stepped. I aimed my light into the opening but could see nothing.

"I don't know how far down it goes, but it's far." I wiped the sweat from my forehead, the dust and dirt on my sleeve leaving a dark smear. A momentary feeling of pride pushed down the buzzing hornets in my head as the realization hit me; I had just saved someone's life. I turned to Karl. "We must be careful."

"Umm . . . I can hear monsters," Elisa said. "And they're getting louder. I think they heard us."

The buzzing returned, the pride evaporating under a cloud of *ANTs* and *what-ifs*.

"Humans, I smell humans," a voice said, the scratchy words floating out of the darkness like a nightmare.

A chill slithered down my spine.

"We gotta hurry." Elisa's terrified words came out in rapid-fire.

"We can't hurry," I whispered. "Caution will keep everyone safe."

*I can't let any of my friends die. I can do this; I can keep them safe . . . even Karl.*

Kneeling, I blew across the ground, my mind focused on the problem and ignoring the *ANTs* for now. The fine dust floated into the air, filling our flashlight beams with a gray haze. Beneath the dirt and grime, I found a patchwork of square stone tiles three feet on a side, each one identical in size and shape.

"You see," I said, "here's the trap."

"Okay, *professor*," Karl mocked. "What do we do? Step on them one at a time and see what happens."

"No, but I have a better idea." I reached out to Karl. "Give me your bat."

"My bat, Number Three? I don't think so."

"They're getting louder." Elisa pointed her flashlight toward me, her voice frantic. "Hurry, please."

Leonard moved to my side. "Give him your bat, Karl, unless you wanna face an army of monsters."

Karl sighed, then handed me the bat.

Carefully, I tapped the nearest tile. The bat pinged.

"You better not scratch my bat."

Ignoring him, I hit the tile harder and then harder, but nothing happened. Turning, I glanced at Leonard. "Hold on to my backpack so I won't fall."

Leonard moved behind and grabbed my backpack. "Okay, I got you."

Carefully, I put my weight on the tile . . . it held.

"Try the next one." Bobby pulled a piece of chocolate from his bag and smeared it on the tile. "This way, we know it's safe."

I nodded, then tested the tiles while Leonard held onto me. In a minute, I'd found all the stable and unstable tiles, a chocolate path keeping us safe.

I handed Karl his bat. "I think you two can now get to the stalagmite and push the top off."

Leonard turned to Karl and nodded. "Let's do it."

Karl glared, then tossed the bat back to me. "Hold this and don't do anything stupid with it."

Leonard and Karl hopped from tile to tile until they stood next to the rocky structure. Both athletes put their shoulders against the heavy stalagmite and shoved. With a loud, grinding sound, the stone inched sideways. The scratchy, gravelly noise reminded me of the gargoyle's voice.

A gremlin suddenly stepped out of the darkness, the creature fat and overweight. A wide leather belt surrounded its rotund belly, sharp stone knives attached along its length. In its left hand, the monster held a vicious-looking whip, this one black as night.

"Watch out." Bobby dove out of the way just as the whip cracked in the air where he'd been standing.

The monster turned to me and flicked his wrist. The whip shot through the air like a vicious snake. I raised the bat just in time to

deflect the attack, the whip grazing my arm, stinging. Fear blasted through my mind as the vicious creature snarled, its hideous pointed teeth smacking together. My heartbeat pounded in my ears, making my head throb. The buzzing filled every crevasse of my mind, the *what-ifs* trying to devour me from the inside. The monster turned toward Elisa and raised its arm, readying for another attack.

*I can't let that happen . . . I* won't *let it happen.*

Something inside me snapped, and the buzzing in my head instantly went silent. The thought of Elisa getting hurt blasted away the *ANTs* and *what-ifs* in my head, leaving only rage. My fear evaporated as every thought went to keeping her safe.

Moving on instinct, I dropped the bat and charged, my entire being laser-focused on that evil gremlin.

The whip cracked, just missing Elisa's face.

I rushed toward the gremlin. As I ran, I reached into my pocket and pulled out a device the size of a cell phone, a static-stunner, two pointed barbs sticking out of the top. I flipped on the power switch just as the gremlin dropped the whip and reached for a stone knife. Sparks danced across the two barbs as I smashed into the gremlin. The sharp points stabbed into the monster's thick hide, bringing a shout of surprise from the Agarthan. Instantly, electricity danced across the gremlin's skin, and the monster shrieked in pain. Like tiny glowing spiders, sparks of electrical power crawled across the gremlin's flesh, muscles convulsing until the terrible creature fell backward, unconscious.

I glanced over my shoulder at Leonard and Karl. "You need to get it done, now!" My voice shook.

"They're almost done," Bobby said, his voice rising with excitement.

The sound of clawed feet scraping the rocky floor of the tunnel grew louder.

"Harder," Leonard said, his voice straining. "Push harder."

The top of the stalagmite moved faster, sliding and griding until it fell over with a crash, revealing a hollowed-out section. Sitting within was an object wrapped in a tattered cloth. Leonard lifted it out and pulled aside the fabric. A carved skull the size of a cantaloupe stared at them, the surface a polished blue with splashes of white here and there, the same as the stone hanging around Karl's neck.

"That's the Skull Key." I held my hands out, and Leonard tossed it to me. "Let's get out of here."

"The Skull of Longing is near," a high-pitched voice shouted. "I can feel it."

"Fly after it, imp," a deep, scratchy voice said. "The Demon Lord of Agartha commands it. Imps, fly after the Skull of Longing. Destroy anyone or anything in your path."

"We need to get out of here." I wiped off the last bit of dust and dirt from the skull. "Bobby, where's the next key?"

Peering at the map, Bobby murmured to himself for a moment, then looked up. "We keep following this passage. Then we go to the—"

Suddenly, three imps and a gargoyle charged out of the shadows.

"Monsters!" Elisa shouted. She moved backward, firing her arrows at the airborne creatures, her shafts missing.

The buzzing exploded in my head. A storm of fear and doubt wrapped around me, suffocating my thoughts, hope feeling forever out of reach. I couldn't think or feel; fear paralyzed my body and mind. My Beast had me in its clutches and refused to let go, my thinking brain a prisoner to my anxiety.

*Will this terror last forever?* My thought made the Beast even stronger. *It'll never end! I can't survive this.*

My arms and legs felt suddenly numb, movement impossible. I tried to speak, but my bone-dry throat made it difficult. *What-ifs* surged through my mind, fueled by soul-crushing panic. I glanced around, looking for escape, but found none; I was doomed. My Beast had me.

"Everyone, fight!" Leonard charged at an imp, swinging his hockey stick at the creature.

The monster darted to the left, but an aluminum baseball bat streaked through the air and pounded the creature.

"Number Three hits a homer," Karl shouted.

The imp fell to the ground unconscious, its horns flickering, then growing dark.

Bobby pulled out his slingshot and fired large marbles at the monsters. His projectiles struck the gargoyle's thick gray hide. It made the monster howl in rage. He fired again, aiming for the creature's head. The marble hit the gargoyle right between the eyes, dazing it for an instant. That moment was long enough for Leonard's hockey stick to come down on the creature's head, knocking it out. It fell to the ground with a thud.

An imp darted toward Elisa. She fired her arrows, but her arms shook with fear, causing each shot to miss. The imp extended a handful

of claws, ready to swipe at her face. This threat snapped me out of my anxiety-induced paralysis. I dropped the Skull Key and activated the lightning-rope. I ran to Elisa. Throwing the end of the rope at the monster, the sparkling tip hit the imp. Painful shocks spread across the little creature, electric fangs finding flesh. Before the monster could respond, Karl hit the imp with his bat.

"Number Three hits another." Karl smiled, pleased with himself. "One more left. Leonard, get the last imp."

Leonard raised his hockey stick, ready to attack when more monsters emerged out of the tunnel, a half-dozen creatures: imps, gargoyles, and a huge demon in the shape of a gigantic half-man, half-raven. They charged forward. The demon leaned his bird-like head back and screeched; the sound turned my blood to ice and made my bones ache. A sense of evil radiated from the monster's dark and twisted form, making every cell in my body cringe. A cold dread spread through me as I stared at the demon's red eyes, fear . . . real fear blasting through me like a hurricane of sharp, jagged things. This wasn't anxiety creating fear for something that didn't exist. No, this fear was genuine, igniting the fight-or-flight response. I definitely chose flight.

"DESTROY THE HUMANS!" the demon screamed.

"Everyone, run!" Leonard shouted.

He turned and ran, grabbing Karl by the arm and pulling him away from the monsters. Bobby fired one more marble, then turned and fled. He grabbed both Elisa and me by the arms and pulled us away.

"Wait . . . the Skull Key." I reached down and scooped up the skull, then followed Bobby.

I glanced over my shoulder. The muscular demon stormed into the passage, his eyes glowing a bright red. I shuddered, then turned and ran, following my friends.

The memory of the Demon Lord replayed itself in my mind. It was a thing that made nightmares afraid, and now its image sat firmly in my brain, ready to haunt me from within.

*What if it catches us? How can we fight that thing? What if . . .* impossible thoughts raged through my mind, my Beast reaching for my soul. I followed my friends, my body functioning on autopilot, but everything felt hopeless. Escape seemed impossible, but still I ran, with sharp claws and pointed teeth hoping for me to stumble.

# Chapter 15 – Escaping the Catacombs

The sound of monsters tore into my courage with sharp screams and jagged howls of rage. I drove my legs hard, trying to squeeze every last drop of speed from them. I glanced over my shoulder as I shifted the Skull Key from one hand to the other. Red light filled the tunnel behind us, the imps lighting the rocky walls with their devilish horns.

The buzzing in my head grew louder.

The passage looked as if it were painted with fire, the walls and floor like glowing coals. It was like staring into the throat of a giant, fire-breathing dragon. The twisting tunnel hid the monsters from sight. But that did nothing to hide their terrifying snarls. The crimson light grew brighter, casting frightening shadows on the rough-hewn walls. With every step, the monsters grew closer.

"Bobby, is there a way out of these tunnels?" Leonard yelled, beginning to run out of breath.

"I'm looking, I'm . . ." Bobby brought the map close to his face.

"Bobby, look out!" Elisa pulled him to the side, dodging a stalactite hanging from the ceiling.

"Thanks." Bobby smiled. "It's hard to run from a blood-thirsty horde of monsters and look at a map at the same time." His smile grew bigger. "I think I found something. There's another passage coming up on the right. It looks like it'll take us to the surface."

The passage widened, then narrowed again as it curved to the left, then straightened out.

"Turn here," Bobby said.

A dark passage pierced the tunnel wall on the right, flashlights barely showing its presence; the narrow path would be easy to miss. We moved into the cramped tunnel, flashlights aimed at the walls and floors.

"Quick, turn off your lights." I switched mine off.

"But we won't be able to see as we run." Karl pointed his light into my face.

"We're not gonna run." Leonard stopped running and turned off his light. "We're gonna hide. Our footsteps might give us away."

"Exactly." I nodded. "Right now, silence and darkness are the best weapons."

Everyone turned off their lights and stood still. The gloom wrapped around me like a suffocating shroud, amplifying my fears and heightening my sense of dread. An image of that terrible demon appeared in my mind, its red eyes staring straight at me.

The sounds of monsters grew louder. I shuddered as my anxiety created worst-case scenarios and played them over and over in my head. I shut my eyes, trying to block them out, but it didn't help. Some of the Agarthans wailed in frustration; others growled and snarled. A whip cracked, causing a high-pitched, painful scream.

My body shook. Sweat trickled into my eyes, stinging. I wanted to wipe it away but didn't dare move. Terror held me in its tight grip.

"Where did they go? You lost them." It was the voice of the gremlin, Krak. "I told you, Fool, to keep an eye on the humans."

The vicious gremlin's whip whooshed through the air, then *CRACK!* An imp screeched in pain.

*They're so close. What if the monsters look for us in here?* The words in my head made the buzzing grow louder, which brought forth more *what-ifs,* causing the hornets to get even angrier—the thought-loop firmly entrenched in my brain.

The buzzing grew louder. I wanted to run, but knew they'd hear me. *ANTs* came to life in my mind as every possible *what-if* hammered away at the last morsels of my courage. My Beast fed on my worries, waiting for its moment to strike. I tried to steal some of Leonard's courage and pretend to be him, but the *ANTs* refused to release their grip on my brain. *That won't help,* one of the *ANTs* said. *You'll never be like Leonard, so don't even bother to try. You're a coward.*

I took in quick raspy breaths as my pulse quickened, my body reacting to the fear. The idea of trying one of the many breathing strategies Dr. Jen had taught me popped into my head, but . . . *Those won't do any good,* my anxiety said. *The Beast is coming.*

"They turned the corner and disappeared," the imp pleaded. "I don't know where they went."

"Keep going, you idiotic monsters." The gremlin cracked his whip again — another scream of agony. "If Malphas finds us just standing around, he'll kill us all. Now MOVE!"

The monsters continued moving past the hidden tunnel. The sound of their clawed feet and the red glow of the imps gradually diminished.

The orchestra of buzzing hornets faded but wasn't gone; danger still lurked nearby.

"Let's go," Karl whispered.

"No, wait." I wiped the sweat from my forehead.

Just then, I heard the hateful voice of Malphas, the Demon Lord of Agartha.

"What?! You lost them?" Malphas bellowed. The demon stood so close to the hidden passage I could hear him breathing.

Goosebumps spread across my arms.

A gargoyle screamed in pain. It was a gravelly noise, like stones being ground together but with a dose of agony added.

"Find them," Malphas commanded. "I want every tunnel searched. The humans have the Skull of Longing; I can feel it. Find them or taste my wrath."

The sounds of monsters filled the air, clawed feet scratching at the ground as they dispersed into adjacent tunnels.

"Just one light," I whispered, my voice shaking. "We need to move while the Agarthans are confused."

Leonard nodded and flipped on his light. Cupping his hand around the edge, he pointed it at the ground and crept through the widening passage. As we went, I moved to Elisa's side.

"You doing okay?" I asked, then shuddered. Shapes in the dim lighting took on monstrous forms. *Is it my imagination, or is there something in the shadows?*

She nodded, her face barely visible in the faint light. "Yeah, how about you . . . the anxiety?"

"It's trying to get me, my Beast, I mean. I hate that the anxiety takes control of me. It makes me feel like I'm letting everyone down, like I'm a failure, as always."

"But is that true, Cameron?" Elisa asked. "You saved Karl from falling and grabbed the Skull Key when we fled, right?"

"Well . . . I don't know."

"I do know. You kept the second skull from getting into the hands of that terrible demon, Malphas."

"I guess." I felt a little stupid now, complaining about how I felt.

"Don't just think about how you feel, Cameron," Elisa said. "Think about the facts around you."

"Now you sound like my therapist."

She smiled and put a hand on my shoulder. "Just remember, I'm here to help

you. Maybe that's all I'm good for. I don't think I've hit anything with my arrows. I love archery, but sometimes I hate it, too."

Gravel crunched under my feet as we walked. It sounded like thunder in the quiet passage.

"Maybe archery isn't your thing," I said.

"That's what I said about gymnastics, 'cause I failed at that." Elisa ducked under a stalactite. "I love archery, but I'm a terrible shot when it's important."

"But I've seen you practice; your aim is excellent."

"Sure, when I'm alone or with a friend." Elisa sniffled. "But when I *have* to make the shot, I miss. And you know why?"

I shook my head.

"Because I'm afraid of failing my father."

"Why is that?"

"Well, every time I shoot my bow, I get an image of my dad in the back of my mind. He's standing there shaking his head, a look of disappointment on his face, like when I quit gymnastics."

"So just ignore it," I said. I felt like a fraud when I said it. It's always impossible for me to ignore my fears, but maybe she's strong enough to do it.

"I can't." Elisa sighed, then leaped over a small boulder in their path. "For some reason, I desperately want the respect he easily gives to my older brother who's at the University of Kentucky."

"The track star?"

Elisa nodded. "When I realized I wasn't good at gymnastics, I told my dad I wanted to stop. He was so angry his face turned red, and he yelled at me. 'Why can't you do it? Just be the best, like your brother.' It was awful; I felt like a total failure. Now, I'm so afraid I'll fail him again that I'm almost afraid to try. My shooting back there was terrible, but I'm used to it. That's what I expect; it's how I shoot in tournaments . . . pitiful. Every time I miss, it just proves I'm the failure of our family." She hung her head down. "I'm pathetic."

"I know a lot about failure."

"What are you talking about? I'm sure you're an A student in every class."

"I don't mean grades; I mean everything else." I sighed, then coughed, our footsteps kicking dust into the air. "The only place I'm any good is on a test or inventing something all by myself. Back home, my anxiety makes everyone think I'm a coward or a baby or just plain weird." I swerved around a pile of rubble in the middle of the passage.

"The only people who accept me and my anxiety are you and Bobby. I'm terrified when I walk through the camp. I'm afraid every time I go to the dining hall. I've failed at many things because of my fear, and I'm always scared. I hate it. So, I know a lot about fear, and I'm gonna tell you something . . . you can beat it. Maybe I can't. My anxiety won't let me, but I know *you* can get past it." I put a hand on her shoulder. "Elisa, you need to realize that you're good enough, just as you are. I've seen you shoot and know how skilled you are; your friends know it too. But *your* opinion is the only important one." I wiped the sweat from my face, trying to keep the salty moisture out of my eyes. "Other people can't make you feel like a failure unless you let them."

"If it's that easy, why don't you beat your fear?" she asked.

"Well . . . umm . . . it's difficult and—" I started to say but was cut off.

"Be quiet," Leonard said. "I see some light ahead."

"I think we're nearing an exit." Karl turned on his flashlight and shone it on his companions.

"Hey, that's bright." Bobby put his hands in front of his eyes.

Karl smiled.

"How do we know if anyone's following us?" Leonard asked. "I hear something back there. It might be an echo, or it might be something else."

We all listened for a moment. The faint sound of claws scratching stone drifted through the passage.

"Poppers!" Bobby said. "I have a bunch of ground-poppers I made in the chemistry lab last week. They're leftovers from the 4th of July, but I wish I had more of the big fireworks with me; they'd be excellent weapons." Bobby reached into his pocket and pulled out a handful of tiny paper objects shaped like teardrops, each with a twisted end. "When something steps on these, they'll explode and make a popping sound. We'll hear when the monsters reach this part of the tunnel. Then we'll know how far behind they are."

"Good thinking, Bobby," Elisa said.

Bobby spread the ground-poppers across the tunnel floor behind us.

"Everyone, be quiet for a change and follow me." Karl switched off his light and turned his back on us.

I could see the end of the tunnel up ahead, silvery moonlight leaking into the passage. But across the exit, a tangle of ivy choked the opening. Through the leafy gap, I saw a tangle

of tall grass and weeds; the passage had dumped us out back in the forbidden grounds near the cave and Crypt. Karl stepped up to the plants, pushed the vines aside with his bat, and then stuck his head out of the tunnel.

Holding the bat sideways, Karl inched forward, pushing the weeds over to make room for everyone.

"Let's get out of here." Karl glanced at his companions and smiled. "Good ole Number Three never fails."

"Number three?" I glanced at Leonard, confused.

"It's Babe Ruth's number; that's what he named his bat." Leonard lowered his voice. "I think that bat is his most cherished possession."

I nodded. "Let's get out of here but stay low and quiet. We don't know if Malphas left any monsters outside."

"Good thinking, Cameron." Leonard slapped me on the back, then stepped out into the moonlight.

Karl pushed forward and stepped out of the passage right after Leonard, leaving Bobby, Elisa, and me to follow.

When I stepped out, I surveyed the surroundings. The moon stared down at us from a cloudless sky, shading the landscape with a silver hue. Countless stars sparkled in the dark canopy like the rarest of diamonds. It would have been a beautiful night except for the horde of monsters trying to kill us.

Crouching, I looked around. We emerged near the cave, the Skull Key over the entrance shading the ground a sickly green. Across the tangle of weeds and grass, the Crypt stood tall and silent.

"Look," Elisa whispered. "Something's coming out of the Crypt."

One of the tiny red imps emerged from the Crypt, followed by the angry gremlin with the leather straps crisscrossing his muscular chest.

"That's the mean one," Elisa whispered. "I think he's called Krak."

I nodded and pushed aside the tall blades of grass and weeds to get a better view.

"You lost the humans while we were following them in the tunnels, Fool!" the gremlin shouted. "They have the Skull of Longing. We need that Skull Key."

"It wasn't my fault, Krak," the imp pleaded. "A lot of monsters followed the humans, not just me."

"Don't make excuses." Krak flipped his whip around, holding the long, leathery thong portion, the wooden handle now like a club.

"No . . . please," the imp begged.

Suddenly, a popping sound emerged from their secret tunnel.

"My ground-poppers," Bobby whispered. "They're coming."

Leonard glanced at the others. "We need to move carefully through this tall grass until we reach the stone wall, then run for it. Okay?"

We all nodded.

"Follow me." Leonard used his hockey stick to part the grass as he crawled across the ground.

Additional pops came from the tunnel.

*More monsters,* I thought, my fear growing.

*Buzzzzzzz,* the bees in my head grew angry.

Suddenly, the imp cried out in pain.

"Let this be a reminder for everyone." Krak swung the handle at the imp, hitting the creature over and over. Other monsters emerged from the Crypt and watched. "The cost of failing our master, the Demon Lord, Malphas, is severe."

"Please, nooooo . . ." the tiny monster begged.

The gremlin beat the imp again and again, the small creature's cries getting weaker and weaker.

Suddenly Elisa stopped and turned toward the gremlin.

"Elisa . . . don't." I reached for her, but it was too late.

Elisa screamed, "NO!" She stood and pointed at the gremlin. "You stop hurting that little guy."

"The humans," Krak screeched. "Get them!"

"Come on, everyone." Leonard stood. "Run!"

I grabbed Elisa by the arm and pulled her toward the stone wall separating the Crypt grounds from the schoolyard. With the Skull Key gripped under an arm, I wove around thick clumps of thistles and through tall grassy barricades, pulling on Elisa's sleeve.

Just then, the monsters emerged from the tunnel behind us and charged across the weedy landscape. Eight monsters surged through the tall grass, imps and gargoyles growling their blood-thirsty cries for violence.

*This is the end,* I thought. *We're outnumbered, and they're probably faster than us.*

Without looking back, we ran for our lives.

# Chapter 16 – The Skull of Longing

We sped through the tall weeds and out the gate that separated the tangled forest of overgrowth from the neatly manicured school grounds.

"Faster," Leonard shouted, his football pads bouncing about on his shoulders. "Karl, take up the rear with me." He glanced at the baseball player. "We have to give Cameron time to hide the Skull Key somewhere within Camp Pontchartrain."

Karl nodded, then slowed, letting Bobby, Elisa, and me move ahead. "Here they come."

A gargoyle leaped into the air and flapped its wings, taking to the sky. The monster picked up speed, then dove at Leonard, its smoking fingers extended. Watching it over his shoulder, Leonard let it get closer, then skidded to a stop and swung his hockey stick. The wood smashed into the gray creature's wing and the gargoyle fell hard to the ground. Leonard hit it one more time across the back, smashing both wings, then turned and sprinted after us.

Karl stopped running, turned, and attacked. He swung his bat at a group of approaching imps. The tiny red demons charged at Karl with claws extended and teeth bared. Their red bodies stood out in the moonlight, making them easy targets. His bat flashed through the air like a bolt of blue aluminum lighting. Karl hit imp after imp, knocking them aside as if they were annoying gnats. Gargoyles charged him. The baseball player slowly moved backward as he struck at the attackers. Number Three smashed smoking hands and extended wings. But for every monster Karl clubbed into unconsciousness, two more flooded out of the Crypt.

A wave of claws and fangs descended upon the baseball player.

Leonard reached Karl's side and used the hockey stick like a scythe cutting wheat. The wooden shaft struck down monster after monster. Imps fell to the ground, wounded, with wings torn and claws chipped.

One imp made it past Karl's bat and slashed at his arm. Its dark claws sliced across Karl's skin, drawing a thin bead of blood. With a kick to the chest, Karl sent the monster tumbling to the ground, then brought his bat down onto the Agarthan, knocking it out. The two captains fought side by side, each watching the other's flank.

I glanced over my shoulder at the two athletes. Soon, the approaching mob would overwhelm them. A buzzing storm of angry hornets filled my head, my Beast closing in.

*I can't let them get hurt,* I thought. *They're like friends . . . Leonard is, at least . . . and I have so few.*

Automatic negative thoughts flashed through my mind like lightning during a hurricane, each image showing how Leonard and Karl might get hurt. *I gotta help them. I* can *do it!*

At that moment, the quartz Chakra stone grew hot on my skin. Light leaked out from beneath my shirt as it glowed, getting hotter, but not burning my flesh. The glow from the quartz leaked into my mind, driving many of the *ANTs* back into the shadows and silencing the angry hornets in my head, allowing me to think. Courage blossomed within my soul, further blasting away the hornets and *what-ifs.*

"Bobby, Elisa, we need to help Leonard and Karl." I skidded to a stop and reached into my backpack. "We can't just leave them there." The hornets grew louder for a moment, but I pushed them aside. Instead, I focused on my friends, the *what-ifs* fading under the glare of the quartz Chakra stone and my courage. "Gather your weapons and follow me."

"Jelly-gun?" Bobby asked.

"Don't be ridiculous," I said. "Leonard and Karl need our help."

Reaching into my bag, I pulled out a handful of shiny spheres; shocker-balls. I was about to put the Skull Key into my backpack when an imp dove at me. Instinctively, I brought up the bag to stop the monster. Its claws sliced into the bottom of the backpack; the bag would never hold the Skull Key now.

With the spheres stuffed into my pockets and the Skull key tucked under an arm, I charged into battle, screaming. I pulled out one shocker and flipped the switch on the bottom, then counted, "one, two, three," and threw it into the air. The gadget sailed over Karl's head, then sprang to life. The lid popped open, and four darts shot out, each fully charged. Two of the sharp points found a pair of imps. Sparks danced across red skin, the electrical charges like glistening bees stinging into monstrous flesh.

It brought the two monsters down.

The sound of something hard zipped past my ear. A gargoyle yelped in pain as something bounced off his head. Bobby moved to my side, his high-tech slingshot in his hand. Loading two marbles into the weapon, he fired at the airborne

109

creatures, his aim deadly accurate. Firing as fast as he could load the pouch, Bobby pummeled the monsters. Marbles bounced off skulls, pierced wings, and slammed into an eye or two.

I tossed another shocker-ball into the air, this time over Leonard's head. The tiny darts found a gargoyle and an imp, the stunned monsters plummeting to the ground. I threw another and another as Bobby kept firing his marbles at the Agarthans. Karl's bat pinged again and again as a loud *thwack* sounded from Leonard's hockey stick.

Elisa fired her arrows at the imps and gargoyles in the air, her arm shaking violently. She couldn't aim, her arrows flying wide, missing the targets.

"How about you hit something?" Karl glared at her. "I could use some help."

She gripped her bow tight and fired again, the arrow, like all the rest, missing the monster.

But with Karl's bat, Leonard's hockey stick, Bobby's slingshot, and my shocker-balls, we held back the flood, for now. It seemed as if we were winning until . . .

"Cameron, that huge demon is coming!" Elisa shouted.

I knew it had to be Malphas.

The Demon Lord of Agartha emerged from the Crypt. He extended his dark wings and took to the air. Flying over the battle, the demon glared down at the five of us, his scarred beak pointed at us like the tip of a deadly spear. Malphas leaned forward and dove straight for Karl. The monster extended his muscular arms, the shining talons at the end of each finger glistening in the moonlight.

"Karl . . . look out!" I shouted, but Karl couldn't hear me. The growls and shouts of the monsters around him drowned out my voice.

I ran over and grabbed the back of his jersey, pulling him backward. "Leonard, we have to retreat."

"What are you doing!" Karl shouted.

"We gotta run." I pointed at the streak of terror descended from the night sky. "The demon . . . THE DEMON!"

Karl spotted the monster plummeting toward him and gasped. Turning, he fled from the imps and gargoyles.

Leonard turned and ran. He reached out to me, trying to take the Skull Key from my grasp, but Malphas hit the ground like a meteor, causing a shock wave to ripple across the ground, knocking us backward. I tumbled to the ground, hitting hard, the blue skull rolling from my grip. Leonard lunged for it but was too late. Malphas had it in his clawed hands, a vicious smile painted across his hideous face.

"Thank you for finding my Skull Key, Earthers." Malphas glared at me, then glanced up at the moon. "Next time we meet, it will cost you your life. Fortunate for you, human, time is short."

I looked to the west. The moon kissed the horizon, the edge sinking below the roofline of distant houses.

"Agarthans!" the demon shouted. "Return to the doorway. The moon is about to set."

The monsters retreated toward the cave, picking up their fallen comrades. They all rushed into the dark opening, a sense of panic painted on their faces. Another gargoyle flew out of the Crypt with a quartz skull held in its hand. It flew straight toward the cave and pressed it into the stone arc over the entrance. Instantly, the skull gave off a flash of light and glowed white.

"They got another one," Bobby moaned.

Malphas smiled, then took to the air, the blue Skull of Longing in his hands. He flew to the stone arch over the cave and placed the skull next to the glowing quartz one. Instantly, the blue skull flashed, then gave off a sapphire hue, painting the grass and weeds. The demon stepped into the cave and disappeared.

"We lost." Leonard dropped his hockey stick and knelt, breathing hard.

"No thanks to her." Karl glared at Elisa. "You ever hit anything with that toy? I think you should go back to bow and arrow school. No, maybe pre-school instead."

"It's not a toy." Elisa sniffled as she wiped away a tear. "It's just that . . . sometimes I get nervous . . . and umm . . ."

"Umm . . . great answer." Karl turned to me. "Is it so hard to hold on to one skull?"

"The impact of that demon sent me flying. It rolled out of my hands when I hit the ground." I glanced at Leonard, hoping for support.

The football player said nothing.

"If I hadn't pulled you back, the demon would have . . . ." I lowered my gaze.

"So, you just gave them the thing we were supposed to be protecting." Karl glared at me. "Good job, Techie."

"It'll be okay, Cameron," Leonard said.

"How do you know?" I snapped.

The football captain shrugged. "I don't."

"This is my fault. I did nothing to help." Elisa dropped her bow and quiver and walked away from the group, heading toward the stone wall at the edge of the grass.

"Elisa, wait." I ran after her, then walked to her side. "This wasn't your fault; it wasn't anyone's fault. The Agarthans got another skull. So what?" I put a hand on her shoulder. "We only need to keep one skull from them, and we win; any more is just a bonus."

"Don't you get it?" Elisa wiped tears from her face, then glared at me. "This was me failing, *again*."

We reached the stone wall and sat, dangling our feet in the weeds.

"It wasn't your fault." I grabbed her hand. "They outnumbered us. If you had hit some monsters with your arrows, that demon would have still taken the skull, and maybe killed some of us as well." I glanced at the cave entrance, the three skulls glowing brightly. "The Demon Lord is too big and too terrifying. No one can stand up against a monster like that."

"Then what? We should just give up?"

"No, we have to keep trying. If we give up, it guarantees the outcome. We can't just surrender; we must keep fighting."

"Those are fine words." She turned toward me. "But why do you give in to your anxiety and let it take over?"

"That's different. It's—"

A moan drifted out of the weeds.

"Someone's hurt." She stood and turned toward the sound. "Come on."

Elisa leaped off the wall and ran through the weeds, heading for the Crypt and the groans of agony. I followed her, letting the weeds and thistles whip across my pants. When she reached the entrance, Elisa skidded to a stop and knelt.

"Who is it?" I asked, then was shocked at what I saw.

The little imp with the broken horn, the one I'd seen from the ropes course, lay on the ground. Ugly bruises covered his red skin, and dark blood dripped from an angry gash on his arm. The imp moaned, clearly in pain, but unconscious.

"We need to help this little guy," Elisa said. "At least this is something I can do without failing."

"But it's an imp . . . a monster . . . our enemy."

"This little guy isn't our enemy." Elisa knelt and scooped the demon up in her arms, then stood. "His master, the demon, Mal-something."

"Malphas."

"Right, Malphas." Elisa nodded. "He's our enemy. This little guy is just a pawn who's been beaten nearly to death. Maybe he can give us some information about the other monsters of Agartha." She glanced at Bobby, Karl, and Leonard. "We're gonna take him to the barn and help him."

Without waiting for a reply, Elisa walked through the thick weeds toward the gate, the creature's pointed tail dangling over her arm.

"What have you got there?" Bobby asked.

Elisa walked past the other three, heading for the barn. "Someone who needs help."

"We have a prisoner." Karl smiled.

"He's not a prisoner," Elisa scowled at the baseball player. "He's gonna be an ally, so all of you leave him alone. I'm taking him to the barn and help him get back on his feet again."

"But Elisa, what if he doesn't want to help us?" Leonard jogged to her side, then walked with her. "What if he wants to kill us like all the other monsters?"

"Then I'll let him go. But until then, he's under my protection." She turned away from Leonard, flinging her blond hair through the air.

I glanced at Bobby and sighed. "Come on, let's help her."

"Absolutely." Bobby nodded. "Did you see what that gremlin was doing to this little imp? That gremlin—"

"I think his name was Krak," I said.

"Right. That gremlin, Krak, beat on the imp with that vicious whip." Bobby glanced at Elisa, then back to me. "Krak is like every bully who has ever picked on us. We aren't gonna stand for that."

"No, we aren't." I nodded to my friend. "Come on; follow Elisa." I glanced at Karl. "Are you coming with us?"

The ball player smacked his bat into the palm of his left hand. "You bet. When that monster wakes up, it'll give us some information or feel Number Three's wrath. And when it's done answering my questions, maybe I'll bonk it on the head a couple of times, just for fun."

"Don't act too quickly with that bat." Bobby glanced at the imp hanging limp in Elisa's arms, then gave Karl a mischievous smile. "An ally is better than an enemy."

Karl shrugged, then headed for the barn, Leonard following close behind. I glanced at the moon, the last sliver of its lunar face slowly ducking behind the western horizon.

"The Super Blood Moon is tomorrow," I said to myself. "I hope we can survive this."

A shudder slithered down my spine as I ran to catch up with the others, icy fingers of dread grasping my soul and starting to squeeze.

# Day of the Super Blood Moon Lunar Eclipse

## Chapter 17 – Friend or Foe

I woke from a fitful sleep, every muscle in my body complaining of abuse. Nearby, the imp slept on a cot, the creature's wounds bandaged as best as we could.

We brought the imp back to the barn and found a large room in the back, eight cots with pillows and blankets distributed across the floor. The gardeners who came to the camp periodically to run the fleet of riding mowers probably used this room. Each of us chose a cot and instantly fell asleep, someone always taking a turn watching the Agarthan in case he woke during the night.

I sat up and found Elisa sitting next to the creature, a worried look on her face. She dipped a cloth into a bowl of water, then rung it out and placed it on the monster's forehead. The imp stirred, then slowly opened his eyes. Instead of glowing red, like Malphas's, his eyes were gray and peaceful.

"Are you okay?" Elisa placed a gentle hand on the monster's broken horn. "Does it hurt much?"

The imp looked up at Elisa and then glanced at me, eyes darting back and forth. He shook his head, dislodging her hand from his horn.

The other kids woke and gathered around the imp, Karl, with his bat, standing menacingly nearby.

"Where am I?" The monster stood and moved backward, bumping into a cabinet. "I must get back to Agartha before the moon sets."

The imp flapped his wings and ran toward the door, but Leonard stepped forward and caught the imp just as it was lifting off the ground. He wrapped his arms around the creature and held it tight to his chest, arm and wings pinned to his body.

"I must get back to Agartha before the moon sets, or I'll die." The imp struggled in vain against Leonard's muscular arms, then gave up and stopped thrashing about.

"First, you're gonna answer a few questions." Karl moved closer to the imp and glared. "Then we'll see what happens next."

"Don't let him scare you." Elisa stepped between Karl and the imp. "Your name is Rylee, right? I heard that terrible gremlin, Krak, say it once."

Rylee glanced from Karl to Elisa. "Yes, I am called Rylee." He looked down at his arm and found the bandage wrapped around his wound. "You tried to heal me . . . why?"

"If we see someone suffering, we offer assistance, and you needed some help." Elisa smiled at the little imp.

I moved closer to the creature. "Why do you think you'll die when the moon sets? What does the moon do to you?"

"I don't know." Rylee glanced at Karl again, the baseball player frowning, then back to me. "The Master said it, so it must be true."

"Who is your master?" Elisa asked.

"The Demon Lord, Malphas. He rules all of Agartha, and everyone is controlled by his demon-magic. They do as he commands."

"What does Malphas want?" I moved closer to the imp and put a gentle hand on the creature's shoulder.

"My master seeks the seven Skull Keys," Rylee said.

"We know that already." Karl pushed the tip of his bat into the tiny imp's chest. "You'll have to do better than that if you want to return to your precious Agartha."

I shoved the bat away, then patted the imp on the shoulder again. "It's okay. Don't let him scare you, Rylee. Please tell us, why does your master want the Skull Keys?"

"I don't . . . know." The imp's high-pitched voice quivered. "The Demon Lord never tells us why we must do something. He commands, and we obey. We have no choice."

"What do you mean, you have no choice?" Elisa stepped up to Karl, put a hand on his bat, and forced it away from the imp.

"Malphas can control anyone he gazes upon. His red eyes take control of anyone who looks back at him. My eyes glow red because I'm under his control. I must get back, or he'll be angry." The imp struggled in Leonard's grasp but still couldn't get free.

"But your eyes aren't—" Bobby said but was interrupted by Karl.

"We need to know how to stop him first, and then we'll let you go." Karl glared at Rylee.

"You cannot stop him. The Demon Lord of Agartha destroys all enemies and takes what is theirs. You've already lost; you just don't know it yet."

Light from outside leaked into the room through the window mounted in the door. It grew brighter as the sun rose.

"The moon . . . the moon!" Rylee wailed as he struggled within Leonard's grasp. "Something is wrong. Please . . . let me go, or I'll die."

Elisa nodded.

Leonard set the imp on the ground, then opened the door. The tiny creature took off running through the barn. He flapped his small wings and floated into the air. When he reached the large barn doors, both open, Rylee stopped in midair and hovered there. The morning sun bathed the school grounds with its warm radiance, the cloudless sky showing a canopy of blue stretching to the horizon.

"It has set. The moon is gone. I'm going to die." Rylee fell to the grass with a thud.

Elisa ran to him. "Rylee, are you okay?"

"I should be dead. The moon has set, yet I'm still alive." The imp glanced at the mirror hanging from one of the doors and took to the air, floating to it. "My eyes . . . they no longer glow." He reached up and carefully rubbed his eyes. Blinking, he gazed into the mirror again. "His hold over me, it's gone!" The imp smiled a toothy smile, creepy and joyous all at once. "I am no longer a servant of Malphas, Demon Lord of Agartha. I am myself again. It's been so long. I don't know who I am."

"You're Rylee, and you're surrounded by friends." Elisa reached down and took the imp's hand. Its long claws gently wrapped around her fingers.

"This is why Malphas makes you afraid of the setting moon," Bobby said. "He doesn't want his army to realize that freedom is just within their grasp." He reached into a side pocket on his backpack and pulled out a box of Gummy Bears. Pouring a couple into his hand, Bobby offered them to the imp, then popped one in his mouth. "Try it."

The imp took the candy and held it up to his little nose. He sniffed it, then took a small bite, his pointed tail flicking about. "Sweet." The creature put the whole thing in his mouth and smiled. "Rylee likes."

He held out a clawed hand for more. Bobby poured a dozen of them into the imp's hand. Rylee shoved them all into his mouth.

"Slow down, Rylee." I rushed forward. "Besides, I want some; don't eat them all."

Bobby handed the Agarthan the box of candy after gobbling down a few more.

"Don't worry. I always have more Gummy Bears; they're my favorite."

Rylee chewed the candy, a smile spreading across his red face. "I'm free, and you are friends?"

Elisa and I nodded.

"Even the great warriors." He pointed to Leonard and Karl.

Leonard nodded as well, then elbowed Karl in the ribs, who rolled his eyes, then nodded.

"Sure, I'll be friends with a monster from a parallel universe; why not?" Karl laughed. "I don't have any real friends anyway. I might as well have a monster for one."

Just then, a young girl approached the barn carrying a cardboard box.

"Rylee, hide," I said.

The imp continued to stare into the mirror, transfixed. I stepped between the monster and the mirror, breaking Rylee's gaze. The imp looked at me.

"Hide behind the mowers." I pointed to the line of green metal beasts.

Rylee nodded and floated through the air, hiding behind one of the lawnmowers.

"Mrs. Chakoté said I should bring this to the barn in the morning." The girl set the box on the ground, then turned and headed back toward the buildings on the other side of the lawn.

"I smell bacon." Bobby moved to the box and lifted out a paper bag. Stuffing his hand inside, he pulled out a bagel sandwich, eggs and bacon trapped between the round bread.

Rylee flew to Bobby's side and sniffed. "What is that smell?"

"It's humanity's greatest invention." Bobby pulled a piece of bacon from the sandwich, folded it in half, then in half again, then did it one more time, forming a bacon cube. Bobby smiled, then popped it into his mouth.

Rylee stared at Bobby, the little imp's mouth starting to water. Pulling out another piece of bacon, Bobby formed the yummy cube and handed it to Rylee. The imp sniffed it cautiously, then gobbled it down.

"That's good," the monster said with a smile. "Is there more?" The imp peered into the box, then took to the air and floated backward, pointing with a clawed finger. "Something glows."

I reached into the box and pulled out a cloth-wrapped object. Removing the covering, I found a dagger, seven colorful stones mounted into its handle, the blue, green, and clear stones glowing

118

faintly. The blade, made of dark metal, almost black, had a blunt tip, the edge rounded and dull. When I grasped the handle, each stone flashed, giving off a splash of color.

"Ahh . . . the Dagger of Stones." Rylee hovered closer to me. "That is the only thing that can remove a Skull Key from the doorway linking Earth and Agartha, but it can only be used once. After a Skull Key is dislodged from the doorway, the dagger will dissolve and become useless. It must be used wisely, for you have only one chance."

I held the dagger up to my eyes.

"The first person who touches it is the only one who can wield it." Rylee looked at me. "The Blade of Stones is now yours."

I shuddered. "I don't want a dagger."

Rylee shrugged. "It doesn't matter what you want . . . it's now yours. You should use this powerful weapon only in the direst of circumstances."

I shuddered again, slipped the knife under my belt, then grabbed a bottle of water from the box and took a drink.

"There's a note in the box." Elisa grabbed a folded piece of paper, then distributed the remaining sandwiches. She pulled a piece of bacon from between the bagel halves of her sandwich and tossed it to Rylee. The imp floated into the air, skewered it on a claw, and then gobbled it down.

Elisa smiled at Rylee, then read the note.

> Kids,
>
> I see by looking at the Chakra stones on my cane that the Agarthans have found three Skull Keys. This is not good. With three stones in place, larger monsters can move through the gateway and come to Earth. Undoubtedly, more monsters will search the tunnels and caves under the Crypt. They'll likely find the rest of the skulls. The Order of the Stones is on the way; you just need to hold out for a little while longer.
>
> With three skulls already found by the Agarthans, it would be best to focus your efforts on the most powerful of the Skull Keys, the black onyx Skull of Fear. Anyone who touches this Skull Key must confront their fears. Only the strongest have proven able to do this. Find the Skull of Fear and keep it safe.

The Order hid it in the Cave of Soles, which is a clue to its location on the map.

Find the Skull of Fear and keep it from the monsters of Agartha. I have left you the Dagger of Stones to help, just in case Malphas gets all the Skulls.

Right now, everything depends on you. I have faith you're all up to this challenge. If you aren't, then death and destruction will greet us all.

Good Luck.

Mrs. Chakoté, Order of the Stones

"Cave of Soles . . . what does that mean?" Karl asked.

Leonard turned to Bobby. "Pull out the map. Let's see if it shows a cave."

Bobby took out the map and unfolded it, setting it on the hood of a riding mower. "The problem is, there are lots of caves. Which one is the Cave of Soles?"

I pointed to the map. "It's that one."

"How do you know?" Karl pushed his way to the map and stared at it.

"She spelled it S-O-L-E-S, right?" I asked.

Elisa nodded.

"That cave is shaped like the bottom of a shoe." I looked up from the map and smiled. "That's the one."

"Okay then, let's get the Skull of Fear." Bobby folded up the map and shoved it into a pocket.

"I can help." The imp floated into the air and landed on the mower. "You're my new friends. Malphas will do terrible things if he gets all the Skull Keys."

Elisa glanced at me. "You sure we can do this?"

I shrugged, then shuddered. A faint buzzing emerged from the dark places of my mind; the Beast was awakening.

Leonard stepped forward and spoke softly, the sadness in his eyes fading a bit. "There are no great people in this world, only great challenges which ordinary people rise to meet." He paused for a moment to let them all digest the words. "That's a quote from a famous Admiral during World War II, Admiral William Halsey." Leonard moved to my side and put an arm around my shoulder. "I don't know if we're great people, but we *will* rise to this challenge, right, Cameron?"

"Ahh . . . umm . . . sure, I guess."

"That was *way* too much confidence, Poole," Karl said sarcastically. "Like, wow." He grinned a mischievous grin.

Bobby cleared his throat, then stood tall and spoke. "Let the overwhelming size and devastating strength of our enemy not deter us from our task." He looked at his companions and smiled. "How about that one?"

"Overwhelming size?" Leonard asked.

Elisa shook her head. "Devastating strength . . . really?"

"I think you might have missed on that proclamation, just like the others, Techie." Karl laughed. "But I liked it." He picked up Number Three and headed out of the barn. "Let's go. We have a date with some terrifying monsters."

Leonard glanced at me, an eyebrow raised with an unasked question. I returned the expression with a shrug, then gathered my things and followed, the rest of the kids donning their bags and weapons.

"Wait a minute." Bobby dashed into the back room. He pulled a bed aside and pried up a loose board from the floor. Reaching into the darkness, he withdrew multiple boxes of candy. "This is an emergency stash; I have them hidden throughout the school." He shook a box of Hot Tamales and an envelope of Pop Rocks. "I can't go back into those spooky tunnels without something spicy for my tongue."

"What are they?" Rylee asked as he sniffed the box.

"I'll show you later, Rylee, that is, if we survive." Bobby laughed as if it were the funniest thing he had ever said.

I shuddered and headed back to the barn's entrance.

As we walked through the barn, Rylee spotted the mirror mounted to the door and hovered in the air, unable to look away.

"Rylee, come on," I said, but the monster didn't respond; the imp was transfixed by his reflection.

Stepping up to the mirror, I put myself directly in front of the imp, blocking his view.

"What happened?" Rylee glanced about, afraid.

"You just got stuck in front of the mirror." I reached out to the monster. "Close your eyes and hold on to my hand." I led the imp out of the barn.

When we were clear, Rylee opened his eyes and flew ahead, watching for monsters from high in the air.

I looked back at the barn door and Mr. Wallace's mirror. Something about it tugged at the back of my mind, like a memory fading away. All I could think about was the art studio at Camp Pontchartrain, but that didn't make any sense. With a shrug, I let the thought go and caught up with my friends, trying to ignore the *what-ifs* surfacing from the depths of my mind.

But as I walked toward the Crypt, I felt as if we were approaching the edge of a deadly cliff, and we were all about to plummet to our doom.

# Chapter 18 – Cave of Soles

I glanced at the glowing skulls mounted over the cave entrance. They cast a harsh glare on the ground, making the cave seem even spookier than usual. My mind conjured up images of various mythical creatures storming out of the dark opening, each trying to kill us all. The *ANTs* and *what-ifs* awakened the buzzing hornets in my mind, bringing them to life. My anxiety grew as the thought-loop strengthened, fears feeding themselves and growing stronger.

*'Some fears are real, Cameron'*, Dr. Jen's voice said in my head. *'Your body can respond to those fears to keep you safe. But the fears your anxiety creates, they try to deceive you . . . they're a lie. Think about them logically, challenge them, and you'll see the ANTs make no sense.'*

Would the monsters come charging out of the cave right now? Probably not. The positive self-talk was trying to chisel away at my anxiety. But logic didn't seem to help with the buzzing in my head. It didn't matter if the fear seemed illogical or insane; it felt real to *me*. That's why they're so difficult to ignore.

The buzzing grew louder as we neared the Crypt.

*Is this fear gonna stop? Will it keep growing?* Sometimes, it felt like the terror would last forever. I knew this also to be a lie, but that's how it felt; it was the worst thing about anxiety. In those moments, when my Beast had control, it seemed endless . . . a lifetime of eternal terror ravaging my soul. None of Dr. Jen's strategies seemed to help when my Beast had me firmly in its grasp.

The buzzing grew louder, the hornets getting angry. The more I thought about the fear, the worse it became. My body shook for a moment, arms and legs feeling weak . . . like spaghetti.

A hand settled on my shoulder. I turned and found Elisa there, a look of compassion on her face.

"You can't focus on it," she whispered. "Try to distract yourself. Make an alphabetical list of adjectives."

"Adjectives?" My mind thought about the challenge.

Facing the Beast Within

"You know, a word that describes a person, place, or thing," Elisa said. "Usually, you can put the word *very* in front of an adjective to test it."

I sighed, annoyed. "I know what an adjective is."

She smiled and shrugged.

*Let's see . . . adjectives . . .*

*A – agonizing, B – brutal . . .* the buzzing seemed to diminish a bit.

I glanced back at the glowing Skull Keys. The furious hornets grew louder again.

*C – cruel, D – destructive . . .* the buzzing decreased. *E – empty, F – frightening, G – ghastly.*

The buzzing grew softer, my Beast slowly settling back into the dark places of my mind.

*H – hateful, I – isolated, J – jealous . . .* the buzzing nearly disappeared as the *what-ifs* faded away, allowing me to think.

I glanced at Elisa. "Thanks . . . again."

"No worries," she said with a smile. "We're in this together. And besides, we're friends. We'd do anything for each other, right?"

I nodded. "Right."

We reached the Crypt and entered the terrifying structure, moving through the catacombs as quickly as possible. The glow from Rylee's horns filled the tunnels with crimson light, making it easy to avoid obstacles and small holes in the ground. We walked for a couple of hours, following the maze of underground passages and pausing only to drink water or eat some of the food we'd brought. Before long, we reached the location where we found the second skull. Avoiding the stone tiles on the ground, Bobby led us past the decapitated stalagmite and continued through the passage. After a couple of hundred yards, Bobby turned into a tunnel on the left and followed it down a steep incline, going deeper into the stony flesh under the camp. The air grew stale as if another living creature hadn't set foot here for decades.

*Is there enough oxygen down here?* I thought as I took in raspy breaths. I wanted to wipe my tongue, the perpetual dust floating up from our footsteps coating our mouths and the insides of our noses.

"We need to rest," Elisa said. "Walking until we're exhausted isn't a good plan."

Leonard nodded. "She's right. Bobby, how far is the Cave of Soles?"

Bobby sat on a nearby boulder and pointed his flashlight at the map. "It's still far away. We need to switch tunnels multiple times, and the passages zigzag back and forth, probably to confuse the monsters." He reached into his pocket and pulled out a box of candy, Hot Tamales. "Rylee, try these." Bobby poured some into Rylee's hand.

The imp stuffed the candies into his mouth.

"Slow down, Rylee," I said. "They're—"

"Hot." The imp grinned. "Rylee likes." He extended a clawed hand to Bobby who just handed over the box. "They taste like the fire mushrooms from back home." The imp lowered his gaze to the ground.

"Don't worry, Rylee. You'll get home, eventually." Elisa sat on the ground next to the Agarthan.

"I know, but what will home be like?" Rylee skewered a candy with a claw, then poked another one and another until he had a Hot Tamale on the end of each finger.

"Tamale fingers," Bobby nodded and smiled. "Nice."

Rylee sucked the candies off each claw and chewed.

"What do you mean, Rylee?" I sat next to Elisa, glad to be off my feet.

"Well, if I go back to Agartha, what will change? Malphas will be the ruler, and he'll use his demon-magic to control me again. The Demon Lord will force my brothers and sisters into the army when they're old enough. There will be no freedom like what I've tasted here, only sorrow."

"Maybe there's a way to bring freedom to your people while we're stopping Malphas." I glanced at Elisa and Bobby. They both nodded in agreement.

"Hold on." Karl stood and held his hand out as if stopping traffic. "How about we focus on one impossible quest at a time?"

Rylee's posture slumped.

Karl glanced at his companions, their angry stares all focused on him. "But, if the opportunity arises, we'll also free the Agarthans. What do you say to that?"

Rylee raised his head and gazed at Karl, then nodded and smiled.

"Let's get going." Leonard stood and put on his shoulder pads. He extended a hand to Elisa, pulling her to her feet, then did the same for others. "Lead on, Bobby."

Glancing down at the map, Bobby checked the directions, then started at a brisk pace. We walked for hours, only stopping for water. Our only sense of time was the exhaustion our bodies felt. Suddenly, Rylee screeched. "I feel the moon rising." He glanced at Elisa. "Give me a mirror, quick."

Elisa pulled a mirror from a pocket and handed it to him. The imp opened the compact makeup mirror and stared into it, instantly transfixed by his reflection.

"Rylee . . . Rylee." Elisa knelt and gently shook the imp.

Turning, Rylee looked at Elisa, a smile on his red face.

"What are you looking for?" she asked.

His smile widened. "My eyes. I wanted to see if they started glowing with the rising of the moon. If they were red, it would mean . . ." He glanced at the mirror again, mesmerized into silence by his own image.

Elisa closed the mirror and took it from the imp's hands. She shook him again. "What were you saying?"

A tear trickled from one of Rylee's dark eyes. "I'm free . . . I'm truly free." He turned and faced Elisa. "I was worried I'd become the Demon Lord's servant again when the moon rose, but my eyes aren't glowing. I'm still me." The imp flapped his wings and floated a couple of feet in the air. "This is a great day."

"Well, it's gonna turn bad really quick if we don't find this Cave of Shoes." Karl tapped Number Three on the ground in annoyance. "My gramma could walk faster than some of you. Let's get moving."

We continued. As we walked, voices percolated out of the shadows, angry voices with a thirst for violence dripping off every word.

"They're here." Rylee's voice shook with fear.

"We need to hurry." Leonard glanced at me. "Bobby, move faster."

With Rylee's glowing horns enveloping the party in a circle of crimson light, we ran through the passages, heading for the Cavern of Soles.

"Wait . . . stop." Leonard skidded to a stop and reached into his shirt. He pulled out his Chakra stone pendant and held it by the cord. The purple Amethyst stone glowed as if electrified from within. The color drained from his face. "They got another one."

"That will mean more monsters," Rylee said in a soft, scared voice, "and bigger ones, too." The tiny imp shuddered. "Banshees . . . he'll send banshees, I'm sure of it."

"What are banshees?" Bobby asked, his voice shaking.

"They're creatures of hate and malice." Rylee glanced at Bobby. "Imagine an evil spirit with a voice able to split stone and drain a creature of life. When they aim their screech at you, agony envelops your body." The red in his face faded, fear driving the color from his skin. "Back on Agartha, banshees hunt imps for sport. They're our enemies and our nightmares."

126

"Don't worry, Rylee. I'll protect you." Bobby pulled out his high-tech slingshot, the metal painted midnight black. "I'll let them taste the sting of my friend here." He shook the weapon, the thick elastic bands dancing about.

"This is a great little chat, but less talk and more walk." Karl gave Bobby a gentle shove. "Let's get there."

Bobby nodded and took off running, his eyes glancing at the map now and then.

The sounds of clawed feet on stone grew louder as we ran.

"They must be able to sense the location of the Skull of Fear," I said.

We ran as fast as we could, but the uneven ground and occasional holes made speed dangerous.

Rylee reached to the back of his neck and scratched his skin with one of his claws. The sharp tip gouged his flesh.

"What are you doing, Rylee?" I asked.

The imp stopped scratching and stared at his claw, a small stain of red covering the tip. "My skin itches like tiny needles digging into my flesh." Rylee shuddered. "It's the banshees. They do that to us. It has something to do with their magic. I can feel them; they're getting closer. We need to move faster."

"We're almost to the Cave of Soles," Bobby said, his nose in the map. "But the map says something I don't understand. It says, 'The threads of time, if broken, can be unforgiving.' Does that make any sense?"

"It means nothing," Karl snapped. "Just keep going. Or do you need me to lead so you won't mess it up?"

"Thanks for your confidence, Karl." Bobby shook his head. "I can do it. In fact, the Cave of Soles is up here on the left."

Bobby reached an intersection and went left. The tunnel brightened as if sunlight somehow leaked in. A hundred feet ahead, the passage opened into a vast cavern. Before Bobby could enter the cave, I shouted.

"Stop . . . there's a trap." I grabbed the barrel of Bobby's jelly-gun, the weapon slung over a shoulder, and yanked him back.

"What's the problem?" Bobby skidded to a stop. "I don't see any stone tiles, like at the second Skull Key."

"I see something." Leonard held his hockey stick in front of him and slowly lowered it to the ground. "There's a tripwire an inch off the ground."

"Press on it, and let's see what happens." Karl moved back, leaving Leonard and me near the entrance.

Leonard extended his foot and pressed down on the wire. Instantly, an arrow shot out of a hole at chest height and flew across the tunnel, slamming into the opposite wall. "If I'd been standing on that wire, it would have gone right through me. We need to disarm them." Leonard turned to me. "Any ideas?"

"Yeah. Hand me your stick." I took the hockey stick, then laid it on the ground, across multiple wires. I then picked up a large rock and tossed it on the wooden shaft, slamming it to the ground. Instantly, a half dozen arrows streaked out of small holes, stabbing the opposite wall. I pulled the stick back, then pressed it on the tripwires again. This time, nothing happened. "Okay, I think it's safe."

"What if we missed a wire?" Elisa asked, her voice shaking.

The sounds of monsters drifted out of the darkness behind us, snarls and growls getting louder.

"I'll go first with the hockey stick on the ground in front of me." *I can do this,* I thought, the words sounding weak and pathetic in my head. But when I glanced at my friends, I knew I wanted to keep them safe… I had to try. *It's okay if I'm afraid*—the thought pushed back on the *ANTs* trying to claw their way into my mind—*as long as I'm trying to be safe.*

Stepping forward, I slid the blade of the stick across the ground. It caught two more tripwires. Arrows flashed through the air, struck the opposite wall, then clattered to the floor. Finally, I made it to the entrance of the Cave of Soles.

When I stepped into the massive cavern, a strange feeling spread through me, something eerie and terrifying. It felt as if every nightmare I'd ever experienced waited for me in the darkness, each of them hungry and wanting to feed. Something in the chamber whispered to the dark places of my mind, awakening slumbering fears. Images from past terrors surfaced in my brain for a moment, monsters and demons hiding in the shadows, then fading away. Memories of bullies humiliating me in school played through my head, one after another, only to disappear and be replaced by another. It was as if this cave held all my fears.

I glanced at my friends and could tell they felt the same thing. I wanted to run away but knew I couldn't. The sounds of monsters in the passage behind us told me we had no choice.

I abandoned all hope and entered the Cave of Soles.

# Chapter 19 – Skull of Fear

A lingering sense of dread nibbled at the edge of my senses like the echo of a terrible nightmare. Stepping into the vast cavern, I shuddered. The chamber looked massive, about the size of a football field, if not larger. It curved a little, thinner at the center, and with rounded ends. Bats fluttered around the cavern, their tiny black shapes clinging to the ceiling, giving the granite roof a velvety appearance.

Massive stalagmites grew from the ground like giant spikes driven up by some subterranean beast. Their stalactite companions hung from the ceiling, stony fangs waiting to devour the unwary. Water dripped from cracks overhead, splashing down onto the cavern floor. Tiny rivulets of water zigzagged their way across the uneven floor, flowing to the center of the cavern. The small streams combined, forming a three-foot creek trickling from one end of the cave to the other.

I noticed a few torches positioned throughout the cavern, all covered with cobwebs and dust. They probably hadn't been lit for a century, if not more. One torch rested in a holder near the entrance.

"Let's light that thing." Karl bent over, picked up the torch, and then produced a packet of matches.

I didn't want to know why he carried a matchbook with him.

He handed me the torch, struck the match once, then again, bringing it to fiery life. Karl touched it to the torch, and instantly it caught, the oil-soaked rope wrapped around the end still able to burn.

Sunlight streamed in through a hole in the ceiling, the rays sparkling off coins spread across the floor. That light, mixed with the radiance from the torch, encircled us with a warm glow.

"Look at the money on the ground." Bobby moved into the circle of light and picked up a quarter, then stared up at the hole in the ceiling. "I bet we're under that old, dry well just off the camp grounds, you know, near the New Canal Lighthouse."

"If that's true, then half of this cavern must be under Lake Pontchartrain." I stared up at the rocky ceiling, expecting it to cave in because of the tons of water overhead. The image of a tidal wave flooded through my head and washed away much of my courage, leaving behind only buzzing hornets and fear.

*The fears are a lie,* I told myself, but it did little to push aside my growing terror.

Grabbing the map from Bobby, I stared at it. "There's a tiny mark at the far end of the cavern," I said in a weak voice. "The skull is probably there."

"Then let's go find it." Leonard followed what looked like a path along the cavern's wall, wending its way around stalagmites eight feet tall, if not higher. Piles of stones lay strewn across the cavern floor; the debris had fallen from the ceiling long ago.

I took a deep breath. The air lacked the dank, dusty taste of the tunnels and catacombs. Fresh air came in through the well piercing the high ceiling overhead, a welcome relief.

The rest of the party followed Leonard. Angry voices and hungry growls drifted into the chamber, filling the shadows with dread. The feeling of something dark and dangerous seemed to float through the cave like a dreadful mist, a failure yet to happen.

*Something is waiting for me,* I thought. *Something terrible.*

Everywhere I looked, I saw imaginary creatures hiding in the darkness, waiting with pointed claws and hungry teeth. Rylee flew high overhead, his horns painting the cavern's walls a soft red. The light from his horns and my torch pushed back on the darkness, helping with my fear, but not much. I went through the list of adjectives again, driving the thoughts from my head.

"I think I see it." Elisa pointed to the rocky column with her bow. "The skull . . . it's over there."

I turned and saw it. A midnight-black skull sat atop a stone pedestal, the dark skull's surface reflecting the scant rays of light bouncing throughout the cave. A sense of waiting doom seemed to emanate from the polished skull.

"Let's grab it and get out of here," I said, my voice quivering.

I wove my way around boulders and piles of stone, heading for the granite pillar. I stepped through the chilly stream, water soaking my shoes and splashing my pants. The pedestal stood waist-high. It looked like a carved piece of granite, with seven Chakra stones embedded in the side. The green, clear, blue, and purple stones gave off faint splashes of color, each representing our failures in this conflict. I walked up to the black skull and searched the ground for traps but found none; *was this skull free for the taking?*

Elisa notched an arrow to her bow. The sounds of monsters grew louder. Suddenly, she reached into her shirt and pulled out her pendant. The orange Carnelian Chakra stone glowed as if lit with an internal fire. "They got another one."

The orange stone of the pedestal came to life.

"We need to hurry." Karl tapped his bat on the ground, Number Three making a pinging sound.

"I'll do it." Leonard set his hockey stick on the ground and stepped up to the pedestal. Reaching out, he grabbed the skull with both hands. Instantly, Leonard screamed and fell to his knees, his hands still grasping the carved stone. Tears streamed down Leonard's pale face, his eyes darting about. The muscles in his neck went tense as he clenched his jaw, trying to hold in a scream.

"No . . . not that," Leonard mumbled, then groaned. "Not my mother; please no." His breathing grew rapid, his gasps for air sounding ragged and strained. "I'll do what you say, just . . . don't do it . . . not again, please."

A sorrowful sob leaked from him as if he lacked the strength to do anything else. Leonard's eyes grew wide with terror as his mouth opened into a silent scream. Finally, he collapsed to the ground and dropped the skull, the polished black stone rolling a few inches away.

Elisa rushed to his side. "Leonard, are you okay?"

Leonard wiped tears from his cheek and glanced about, looking for threats. "I'm back? Is it over? How long was I gone?" He turned to look behind him, then to the left and right again, as if confused.

"What happened?" Bobby asked.

"The Skull of Fear spoke to him," Rylee said.

"What do you mean?" I knelt next to the football player and checked him for injuries.

"The skull knew every one of my fears. It showed them to me like nightmares, but they came to life around me all at once." Leonard shuddered, then climbed shakily to his feet. "It felt as if I was stuck in those nightmares forever. They occurred over and over . . . one terrible thing after the next." His voice shook. "It was the most terrifying experience of my life."

Leonard turned away, his body still shaking. He looked as if he were broken, the echo from those terrible moments probably still reverberating through his mind.

"The Skull of Fear protects itself." Rylee flapped his wings and rose into the air, his

horns glowing brightly. "It will not stop the Demon Lord. Malphas knows no fear."

"We have to do something." Elisa glanced at me with uncertainty in her eyes.

*I should grab it,* I thought. *Fear is like an old friend who refuses to leave me alone. I failed at stopping the monsters from finding the other Skull Keys; I can't let them have this one.*

"I'll grab it." I stepped up to the pedestal.

"Cameron, no." Elisa rushed to my side.

"If anyone here knows about fear, it's me." I wiped the sweat from my brow, glanced at Leonard, then turned to Elisa and lowered my voice to a whisper. "I won't let what happened to Leonard happen to you or Bobby. You're my best friends." I glanced at Karl, but the baseball captain turned away.

I sighed. My heart pounded in my chest, getting faster and faster. The buzzing started up in my head; the Beast was awakening. "Here goes."

I picked the skull up off the ground. Instantly, the buzzing in my head became a firestorm of fear. Every failure I'd ever experienced came back to me hot and jagged. I shut my eyes, trying to hide from the terror, but of course, it didn't work.

Every bully who'd ever tormented me appeared at my side. The thrown milk cartons and mashed potato bombs in the dining hall pelted me from all sides. I was stuffed into lockers, tripped, shoved, and elbowed by every tormentor I'd ever had to face. And then they happened, again and again, an unstoppable cycle of abuse. *What-ifs* flooded my mind as images of that terrible demon, Malphas, appeared in the nightmares. The imaginary Demon Lord tore at my friends with razor-sharp claws, hurting them over and over again.

*"Cameron . . . help us,"* Nightmare-Elisa screamed.

*"Make it stop,"* Nightmare-Bobby shouted as Malphas tortured him.

They screamed in agony in my mind, each of them reaching out to me for help. But I couldn't do anything; I'd let them down again. An overwhelming sense of failure washed over me, a feeling I knew all too well.

The ability to think vanished as the buzzing in my head grew even louder. My Beast was now in control. But I didn't crumble, for this was something I'd faced every day. I was used to failure and fear. They were like old companions I could never avoid. And because I knew the face of my Beast, I could withstand the onslaught, my mind still functioning just a little . . . just enough.

I started counting by sevens. Then I listed all the animals I could think of that had fur.

*The ANTs are a lie!* I screamed within the nightmare.

*It won't last forever. It won't last forever.* I repeated the mantra as if it were a magical spell.

I listed the titles of every book I'd read, then ranked the Transformer movies from best to worst. Struggling to control my mind, I tried every possible way to distract myself. The Beast tried to take bites out of my courage, but I had no courage left and nothing to lose. This was just an ordinary day of torment for me. No, *every* day of torment all brought together. I'd survived them before, and I could survive them now.

*It won't last forever,* I thought, trying to believe it. *These fears are a lie . . . they're all lies.*

And then I examined these fears . . . did they even make sense?

*I'm not in the dining hall—how can the bullies be picking on me? Is Malphas right in front of me?* I challenged each fear, considering the most likely thing to happen around me instead of the worst-case scenario. Staring each nightmare in the face, I confronted the facts surrounding them. They made little sense. There was no pit of lava to fall into; the soccer team wasn't going to attack me; no one was about to publicly humiliate me.

*They're a lie* – but my fear still grew.

I thought about Elisa and the courage she showed throughout this terrible adventure. *Maybe I can be like her, or maybe like Karl.* Focusing my thoughts, I imagined myself to be them, confident and strong, the fear bouncing off them as if they wore steel armor.

The buzzing decreased a little.

Gritting my teeth, I forced the images back where they belonged, in the worry part of my brain. The logic part of my mind slowly came forward and took control. It acknowledged each fear, but instead of giving into its power, I let it fade into the background where its fiction belonged.

The buzzing grew softer as the coping strategies filled my mind, pulling my focus from the *what-ifs* and *ANTs*. My Beast screamed as its power over me faded. Its presence gradually submerged into the dark places within my soul, waiting . . . always waiting. Without warning, my Beast could burst forward again,

its prison cell in my mind held shut by the finest thread. I had to be careful. Slowly, I opened my eyes and faced Elisa, my face ghostly white.

"Are you okay?" she asked.

I nodded. "Barely. Let's get out of here before it's too late." I slowly stood, my legs wobbly, feet dumb and clumsy, the post-anxiety fatigue hitting me hard.

Just then, a terrible screech filled the Cave of Soles. Malphas stepped into the chamber, followed by golems, gnomes, and floating pale-white spirits I assumed were the banshees Rylee feared so much. Next to the Demon Lord stood the vicious gremlin, Krak.

"Not him," Rylee moaned.

The monsters blocked the only exit; we were trapped. The Demon Lord pointed across the cavern at me and screamed, "The humans have the Skull of Fear. Take that skull and let none leave this cave . . . alive."

And then the monsters charged.

# Chapter 20 – Trapped

A group of dirt-brown creatures rushed across the cavern floor, each six to seven feet in height, with massive arms and fists the size of boulders. Made from soil, stone, and old branches, the creatures moved clumsily, rage carved into their brown faces. Behind them flew a squad of gargoyles, their gray skin merging with the granite of the cavern, eyes glowing blood-red.

"The tall ones are golems," Rylee said. "Very strong, very dangerous."

"How do we fight them?" Leonard asked.

"You . . . don't." Rylee's voice shook. "You run."

"If you haven't noticed, imp, there's no place to go." Karl shifted Number Three from his left hand to his right.

"Stay together," I moaned, the terror caused by the Skull of Fear making it difficult to speak. "Help each other."

"He's right." Leonard nodded. "We work together and watch each other's back. United, we're stronger."

Behind the golems and gargoyles floated a group of banshees. Each had the pale white face of a beautiful woman, their skin smooth, like the finest china. Lifeless, black eyes peered from those serene faces, inky holes in an alabaster mask. The dark eyes oozed with a hatred for all living things, the coal-black pits yearning for violence. A white, tattered robe hung off their bodies, skeletal hands sticking out of sleeves. The bony appendages added to their terrifying presence. Everything about the banshees suggested an unquenchable thirst for violence as if their only purpose in life was to devour hope. They were the embodiment of evil. Goosebumps crept down the back of my neck when their terrible gaze fell on me. My whole body shook, and I looked away, hoping never to peer into those awful eyes again.

Below the banshees walked a group of gnomes. Dressed in bright colors with pointed conical hats, they looked like the garden gnomes people used to decorate their flower beds. But nothing about these four-foot-high gnomes seemed decorative. Their scarred, wrinkled faces and stained, pointed teeth gave the tiny creatures a malicious appearance, danger wrapped in bright colors.

The banshees and gnomes moved to the center of the cavern and waited for their master as the golems and gargoyles charged.

I felt my mouth become bone-dry as the army of monsters moved closer, their red eyes burning with hatred and a need for violence. I thought my heart might leap out of my chest as my pulse raced. The hairs on my arms stood up straight, fear leaching through my body.

Malphas took to the air, flapping his midnight-black wings. He landed atop a tall stalagmite and glared at us. "Agarthans, hold."

The attacking monsters stopped twenty yards from us and turned toward the Demon Lord.

Malphas ruffled his feathers, then stared at us. His eyes glowed as a high-pitched whine filled the air.

"All of you, look away," Rylee said.

I closed my eyes, as did the others. A faint high-pitched whine came from the demon, growing louder.

"He is trying to capture our will." Rylee's voice shook with fear. "Wait until the buzzing stops."

We kept our eyes shut as the high-pitched whine from the Demon Lord stabbed at our ears, the monster's demon-magic trying to pry open our eyes. But we kept our eyes shut, denying Malphas what he wanted.

The demon screamed in frustration as the buzzing abruptly ceased. "Golems, gargoyles, destroy them." He glanced down at the gremlin. "Krak, get that traitorous imp. Make him suffer."

Krak nodded as he gripped the handle of his whip.

The monsters charged. When the first golem reached the trickling stream, it leaped over, an expression of concern on its dirty brown face. It glared at the kids and gave off a deep, angry growl. "Kill the pathetic humans," the monsters grumbled.

"Pathetic? Who you callin' pathetic?!" Karl screamed in rage and charged at the golem.

"No, stay together," Leonard shouted, but the baseball player wasn't listening.

Karl attacked the nearest gargoyle. The monster swung at Karl's head with a clenched fist of dirt and stone. Karl ducked, then struck the monster's knee. His baseball bat smashed into the leg and sank in as if he were hitting something made of soft clay. Karl tugged at the bat, pulled it free, and ducked under another attack.

The monster stared down at the injured leg and growled, then kicked at its prey. Karl rolled out of the way, then stood and struck at the same leg again. He hit it repeatedly as if chopping down a tree. Finally, the bat went through the leg, and the golem tumbled to the ground. It tried to grab Karl's ankle, but Leonard was there before it could get a grip. He kicked the monster hard, again and again, driving it away from Karl. Hitting it with his hockey stick one last time, Leonard pushed the golem into the stream. Instantly, the dirt holding the creature together turned to mud. The monster screamed in terror as its body slowly dissolved, becoming a cloud of brown sludge flowing downstream.

"Leonard, duck!" Bobby shouted.

The Techie fired a barrage of marbles at a gargoyle closing in on the football captain. The projectiles struck the monster in the chest and head until one pierced through a wing, causing it to fall to the ground with a thud.

Leonard struck it with his hockey stick, knocking it out cold.

More golems leaped across the stream, each staring down at the pile of mud and sticks that had been their comrade moments before.

Krak ran toward Rylee, his whip flicking this way and that. Rylee cringed, backing away. The gremlin leaped over the stream as the other kids were busy with the golems and gargoyles, a look of evil delight in his red eyes.

"Hello, Fool. I see you're still alive, somehow." The gremlin flicked his whip, the end just missing Rylee's head.

"You don't understand, Krak. When the moon sets, we don't die. We—"

"Save your words, Fool. It's time for you to meet your pathetic end."

The gremlin charged at Rylee, whip ready to strike. Suddenly, a hail of marbles flew through the air, hitting the gremlin in the chest and head. An arrow streaked next to the monster, driving it back. Elisa stepped to Rylee's side, her arm shaking. She fired again, the arrow missing its target, but the next one found the gremlin's leg. The blunt tip sunk into flesh, causing the monster to howl in pain. Bobby moved to Elisa's side and fired his marbles, hitting the gremlin in the head.

Outnumbered, Krak turned and fled just as another golem approached, the strong, dirt-brown arms swinging at the three companions. But before the monster could get close, Leonard was there with his hockey stick, striking at the monster's leg. The stick bounced off pieces of wood in the golem's knee, causing the creature to lose its balance. The monster fell to the ground with a thud. Bobby rushed forward and kicked the golem hard, pushing it into the stream. The

terrible Agarthan dissolved into mud and sticks.

A gargoyle streaked toward Karl, smoking claws extended. Karl ducked, the claws just missing his face. Spinning, he struck the monster in the back, knocking it out of the sky. It fell into the stream and instantly turned to stone.

"The water," I moaned. "It hurts the gargoyles."

"He's right." Elisa pulled back on her bowstring, her arm shaking. She fired at a gargoyle, the shot flying wide to the left.

"Elisa . . . look out!" I yelled.

She turned and fired at a golem charging toward her. The arrow struck the monster in the dirt chest but had no effect.

Bobby scooped up a handful of water and threw it at the golem. The monster skidded to a stop, an angry snarl on its terrifying face. It turned and charged at Bobby, who just stood there, motionless.

"Bobby, run!" Elisa shouted.

But the Techie held his ground. The golem charged straight at him. When the monster was only a step away, Bobby dropped to the ground.

"Bobby-boulder!" he yelled as he tucked his body into a ball and rolled into the golem's feet, his weight taking the monster's legs out from under it.

The golem fell into the stream, screaming.

Leonard stepped into the stream and splashed water into the air, pelting gargoyles and soaking golems.

Karl dipped his bat in the water, then attacked the golems, creating piles of mud with every swing.

Gargoyles fell to the ground as splotches of stone spread across their gray wings. Bobby and Elisa carefully dragged the wounded monsters into the stream, the water petrifying their flesh.

I tried to help my friends, but when I reached for my lightning-rope, the Skull of Fear turned it into a deadly snake. I knew this to be a lie, but it looked so real my arm refused to grab the weapon and turn it on. My breathing became short and raspy as I looked for some way to join the battle. My legs felt heavy as if filled with sand, feet anchored to the ground. I tried to move, but it was impossible. It took every thought and effort just to keep from dropping the Skull, my fears and anxiety barely under control.

"Gargoyles and golems, you're pathetic," Malphas shouted. "Banshees, end this battle . . . now!"

The banshees floated toward us, their tattered robes fluttering in an unseen breeze. One of them moved in front of the rest and glared down at us. The flying monster took a huge breath, then opened her mouth. Her beautiful, white face suddenly changed to that of a wretched hag, her skin mottled with scars and open wounds.

And then she screamed.

It was as if a thousand rusty knives tore into my flesh. Agony wrapped around me like a thorny blanket. I felt burning heat charring my skin while, at the same time, a chilling cold bit into my nerves. The pain felt overwhelming, replacing my fear with anguish.

The banshee grew silent, her face morphing back to her beautiful, pristine form. She smiled at me, her dark eyes devouring my courage. She took a deep breath and readied for another scream. I dashed to Bobby's side, my friend still on the ground. Reaching into his pocket, I pulled the box of Gummy Bears out and stuffed one in each ear.

Just then, the banshee screeched again. Rylee and the other kids yelled in agony as they writhed on the ground, but not me. With my left hand clutching the Skull of Fear, I picked up my lightning-rope, turned it on, and flung it at the banshee. The sparkling end wrapped around the creature. Electricity danced across the banshee's body like a swarm of sparkling flies. Her screech changed to a cry of pain as the electrical charges stabbed at her body. The monster took one last breath, then fell to the ground, unconscious.

"What kind of magic is this?!" Malphas bellowed.

The Demon Lord glared at me, then tilted his head back as if staring at the high ceiling overhead. The monster's dark feathers sparkled, the dance of white light on his body getting brighter. And then the demon screeched. Instantly, the shimmering light on his feathered body burst outward, the shards of his fear-magic passing through everyone in the cavern, monster and human alike. We all fell to the ground, our minds consumed with horrific terror.

I was drowning in a tide of panic. I could barely breathe under the weight of the overwhelming fear, terror crushing my chest and growing heavier by the second.

I dropped the Skull of Fear and curled up into a ball, trying to disappear. My Beast, empowered by Malphas's magic, bit into my soul with remorseless fangs, devouring my ability to think. My skin felt numb, though every muscle in my body ached. Deep within my stomach, something churned, acid and fear threatening to make me sick. The pounding in my ears grew louder and faster as my heart beat out of control. I clenched my teeth to

keep them from chattering as the horror of Malphas's fear-magic cut through me. Paralysis gripped me as every terrible event, every nightmare, every *what-if* blasted through my mind in an inferno of panic, each amplified by the magic of the Demon Lord.

*What if this never ends? I'll never survive this . . . I'm not strong enough . . . I'm just a failure.* Everything felt hopeless.

Malphas smiled, then took to the air as everyone in the cavern writhed and wept. With just two flaps of his wings, Malphas landed in front of me. He shoved my body aside with a clawed foot, the long talons on his bird-like feet tearing into my shirt and scratching my skin. Malphas picked up the Skull of Fear and smiled.

"Thank you, Earther. I'll think of you when I add this Skull Key to the doorway." The Demon Lord laughed, then leaped into the air, flying to the entrance. He released his fear-magic, and the glistening sparks of horror dissolved away.

As the terror dissipated, I slowly climbed to my feet. I picked up the lightning-rope and readied for the next attack.

"Agarthans, follow me." The Demon Lord's voice echoed through the chamber.

The monsters turned and headed toward the cavern entrance, leaving my friends and me bewildered.

"I think we'll leave these humans in here." Malphas chuckled a malicious laugh. "Let them starve to death. That'll teach them not to interfere with my plans." The demon glanced at his army as they filed out of the cavern. "We'll soon have all seven skulls. When that happens, I'll bring the largest monsters from Agartha." The golems stomped their muddy feet on the ground, gnomes giggled, and gargoyles smiled. "The devastators, annihilators, crushers, and destroyers will spread across this world, leveling Earth's cities so we can rebuild. Agartha is nearly dead, my friends, but Earth has the resources to allow us to thrive." He held the Skull of Fear high in the air. "Soon, Earth will become the new Agartha, with every human as my unwilling servant."

The Demon Lord laughed a vicious laugh as he led the monster army to the cave entrance.

I reeled in my lightning-rope and readied myself for an attack. Leonard and Karl moved forward, stepping over the piles of muddy golems and stony gargoyles, weapons at the ready. Elisa fitted an arrow to her bow and pulled back the string, her arm shaking with fear. Bobby loaded his slingshot and stepped through the stream, Elisa and I doing the same. Rylee floated overhead, the light from his horns shading the ground with a crimson hue.

I pulled the gummy bears from my ears and tossed them aside. Just then, a loud screech pierced the air.

"Banshees again?" Bobby asked.

Rylee descended to the ground and shook his head. "Yes, but they're not aiming at us."

The air shimmered near the entrance as the banshee's voice carved away at the walls and ceiling. Chunks of stone and dirt fell to the floor, choking the air with dust. An avalanche of granite tumbled into the cavern, the thunderous crash making us cover our ears. The ground shook as cracks spider-webbed their way across the walls and ceiling until, finally, near the entrance, a thunderous explosion of stone, gravel, and dirt filled the air.

The angry hornets came to life in my mind as sweat trickled down my forehead. A rapid pulse pounded in my ears, but the crash of stone made it impossible to hear. My Beast emerged from the darkness of my mind, wrapped its thick arms around my soul, and squeezed; terror overwhelmed everything.

*What if the whole thing caves in?* The thought amplified my fear, letting the worry part of my brain look for the worst possible thing to happen, no matter how unlikely.

The ground rocked, and dust billowed into the air.

*Will we be buried in stone? What if the ceiling is breached?* The buzzing became a constant drone of thunderous noise in my mind. I wanted to hide but knew avoiding the fear would do nothing.

*Lake Pontchartrain could come pouring in and drown us? What if ... ANTs* flooded through my mind, triggering another thought-loop of fear, amplifying the *ANTs,* which in turn boosted the volume of my fear. The loop continued without slowing, my panic feeding the Beast.

*'Stay in the moment . . . the ANTs are a lie, challenge them . . . the anxiety will end . . .'* Dr. Jen's words tried to cut through the banshee wails and falling stones, but my Beast refused to weaken its grip on my soul. Terror consumed every fiber of my being.

I tried to challenge my fears, but the roar of falling stones and the tremors pulsing through the ground made it impossible. Focusing on Dr. Jen's teachings, I imagined the most likely scenario instead of the worst, but it felt like the world was falling down upon us. I tried 4 – 7 – 8 breathing. Dust choked my throat and

made me cough. With a shudder, I collapsed to the ground and awaited my fate.

And then the screeching thunder stopped, the banshee's voice finally silent. When the dust cleared, we found a massive pile of rubble clogging the entrance to the Cave of Soles. The barrier of rock stretched to the ceiling, stones of various sizes, most too heavy to lift. But even if we could move them, the dangerous climb up the pile of rubble seemed impossible. A fall from the top would break limbs, if not a neck.

We were trapped.

I turned to my friends. The expression on their faces matched how I felt. We were defeated and would likely starve in this cavern.

This was the end.

# Chapter 21 – Facing the Beast

I stared at the impossibly high wall of debris, a feeling of hopelessness pressing down upon me like the weight of a thousand broken dreams. I looked at my friends as we approached the avalanche. As one, we stared at the stony obstacle in our path, trapping us in the Cave of Soles. One after another, we lowered our heads in defeat.

A tingling sensation spread across my chest. Reaching to my belt, I withdrew the Dagger of Stones and held it out. The red jasper Chakra stone glowed as if surrounded by a crimson haze.

"They've found the sixth Skull Key, the Skull of Pain, and have placed it above the doorway." Rylee floated to my side, his wings a blur. "The Demon Lord has the Skull of Fear in his grasp, the seventh key. All he must do is put it in place, and the doorway between Agartha and Earth will stay open after the upcoming Blood Moon eclipse ends."

I sank to my knees and stared down at the dagger. Only the black onyx stone remained dark . . . for now. Buzzing hornets filled my mind, and my head ached.

A feeling of hopeless despair spread across the cave as each of us considered the coming disaster from Agartha.

"I wonder if Leonidas felt this way back in 480 BC?" Leonard's voice rose with curiosity, the sadness from his eyes momentarily eased.

"What are you talking about?" Karl asked.

"You know, Leonidas and the three hundred Spartans under his command. Some say they faced a Persian army of over a million men at the battle of Thermopylae." Leonard turned to us. "Three hundred Spartans stopped the Persian army from going through a narrow pass for a while, keeping them from spreading across the countryside of Greece."

"How did the battle end?" Bobby asked. "Did the Spartans defeat the Persians?"

"Well . . . umm . . . no." Leonard took a deep breath and sighed. "They delayed the Persian army, but in the end, all three hundred Spartans perished."

*Facing the Beast Within*

"What's with you and all this history junk?" Karl asked. "You're supposed to be a football player, not a historian."

Leonard shrugged, then lowered his gaze to the ground. "The truth is, I love history, but I have to focus all my free time on football."

"But you're the team captain back at your school, right?" Elisa said.

Leonard nodded. "Just because I'm good at football doesn't mean it's my passion." He glanced at Elisa. "My father thinks I have a shot at being an NFL quarterback. He wants me to focus every second on this. I like football, but I *love* history."

"Does your dad know this?" I wiped sweat and dust from my face.

Leonard shook his head.

"You should just tell him," Elisa said. "It's okay that you don't want to be a professional athlete, isn't it?"

Leonard shrugged. "That's not the way my dad sees it. He thinks I have this gift, and I need to take advantage of it. He always wants me to be the best, which means I have to train and practice all the time so I can be better than any other quarterback . . . I hate it. But I guess none of that really matters anymore." He glanced at me. "You and I are more alike than you realize."

The buzzing in my head faded a bit.

"Between football classes, all I wanna do is go to the library and read about the past," Leonard said. "Camp Pontchartrain is the only place I can do that without my dad finding out." He sighed and sat on a large rock. "One time, I skipped a football practice during the school year to go to the library. My dad found out and was furious. He made me run laps all night long as punishment." Leonard signed. "I feel like I have to do this to please him." He grew silent, head lowered to the ground.

I glanced around at my companions. Defeat showed on their faces; they'd given up, as had I. Failure spread through me like a slowly rising tide, drowning my thoughts.

*The Agarthans will destroy Camp Pontchartrain and New Orleans. I failed everyone.* These thoughts looped through my mind, making my sense of failure and guilt even greater.

*A mountain of stone stands between us and freedom. We'll never be able to get out of here. Everything is lost.*

The buzzing in my head welcomed the *ANTs* as they surged through my brain, but I didn't care anymore. The monsters had won. My anxiety had won. There was nothing left to lose, so there was nothing left to fear. I stopped fighting and invited the Beast in.

144

And at that moment, I saw the *ANTs* and *what-ifs* for what they were . . . lies, made up by my insecurities and poor self-esteem.

The *ANTs* spoke to me, trying to crush the last fibers of my self-worth.

*Yes, I'm the smallest sixth-grader at the Camp,* I thought.

*Yes, I'm a geek who loves technology.*

*Yes, I struggle with anxiety.*

*But so what?! None of this makes me a bad person* . . . "It just makes me who I am," I whispered.

The *ANTs* attacked again.

*I'm not a loser—I'm just good at different things than other kids.*

*More monsters aren't about to attack—the entrance is blocked.*

*The ceiling isn't about to cave in—this cave has been here for centuries.*

The *what-ifs* tried to feed my Beast, stabbing me with fear after fear . . . but I didn't care anymore.

For an instant, I tried to imagine myself to be Leonard, strong and confident, hoping his courage would drive away the *ANTs*. But at that moment, I realized I didn't need Leonard's courage. I'd looked up to him for many years, hoping for the hopeless dream of being strong and courageous like him. But Leonard had his own problems; we all did. And that thought made me realize we have more in common than I ever realized.

Deep down inside myself, I had my own courage. I just needed to find a way to bring it to the surface.

*I can't control everything, only the things within my ability.* That thought caused many of the *what-ifs* to vanish, their presence no longer important.

*I can only be the person I believe in.* I was done comparing myself to others and trying to be like them. *I don't need to be like Leonard, or Karl, or anyone else.*

*It was time I tried to be like me!*

*Beast, I've let you take over my life . . . BUT NO MORE!* My thoughts were daggers stabbing at my fears and insecurities.

Within my mind, I faced the Beast and saw it for what it was . . . a lie trying to devour my self-esteem until I hated everything about myself. The *ANTs* and *what-ifs* that stalked me for so long, that had amplified my fear and fed my Beast . . . they suddenly seemed so ridiculous.

*It's okay if I'm afraid of a monster or some real threat, but the ANTs and what-ifs don't even exist. They're like smoke obscuring everything around me, making it difficult to see.*

I imagined a breeze blowing through my mind, carrying with it that mist of *ANTs* and *what-ifs.*

The buzzing grew quiet in my mind.

The worry part of my brain finally let go of the logic part, and I could think.

I let my doubts and worries wash over me like an ocean wave, then recede, each acknowledged for what they were—a lie. New strength blossomed within my soul, shining the bright light of courage on my Beast, forcing it to slink back into the shadows where it belonged.

*THIS ISN'T OVER,* I yelled in my mind. The quartz Chakra stone hanging around my neck grew warm as its song resonated in my head. Courage detonated within me, a supernova of faith and strength.

Standing, I faced my companions. "My dad has a poster in his workshop."

"That's great to know, Poole," Karl said. "How does that help us?"

I raised my hand, silencing him. "It's a quote from Thomas Edison. It says, 'Many of life's failures are people who did not realize how close they were to success when they gave up.' That's us right now."

"Cameron, you think we're close to success?" Elisa looked up at me with moist eyes.

I nodded. "I've given up so many times; I expect failure before I've even tried." I turned to Leonard. "I once heard a quote from Abraham Lincoln about falling down, but I don't remember it. Do you?"

Leonard nodded, his eyes brightening again as they did whenever he talked about history. "Lincoln said, 'I am not concerned that you have fallen — I am concerned that you arise.'"

"What did he mean by that?" Elisa asked.

"He meant it's okay to fail as long as you get up and keep trying." Leonard stood, courage beginning to blossom within his eyes. "President Lincoln had lots of reasons to give up in his life. His family was forced out of their house when he was seven. His mom died when he was ten. Lincoln failed at business and lost eight elections before becoming president, but he never gave up. He always got up and kept going."

"Exactly." I stood and faced my friends. "Look at us, here in the cave. We've given up when we should try to stop Malphas."

"What do you suggest? We lift the thousands of rocks that block the tunnel and just toss them out of the way. Look at the height of that pile of rocks. It would take a year to clear them all away." Karl kept his eyes on the ground.

"Karl is right." I nodded. "We can't move all those rocks, but we can move just a few. All we need to do is make a small hole to wriggle through."

"But look at how big they are," Elisa said. "None of us are strong enough to lift them, not even Leonard."

"We won't use muscles to lift them." I smiled. "We'll use science."

"But we'd have to start way up there, at the top." Bobby pointed upward. "A fall from that height could be . . . well, you know . . ."

"Fatal," Karl said. "Great idea, Techie."

I smiled. "Yeah, it is a great idea because we're gonna do it together, as friends, each helping the other."

"Friends? I don't have friends." Karl stood and turned away.

"Why is that, Karl?" I moved towards him and put a hand on his shoulder. "Why do you always push people away?"

"Yeah, why do you do that?" Bobby asked.

"It's time you told us what's going on with you, Karl." Leonard pressed.

"You really want to know?" Karl glared at Leonard.

"We *need* to know," I said.

"Okay." Karl sighed. "In my old school, Francis W. Parker School in Chicago, I had friends; at least, I thought they were my friends. But when they saw the opportunity to blame me for something *they* did, they took it. I was expelled from school. My parents said I brought shame to our family and sent me to a boarding school here in New Orleans, far from Chicago and far from home, so I wouldn't embarrass them again." He shook his head, eyes still downcast. "I'm here at Camp Pontchartrain over the summer because my parents don't want me at home."

"So now you insult everyone around you?" I asked.

"I'm new at Camp Pontchartrain and don't know who to trust. I'm not gonna get blamed for something I didn't do, not again. For me, it's safer to have no friends." Karl stood, walked to where he'd set Number Three on the ground, and picked it up. He gazed down at it as if it were a trusted companion.

"Doesn't that get lonely?" Elisa asked.

"Not when I'm on the ball field." Karl stared down at his bat. "When I'm playing

147

baseball, my teammates have my back, no matter what. We can trust each other during a game because we have one goal: to win."

"But after the game?" Bobby asked.

"After the game? Who cares?" Karl said. "And I was fine until Chatoké left that note for me yesterday.

"What did it say?" Leonard asked.

Karl stood, reached into his pocket, and pulled out the crumpled paper. "It's a quote from Mark Twain. It says, 'Anger is an acid that can do more harm to the vessel in which it's stored than to anything on which it is poured.'" He stuffed it back into a pocket and scowled at the ground.

"She's right." Elisa crossed the room and stood next to the baseball player. "Your anger will isolate you from everyone in school and here at the camp. It'll eat you up from the inside."

"I won't be betrayed by a friend ever again." Karl scowled at her.

"You can't live alone with no one to lean on," I said. "It's too difficult."

"I've been doing it for a year now."

"But you're not happy, Karl." I walked to him and stood toe to toe, staring up at the taller boy. "Everyone needs friends, and the funny thing about friendship is, you can get it whether you like it or not."

"What are you talking about?"

"I'm your friend, Karl, whether you want me or not." I smiled.

"Me too." Elisa moved to my side.

"And me," Leonard said.

"Yeah, we're all your friends." Bobby moved next to us.

"Even me," Rylee said in his high-pitched voice, "and I don't even understand what you're talking about."

"There you go." I placed my hand on Karl's arm. "You have five friends. Now all you have to do is take a risk and let us in."

Karl lowered his head and spoke, his words barely a whisper. "I'm not sure if I can."

"Something my favorite author, Ray Bradbury, once said: 'Jump, and you will find out how to unfold your wings as you fall.'" I smiled at Karl. "You just need to do it and take the risk; jump and find your wings."

Karl glanced at us, confused, then lowered his head to the ground. "I think we should get out of here first. I'll figure out *my wings* if we survive." He turned to the others. "Do you have a plan on how to get out of here, Techie . . . I mean, Cameron?"

With a nod, I smiled. "It'll take all of us working together, but we have to go up there." I pointed to the top of the pile of debris. "I'm tired of being the victim. I'm tired of being afraid all the time and just letting things happen *to* me. It's time *I* made things happen. My anxiety has kept me from being the person I wanna be . . . well, not anymore. Giving into fear and accepting failure isn't an option." I stared at my friends. "I won't let Malphas destroy our world and the friends that we love. We may have fallen, but it's time for us to arise; I'm getting us out of here. I'll do it alone if I must, but I'd rather have some muscles up there with me."

"I will help." Rylee floated off the ground, his horns glowing bright red.

"I'm with you, Cameron," Leonard said.

"Me too." Bobby slapped me on the back.

"I'm kinda afraid of heights," Elisa turned to me, "but I'll try."

"Karl?" I asked. "What about it?"

"I guess falling to my death would be better than starving in this cave." Karl shifted the bat from his left hand to his right, then extended his prized possession to me. "I assume you'll need this for the lever and fulcrum stuff . . . you know, *science*."

"Exactly." I took the bat. "We're gonna use your bat and Leonard's hockey stick to pry the stones out of the way." I glanced at Leonard. "It's like how the ancient Egyptians moved enormous blocks of granite to build their pyramids."

Leonard smiled and nodded.

"But what are we gonna do once we get out of here?" Karl asked.

"I have a plan," I said.

"Am I gonna like this plan?" Karl asked.

"Maybe, but it does involve pulling the fire alarm for the camp."

"I like it already," Karl said with a smile.

Bobby stepped forward and raised a hand, then slowly brought it down until it was extended straight out in front of him. He glanced at me and winked. I moved next to him and put my hand on his as Rylee hovered next to me, his little hand on mine. Elisa put her hand on mine, turned to Karl and Leonard, and nodded. The two athletes joined the circle, our hands joined at the center of the circle.

Bobby cleared his throat, then spoke in a clear, dramatic voice. "Our friendship is a beacon that illuminates the darkness and gives us the strength to face our enemies," he

glanced at me, "and our fears, together." Bobby smiled as he cast his gaze around the circle.

Everyone stood there, silent, contemplating his words. Karl pulled in his hand and slowly walked around the circle until he stood right behind Bobby. With a smile on the ball player's face, he patted Bobby on the back.

"You nailed it that time, Bobby." Karl's smile grew even bigger as he started to laugh.

The rest of us joined in, laughing as we gave Bobby high-fives and stared up at the massive wall of granite. Karl moved to the biggest stone, then cupped his hands, making them into a step to help the others up the pile of debris.

"Let's do it," Karl said.

We climbed the pile of rubble, each helping the other ascend the incredibly unstable mound of rock and gravel. And as I climbed, I felt something I hadn't felt since my anxiety took hold of my life . . . hope.

# Chapter 22 – Building an Army

I rubbed my bruised hands and scraped knuckles; the scratches and tiny cuts filled with dirt started to ache. Prying the rocks loose at the top of the avalanche using Karl's bat and Leonard's hockey stick had worked. By working together, we created a small opening in the mountain of stone, escaped the Cave of Soles, and made it out of the catacombs under the Crypt.

Now, we stood near the camp's administrative offices. Light from the full moon shone through the glass doors, casting silvery rectangles on the hardwood floors.

"Are you sure the alarm won't notify the police or fire department?" I glanced at Bobby.

"Don't worry. I took care of it." Bobby smiled. "I disconnected the phone line to the alarm system. They won't hear a thing."

I turned to Karl. "Is the skylight in the gym open?"

The baseball player nodded. "Yep."

"Good, I think it's time." I glanced at my companions. "After this, there's no turning back."

"Do it," Leonard said, his voice, as always, ringing with confidence.

The other kids nodded their agreement.

"Okay." Reaching up, I pulled the fire alarm. Instantly, bells clanged, and sirens screamed across Camp Pontchartrain. Kids of all ages streamed from their cabins, the alarms shocking them awake. "Let's get to the gathering point near the gym."

We ran through the camp, heading to the north end of the grounds. When we reached our goal, we found kids already gathering in front of the gym, sleepy-eyed or wearing headphones. Camp counselors glanced around, looking for smoke, some returning to various cabins, ensuring everyone was out.

"What's going on?" one counselor asked.

"Who pulled the alarm?" Mrs. Seitz, the tennis coach, demanded. She glanced about, looking for answers.

Leonard walked up to Coach Seitz. "Mrs. Chakoté told me to gather the kids in the gym for a special announcement. She said everything would be explained there."

"What? That's ridiculous." Seitz glared at the boy. "We don't use the fire alarms unless it's a drill or emergency. I don't care if she's the camp director; this is wrong. If you see her, you tell her I said—"

"Tell her what?" The sound of an old wooden cane tapping on the ground cut the tennis coach off.

Leonard spun around and found Mrs. Chakoté standing behind him, a scowl on her wrinkled face.

"Mrs. Seitz, please get everyone into the gymnasium. This *is* an emergency." Chakoté tapped her cane twice, signifying the end of the discussion.

Seitz glared at the older woman, then sighed. "Everyone, go into the gym and take your seats." The coach's words pierced through the gaggle of voices.

The other counselors heard and echoed the announcement, ushering everyone into the gym.

Minutes later, the students filed into the gymnasium and climbed into the tall bleachers. As usual, the kids sat with their cliques, soccer players together, runners with runners, a cluster of drama kids . . . a fractured collection of campers casting angry and suspicious glares from one group to another.

Karl moved to the center of the gym with Leonard at his side. The middle schoolers instantly recognized the football and baseball leaders and grew quiet, but the high school kids kept talking, ignoring the younger kids.

"Be quiet!" Leonard shouted.

The students grew silent.

"What's going on?" one of the adult counselors shouted. "Who pulled the fire alarm?"

"I did." I stepped onto the basketball floor and stood beside Karl, who patted me on the back.

Instantly, the students grew quiet, the shock of my confession silencing the crowd. Some pointed at Karl and me, questioning gazes passing from one to the other.

"I think they're surprised that you and I are standing here together," I said.

"That's not the only surprise in store for them tonight." Karl chuckled.

Mrs. Chakoté stepped out onto the court and moved beside me. A hush spread across the student body.

*The kids probably expect me to get blasted by the camp director and are looking forward to watching my destruction*, I thought.

Dr. Jen's voice tickled the back of my mind. *'That's* Future Telling, *and it is never helpful. Focus on the now.'*

I pushed the negative thought aside and stood tall, staring at the kids before me, refusing to look away. Bobby and Elisa moved out on the basketball court and stood with us, looks of grim determination on their faces.

Mrs. Chakoté turned and faced the five of us, then spoke in a low voice. "I see the Demon Lord has all the Skull Keys." She pointed at her cane. Each of the Chakra stones glowed slightly, just like our pendants.

I nodded. "We failed to stop Malphas from getting them . . . sorry," my quiet voice meant only for Chakoté and my friends.

"So, you're organizing the evacuation?"

"No, it's not time to run. It's time to fight." I stood tall and stared straight into Chakoté's ancient eyes. "The younger kids can flee. In fact, we need them too, but we want the high school and middle school kids with us on the battlefield."

"But you can't fight the Demon Lord. Let him burn down New Orleans. We'll get the word out and warn people, and hopefully, we can evacuate the—"

"Mrs. Chakoté," Karl interrupted. "There's more to it than that."

"What?" The old woman glanced at me, a gray eyebrow raised.

The student body started murmuring to each other, but Chakoté tapped her cane on the hardwood floor, instantly silencing the crowd.

I told her what the Demon Lord had said in the Cave of Soles, describing the plan to destroy everything on Earth and put everyone under his control. "Rylee told us it'd take him a while to bring the huge monsters of Agartha to the gateway. We still have a little time, but not much."

"Rylee?" Chakoté asked.

"You'll see." Bobby grinned at the old woman.

Mrs. Chakoté tapped her cane twice on the gym floor again, the sound echoing like a shot from a gun. She turned and faced the students. "There are important things to discuss, and you'll be informed of what's happening soon. For now, I need absolute quiet. Does anyone disagree with me?" She glared at the faces filling the bleachers. No one uttered a word.

"Good." Chakoté gave the kids a grandmotherly smile. "The next person who breaks this silence will most certainly regret it."

She turned back to us. "So Malphas doesn't just want to attack." Mrs. Chakoté tapped the ground with her crooked wooden cane lightly as she processed the information. "He wants to take it all."

I nodded. "We can't let that happen." I stepped forward, chin held high. "It's time to stand up against his violence and push back, no matter what. I've been under my anxiety's control for a long time; I won't let that happen anymore, and I refuse to surrender my freedom to that demon."

Chakoté gave me a wry smile and nodded. "Okay, talk to your army."

I nodded and stepped forward, holding my hands over my head. "We're under attack," I said in a loud, clear voice.

The kids glanced at each other, confused.

"Monsters from a parallel world will soon emerge from the cave near the Crypt. Their goal is to take over Earth and turn us into their servants."

Someone laughed. Karl stepped forward and pointed Number Three at the culprit, instantly silencing him.

"I have a plan to stop them, but I need all of you to help." A buzzing echoed in the distant places of my mind, the Beast trying to awaken. But instead, I thought about my friends and what we've survived so far. I glanced over my shoulder at my companions and smiled, then turned back to the kids in the bleachers.

"If we do nothing, the Earth will be turned into a wasteland, like their own planet. If we do nothing, New Orleans will burn to the ground just like the last time they were here—these monsters caused the Great New Orleans Fire in 1788. I believe this camp was founded on these grounds to prevent the next disaster."

"That's ridiculous," someone shouted. "There's no such thing as monsters or parallel worlds. I supposed you're gonna tell me magic exists, too."

Mrs. Chakoté stepped forward and smashed the end of her cane on the gym floor. A crack of thunder filled the air, the seven Chakra stones embedded in her cane flashing with such intensity that everyone had to shield their eyes, the air sparkling with power.

She glared at the boy. "I think you need to be more respectful and *listen.*"

The students glanced at each other, stunned.

154

"But, come on . . . monsters? Really?" another said.

Chakoté was about to say something when I put a hand on her shoulder.

"Don't worry," I whispered to the camp director. "I got this." I turned to the kids in the bleachers and spoke in a loud voice. "Everyone, don't freak out . . . he's a friend." I looked up at the skylight overhead. "Rylee, how about you come down and meet everyone?"

A red glow filled the skylight as Rylee floated down from the ceiling, his tiny wings flapping so fast they were just a crimson blur. His horns blazed with light.

Kids screamed and shouted, fear rippling through the audience. As Rylee descended, Bobby pulled out a box of Gummy Bears and tossed one into the air. The imp dove and caught the treat, gobbling it down with a smile. Some kids giggled. Bobby threw another in the air, which Rylee easily caught, then extended a clawed hand. Bobby gave the bag of candies to the Agarthan and smiled as the imp devoured them.

Bobby shrugged. "Apparently, imps from Agartha like candy."

Some of the fear in the audience faded. Rylee finally settled to the ground and stood next to us.

"Rylee is a friend who's been helping us battle the Demon Lord, Malphas, and his minions. These monsters aren't evil; they're just under Malphas's control. We have a plan to stop them, but it'll only work if all of you help us."

"You want the elementary school kids to go to war?" one adult asked.

"No, they won't fight, but they'll still help." I crossed to the other side of the floor. "The counselors will take the elementary kids off the camp grounds and head toward New Orleans. While they're leaving, they'll create as much noise as possible. That'll make Malphas think we're retreating, giving us the element of surprise."

"But what can a bunch of middle and high school kids do against an army of monsters?" someone asked.

"We can stand and fight." Karl held Number Three in the air as he moved to my side. "Each of you is part of some team or club. All of you have weapons you're very skilled with; mine is a baseball bat." He pointed at the Icers. "You have your hockey sticks." Karl turned to the Techies. "You have technology. We all have skills; that's why we came to Camp Pontchartrain. It's time we used our skills for something other than just scoring goals."

I looked up at Karl and nodded, then turned to the audience. "You all have a choice. Either you take a risk, stand with us, and try to change the outcome of this war, or do nothing and become an unwilling servant to an evil demon. It's up to you."

The kids glanced at each other, a soft murmur spreading through the crowd.

"I know you're afraid." I stepped forward and spoke at a normal volume, forcing those in the stands to quiet. "Trust me. I know a lot about fear. I have anxiety, and I'm afraid all the time." I glanced over my shoulder at my companions. "But when you're with friends, the fear can be managed if you don't give in. I see the fear on your faces when you look at Rylee or when we talk about fighting a war against creatures from another world. I get it. I'm afraid too. But you need to ask yourself, how will you feel if you back away now and watch your friends suffer?"

*What if they won't listen to me? What if . . . NO.* I let the fears wash over me and recognized them as lies. Instead, I pointed at the wall.

"Think about the lyrics to our camp's anthem, especially the twelfth line. 'For fears that we shall smite . . .' you know how the rest of it goes. I used to think those were just words, but now I realize our founders built the camp here on purpose because of the doorway between our world and Agartha. *We* are the 'golden light.' *We* will 'cast away the darkness,' but only if we 'remain true.' The words in our Alma Mater speak the truth for this moment, right now. And if we do nothing, everything we love, our camp, our friends, even our families and our way of life . . . it'll all be destroyed. We must fight or perish."

I stopped speaking and held a fist in the air, hoping the crowd would cheer, but they were utterly quiet. Some glanced at their teammates, uncertain, while others gazed at the floor, afraid. A held-breath silence engulfed the gymnasium as everyone watched the destruction of my hope.

My heart sank as I lowered my fist, defeated once again. A sense of frustration and disappointment washed over me like a tidal wave, threatening to engulf me. It was a feeling I knew all too well, a feeling of failure that seemed to follow me everywhere. The heaviness spread through me like a disease, my body feeling as if filled with lead. My Beast stirred, happy with my failure. *Why did I think anyone would listen to a loser like me? It should have been Leonard talking to them, or maybe Karl or—*

"I'll fight," a small voice said.

156

I held my breath for an instant, my heart pounding in my chest, hope stirring. I looked up and found a sixth-grade girl standing in a sea of scared faces. Her freckled face and long red hair stood out amidst the blonds and brunettes. She was one of the drama kids.

Helium suddenly replaced the lead filling my body. My arms and legs felt light with anticipation.

"Do you think I can make a difference?" she asked.

"Even the smallest person can be a hero." I glanced at Leonard and Karl, then turned back to the girl. "Never judge a person just by the strength of their body; judge them by the courage in their heart." I stepped toward her section of the stands. "Yeah . . . you *can* make a difference."

"Okay. I'll stand with you, Cameron." The girl made her way to the bottom of the bleachers and stood at my side. She turned and glared at the crowd, daring them to look away.

Just then, the kids from the high school football cabin all stood. "We'll stand with you."

Then the soccer kids took to their feet. "Count on us."

The archers and tennis players stood, then the ice hockey players and the art students, and the . . . Students leaped to their feet and added their names to the ranks of the army as courage blossomed throughout the gym. And for the first time, the patchwork of different-colored jerseys and club shirts were united as one group, the boundaries between cliques and teams erased by a cause and a leader. The kids started chanting my name louder and louder.

I raised my hands, and the crowd slowly grew quiet. "Okay, we don't have much time. The Super Blood Moon will happen soon, and that's when the doorway between worlds will be fully open. Let me explain my plan."

And I mapped out my strategy, explaining key points.

"Don't forget about my jelly-gun," Bobby said, bringing a wave of laughter. A sad expression flashed across Bobby's face as he lowered his gaze to the floor.

When I finished the battle plan, I scanned the faces of the students. The fear that had taken root earlier was blasted away by the fires of courage burning bright in every heart.

A wrinkled hand settled on my shoulder. I looked up and found Mrs. Chakoté standing over me.

"Maybe we *can* do this, Mrs. Chakoté," I said. "Maybe we'll save the camp, no, the world."

She nodded and gave me a warm smile. "Yes indeed, child. And remember, I've called the Order of the Stones. Soon, they'll be here with real weapons. We need to hold the line until then."

"Don't worry, Mrs. Chakoté; you can trust us."

"I *do* have faith, but more importantly, I have faith in you; I always have. I'm confident you'll see this through."

I smiled, and for the first time in my life, I had faith in myself as well. It was a strange feeling, a good feeling.

"OK, everyone, we have supplies to gather and preparations to be made. Once we have everything we need, get into position, and wait for the signal." I held a fist in the air. "We have a war to win!"

# Chapter 23 – The Battle Begins

Raising my head, I caught a quick glimpse of the Agarthans milling about near the cave, then ducked down again, hidden behind the rolling hill of neatly cut grass. The hollow eye sockets in the seven skulls stared across their kingdom of weeds and shrubs, their multi-colored light casting bright-hued shadows from the monsters standing nearby. Sparkling embers of energy danced across leaves and thistles as the magic from the completed doorway spilled across the overgrowth. The combined hues from the skulls gave the forbidden area a harsh white glow, turning night into day.

"Well?" Karl glanced at me. "What did you see?"

"There are a lot of monsters by the cave." I glanced up at the full moon. The smallest piece of its lunar face was cloaked in shadow as the eclipse took its first bite. "Everything is lit up like daytime near the cave entrance."

"Do you wanna change your mind?" Karl's voice was soft and compassionate. "You don't have to do this. I could do it instead and—"

The angry hornets came to life in my mind as I looked at my friends. Beads of sweat formed across my brow as I imagined every possible negative outcome, the *what-ifs* and *ANTs* running rampant. But then Karl placed a hand on my shoulder.

I tried to smile, but fear surged through my mind.

*Are we really doing this? There's not enough of us. We're just kids. No one will follow me into battle. What if . . .*

"Cameron," Elisa whispered. "List the adjectives again."

"Adjectives . . . right." I took a deep breath. "A – astonishing, B – breathtaking. C – cheerful, D – delightful . . ." I glanced at the football captain, a worried expression on Leonard's face. "I'm distracting myself, so I won't focus on my fears." My voice shook a bit. "Fear has a way of making you put a magnifying glass over your worries, creating a larger and more menacing image in your mind. Well, I'm done feeding my fear. Instead of focusing on what *might* happen and getting more afraid, I'm making a list of adjectives that start with the letters of the alphabet to distract myself."

"That's smart." Leonard nodded. "E – epic, F – friendly . . ."

"G – glad," Elisa said.

"H – hopeful," Karl added.

I nodded to him.

"I – ingenious, like me." Bobby smiled.

"J – just," Elisa said in a quivering voice.

"That's not an adjective, Elisa." Bobby thought for a moment. "Maybe J – jealous?"

Elisa shook her head. "First of all, just *is* an adjective if you use it to represent something moral, right, or fair. And second, all these adjectives have a positive meaning, and jealous is very negative."

"That's right." I nodded. "I'm only using positive words as distractions from now on. Sorry, Bobby, jealous is out." At that moment, I realized the buzzing had vanished. My anxiety had submerged into the dark waters of my psyche. I breathed a sigh of relief.

"Feel better?" Elisa asked.

I nodded.

Karl patted me on the back. "Don't listen to those inner voices; listen to mine." He gripped my hand. "You can do this."

"Are you sure?" I asked.

"You can do this because a friend will watch your back." Karl winked. "I guess I found my wings. You're my friend, Cameron; I won't let you fail."

A smile spread across my face, reaching up to my eyes. "I got this."

"I know you do," Karl said, patting me on the back. "Now, let's get it done."

I nodded. "Remember, wait for my signal." I glanced past Karl. Elisa and Bobby lay on their stomachs, hidden behind the hill. Bobby smiled at me and patted the barrel of his ridiculous jelly-gun. Beyond them crouched the rest of the Camp Pontchartrain army, the students murmuring with what was either excitement or nervous fear.

I took a deep breath as if about to do an impossibly high dive into a pool, then stood. Raising my fist, I walked toward the stone wall separating the Crypt grounds from the rest of the school. I jingled a bit with the sound of tiny, muffled bells—tech bouncing about in my backpack. My dark purple shirt merged with the darkness, but the gold C.P. emblazoned on the camp t-shirt made me easily visible.

Bringing my fist down, I pounded my chest twice, then raised it into the air. I did it again, *thump—thump,* raise . . . *thump—thump,* raise . . .

*thump—thump,* raise. The sound caught the attention of the monsters and Malphas, the Demon Lord of Agartha.

The huge demon pointed at me, then said something to a cluster of monsters. A half-dozen vicious-looking gremlins with sharp stone weapons climbed over the rocky wall and charged.

A sharp rapping sound thumped the ground next to me. Glancing to the side, I found Mrs. Chakoté standing beside me, the stones in her cane glowing with magical intensity. She, too, pounded her chest in rhythm with me.

"What are you doing here, Mrs. Chakoté? You should get back."

She looked down at me and gave a pleasant, grandmotherly smile. The gremlins were maybe twenty strides away.

"I couldn't let you have all the fun." The old woman chuckled.

The monsters were now fifteen steps away.

I glanced over my shoulder at my hidden companions, ready to shout for help.

Chakoté put a calming hand on my shoulder. "Don't worry. We can deal with this." She held her cane high in the air, the Chakra stones blazing with intense color. "I haven't been in a battle for maybe fifty years . . . this is exciting."

The monsters were now ten steps away.

I swallowed nervously, my throat dry as a desert, and switched on my lightning-rope. The end danced with electrical sparks. Fear gnawed at the edge of my senses, taking bites out of my courage. But this time, I knew it wasn't a lie. The approaching monsters, with their knives and whips, looked terrifying and dangerous.

I inhaled sharply as my heart raced, each beat sending waves of oxygen through my veins, feeding my muscles as my body prepared for battle. Every muscle coiled tight like a spring, ready to explode into action. The *fight-or-flight* response had taken over. Part of me wanted to run away, which I expected. After all, terrible monsters were charging toward me. But I knew fleeing wasn't the answer. This time, I was choosing to fight.

A faint buzzing sound emerged out of the dark recesses of my mind, my anxiety building. *What-ifs* ricocheted through my brain like balls through a pinball machine.

"No," I whispered. "The *what-ifs* are a lie. I refuse to give them power over me."

Reaching for my quartz amulet, I rubbed the Chakra stone between my fingers. The

feel of the smooth surface reminded me of who I was . . . Cameron Poole, master of my Beast, not a victim.

I pushed the buzzing hornets, *ANTs,* and *what-ifs* aside and instead focused on my strengths.

*I can do this. Electricity and technology are my weapons, and these gremlins are about to feel my sting.*

"I hope I remember how to fight." Mrs. Chakoté laughed, then grew serious when she saw the look of confidence and strength on my face. She smiled a satisfied smile.

"Just stay behind me, Mrs. Chakoté and—" I never had the chance to finish the sentence.

With the gremlins closing in, Chakoté sprang into action, her cane flashing in the dim light. With a powerful spin, she struck the nearest monster. The stones embedded in wood ignited with a brilliant burst of energy. The gremlin flew through the air as if launched from a catapult.

But Mrs. Chakoté was just getting started.

With lightning-fast movements, she whirled from one monster to the next, her cane a blur of colored light as she struck with deadly precision. The Chakra stones flashed with each impact, sending gremlins tumbling across the grass. The old woman moved with the grace of a Kung Fu warrior, her weapon an extension of her body.

I just stood there, mouth hanging open, and watched with disbelief.

In a blink of an eye, the battle was over. Six attackers lay motionless on the ground, bruised and unconscious, painful wounds decorating their rough flesh. Breathing heavily, Chakoté leaned against her cane, her grey eyes scanning the scene with satisfaction. She brushed the wrinkles from her blouse and skirt, then smoothed out her hair and flashed me a smile.

"How did I do?" She smiled.

"What was that?" I asked, stunned.

"I told you I've been a warrior for the Order of the Stones for a long time." She smiled at me. "I can do more than just run a summer camp for kids."

"I guess so," I said, astonished.

"Come on, child, let's go meet our attackers."

I glanced over my shoulder at the other kids. They still hid behind the curving hill of grass, waiting for their turn, but it hadn't come . . . not yet.

We walked forward together, stepping over unconscious gremlins. I bent over and picked up their fallen weapons, then tossed them behind

162

me for another kid to wield. Someone cheered for Chakoté and me but was instantly shushed; surprise was critical.

Mrs. Chakoté patted me on the back as we strode toward the waiting horde. Malphas stood atop the stone wall, his long claws digging into the rocks. I raised my fist high, then brought it to my chest again twice, *thump—thump,* raise . . . I did it repeatedly as we walked until finally, Mrs. Chakoté and I stopped.

"I see you're still alive, Malphas." Chakoté pointed her cane at the demon. "That is indeed unfortunate. My Grandmother, Izabella, told me stories about you; you're much smaller than I expected."

"Is this what's left from the Order of the Stones, an old hag and a skinny runt? How pathetic." Malphas flapped his midnight-black wings, sending weeds and grass into the air, making his monsters shield their eyes. Floating in the air for a moment, he settled back down onto the wall, his eyes glowing red, a faint buzzing coming from the glowing orbs.

"Look down," Chakoté said.

I quickly lowered my gaze as the high-pitched whine filled the air. When the hum from the demon's eyes finally dissipated, I looked up again.

"That was a pathetic attempt at enslaving us, demon. You've gotten sloppy in your old age." Chakoté tapped her cane on the ground, causing the Chakra stones to flash with power.

"Pathetic . . . me?" He pointed at the old woman with a clawed finger. "Let's see if you think my army is pathetic." Malphas turned to his forces. "Monsters of Agartha, these two humans stand in our way. It's time to destroy them . . . now!"

And then, like a tidal wave of claws and fangs, the monsters stepped forward, trampling through the tall weeds and tangled grass. They leaped over the stone wall without slowing, their burning red eyes fixed on their prey. They were coming for us, every last one driven by an unquenchable thirst for destruction. And all we could do was stand there and wait.

# Chapter 24 – Retreat

The monsters moved slowly forward with deliberate menace, likely savoring the thrill of the chase. But we held our ground. Savage growls ripped through the air while ravenous panting intensified with each monstrous step. Many licked their lips as if hungering for the impending violence.

"I hope you have a plan, Cameron." Mrs. Chakoté gripped her cane like a sword and readied herself.

"I got this." I put two fingers to my mouth, took a big breath, and then blew, letting out a shrill whistle that stopped the monsters' advance.

Just then, the Camp Pontchartrain kids stood from behind the grassy hills, fists held high in the air. They brought them down in unison, hitting their chests twice, *THUMP—THUMP,* raise. *THUMP—THUMP,* raise. *THUMP—THUMP,* raise. The thunderous sound filled the air, and some monsters took a step back.

I glanced over my shoulder and marveled at the sight. Instead of groups of kids wearing their team jerseys or club shirts, they all wore a dark purple shirt, C.P. emblazoned in gold across their chest. The collection of cliques and teams had come together as one group, the Camp Pontchartrain Army.

Raising my fist, I joined the rhythmical beat, adding strength to the cadence. The kids stepped forward, then stopped right behind Mrs. Chakoté and me, each holding some kind of weapon. There were baseball bats, hockey sticks, tennis rackets, and lacrosse sticks, as well as rakes, shovels, high-tech gadgets, and the occasional frying pan. Every student had something to push back against the creatures of Agartha, and I knew their strength together was far greater than their collections of teams and groups alone.

Mrs. Chakoté glanced at me and smiled, then nodded and gestured for me to take charge.

I took a deep breath and stepped forward. The buzzing in my head tried to push its way to the surface, but I wasn't letting it. My entire focus was on the monsters before me and how I could protect my friends, no, my family.

Rylee settled to the ground next to me, his tail flicking about, ready for combat.

I pointed at Malphas. "We'll let you go back to Agartha if you turn and leave the field of battle right now. If you don't, you *will* be destroyed."

Malphas laughed. "This is ridiculous. You aren't the Order of the Stones. You're just a bunch of kids." He scanned his monster army with a hateful glare, then shouted, "Attack!"

The monster surged forward, claws, clubs, and stone weapons raised high.

"Earplugs . . . now!" I pulled a pair of earplugs from a pocket and stuffed them into my ears. We'd taken hundreds of them from the woodshop, and now they protected us from the shrill, hateful voices about to attack.

A group of banshees floated to the front of the monster formation and let out their piercing cry. The monster nearby dropped their weapons and put their hands to their ears, many howling in pain, but we were unaffected.

"Mirrors!" I screamed, holding mine in the air for the other kids to see.

Every student pulled a plastic mirror attached to a piece of string out from under their shirts, courtesy of the art department, the reflective pendants resting on every chest. Instantly, the monsters became transfixed, some dropping their weapons.

"CHARGE!" I shouted.

The students surged forward, sticks, bats, rakes, and fists falling upon the monsters as the terrifying creatures struggled to pull themselves from their reflections.

We fought in pairs, each watching the other's back and fighting as a team. The monsters did not. The Agarthans fought like unorganized rabble, some trampling over their companions to reach the students, many still transfixed by their reflections.

I ducked under a spiked wooden club, then flung my lightning-rope at a hideous goblin. Sparks danced across the monster's skin, making it howl in pain. Its eyes rolled back, then it fell unconscious. I sent the rope at another monster, wrapping it around their clawed feet, the sparkling end delivering painful shocks.

As we fought, the landscape grew darker, the Earth's shadow taking bigger bites of the

Moon's mottled face; the lunar eclipse had started.

Reaching into my backpack, I flipped the switch on a shocker-ball and tossed it toward a group of imps. Four barbs shot out and stuck into the tiny creatures' skin, electrocuting them. They fled in agony. I threw another and another, carving holes in the monster formation. My victims either fled or tried to resist the electrical shocks and ended up passing out.

*Thud.* Something whistled past my head. Turning, I found Karl swinging Number Three at a reptilian creature with a long, alligator-like snout and short limbs. I knew it to be a kobold, a creature I'd seen on the Internet. The kobold flew backward, landing in a heap, its skinny arms and legs twitching for a moment, then went still. Swinging repeatedly, Karl took out monster after monster, his bat an aluminum blur.

Leonard streaked past, his hockey stick slicing through the air like a deadly sword. He took the feet out from under a pair of monsters who tumbled to the ground. His teammates jumped onto the fallen monsters, pummeling them with fists and padded shoulders.

Bobby and a group of Techies stood at the back, using high-tech slingshots similar to his. They shot steel ball bearings, the silvery projectiles leaving punishing welts on heads and chests.

Suddenly, a brightly colored something dashed across the battlefield and rammed into me, sending me backward. As I fell, I flung the rope, the sparkling end wrapping around my assailant. I yanked on the line as I hit the ground, knocking the creature off its feet. When I stood, I found a gnome on the ground, sparks licking at its skin. The brightly colored creature thrashed about for a moment, then fell unconscious. Its vicious face seemed locked in a permanent scowl, exposed teeth stained with decay. I kicked the creature's pointed, multi-colored hat; it was rock hard, like a colorful battering ram.

A large group of gnomes climbed over the stone wall and charged at the left flank.

"Leonard, get some football players to the left." I pointed, breathing fast and fierce, then wiped the sweat from my eyes.

Leonard glanced over his shoulder and spotted the flamboyant creatures. The gnomes crashed into a group of soccer players, their tiny feet a blur. The kids fell to the ground, some shouting in pain. In seconds, the football team was there to defend them. They smashed into the gnomes and knocked them off their feet.

Mark Cheverton

I threw the last of my shocker-balls, then dropped the shoulder bag on the ground. Beside me, Chakoté dealt out punishing blows with her cane, her body moving faster than I ever imagined possible for the old woman. Flashes of light came from the Chakra stones, their magic adding to the attack.

Just then, I heard Rylee scream in fright. To my left, I spotted my friend standing before that horrific gremlin, Krak. The monster had his whip out and swung it at Rylee, a vicious snarl on his scarred face. The imp dodged to the left and right as he floated in the air, avoiding the end of that terrible weapon. I ran toward my friend but knew I was too far away to help.

"Rylee, don't give in to fear!" I shouted. "Stare it in the eye and refuse to yield."

"Take control of my fear?" The imp glanced at me, then turned to Krak. Rylee quivered with fright. "I fear that whip."

"Good," the gremlin said. "You're gonna get a taste of it right now."

Rylee scowled, the fear painted across his red face changing to anger, then fury.

Krak swung the whip at Rylee. But this time, instead of retreating, Rylee leaned to the side and extended an arm. The whip hit his forearm and wrapped around it like a snake. Before Krak could yank it back, Rylee grabbed the whip with both hands and pulled.

"No, you don't." Krak pulled on the handle, trying to bring the imp closer.

Rylee flapped his wings and flew backward with all his strength. The gremlin dug in his heels, pulling back with all his might. Suddenly, Rylee changed direction and flew straight at the gremlin, the claws of one hand extended, aiming at the monster's face. Krak instinctively raised both hands to protect himself, releasing his grip on the whip's handle. Rylee took advantage of this and swooped straight up, pulling the whip out of reach.

"Noooo!" Krak yelled.

Rylee pulled the whip in and held it by the thick cord, the handle dangling from the end. He then flew to the ground and approached the gremlin. Krak held a stone knife before him, but Rylee swung the whip's handle at him, smashing the gremlin's hand and breaking bones.

Krak screeched in pain and dropped the knife, then stepped backward. Rylee lunged forward and swung the handle like a club,

167

striking one of the gremlin's knees. Krak fell to the ground.

"Please have mercy." The gremlin tried to crawl away.

Swinging the whip, Rylee brought the handle down upon the gremlin, hitting Krak on the shoulder. The monster screamed in pain. Rylee moved closer, standing over the gremlin, the whip held high in the air, his eyes boring into the gremlin's glowing orbs.

I finally reached my friend's side. "You don't have to kill him."

"Krak would have killed me if I hadn't stood up to my fear."

"I know, but you aren't a killer. You're good; you're not vicious or evil." I put a hand on Rylee's arm. "Don't become what you hate."

Rylee glanced at me, then back down to Krak, the gremlin's eyes glowing red. He lowered the whip, then leaned down and spoke in a soft voice, Rylee's words hard as stone. "If I ever see you again, Krak, I *will* kill you. Go back to Agartha and do no harm."

"Yes, Rylee. Thank you, thank you. But the Demon Lord, he commands me."

"If he can't see you, he cannot tell you what to do," Rylee said with a sneer. "Now, begone before I change my mind."

The gremlin nodded, climbed to his feet, and limped back toward the cave.

I patted Rylee on the back. "I'm proud of you."

"Thanks."

Glancing to the left and right, I saw the kids of Camp Pontchartrain holding the line and even pushing the monsters back a bit.

Malphas saw this as well and screamed in rage. He then shouted some commands over his shoulder and smiled. A flood of golems and gargoyles took to the battlefield. They flowed over the stone wall like a brown and gray tidal wave. The gargoyles flew high into the air, each holding large stones in their hands, while the golems, with their long legs, strode across the ground, shoving aside their comrades as they closed in on the students. There were at least sixty of them, if not more, each with a vicious snarl on their terrible faces.

"If those monsters reach the battle line, they'll overwhelm us," Karl shouted from a few feet away.

I glanced to my left and right and knew it was time. "RETREAT!"

Karl echoed the order. "Retreat! Fall back . . . fall back!"

The kids moved backward, trying to keep their distance from the massive group of gargoyles and golems.

I lashed out at monsters with my lightning-rope as I walked backward, hoping I wouldn't trip. But as I retreated, I watched student after student take injuries from the Agarthans. With their glowing, red eyes, the vicious creatures hungered for victory, and they could nearly taste it.

"Cameron, what do we do?" someone asked. "We can't keep retreating. We gotta fight." It came from one of the high school football players.

"Keep retreating!" I shouted. This was part of my plan, but if this didn't work, it would be the end of us all.

"I hope everyone is ready," I whispered. "If not, we're all dead."

# Chapter 25 – Stealing the Skull

I turned and looked for Bobby. He stood to the side, firing handfuls of ball bearings at banshees.

"Bobby . . . NOW!"

Nodding, he stuffed his slingshot into his belt, then pulled a long cardboard tube from under his shirt, a Roman candle. Lighting the leftover firework, he held it high over his head. The fuse burned down, but nothing happened.

I clenched my teeth. "This *must* work." My heartbeat sped up.

Still, nothing happened. The monsters moved closer as darkness cloaked the landscape. The Earth's shadow had completely devoured the Moon.

Beads of sweat trickled down my face. "If it doesn't go off in another second, we might need to—"

A blazing red ball erupted into the sky, quickly followed by shimmering green and brilliant yellow. The Roman candle exploded into a kaleidoscope of color as it launched more colorful balls of fire into the sky, illuminating the darkness with its dazzling display.

That was the signal.

A deep rumbling sound filled the air, echoing like thunder across the land. The monsters halted their advance and glanced at each other, confused.

The ground shook just a little. It caused a wave of uncertainty to ripple across the monstrous ranks. The grass trembled a little more as a mechanical roar filled the air. A cheer erupted from the students as a line of riding lawnmowers charged across the ground, their motors like the deep-throated roar of some ferocious beast. Drama kids drove the metal beasts. Art and writing students hung off the back of the mowers, one holding a super soaker while the other gripped handfuls of fireworks left over from the 4th of July.

"Yeah!" the kids cheered as the mowers crashed into the monster formation.

"Don't get the gremlins wet," I shouted. "Focus on the golems and gargoyles."

The lawnmowers sped toward the golems, the water crew using the super soakers with deadly accuracy. Splashes of artillery fell upon the golems, turning the animated creatures into puddles of mud and sticks. Water balloons sailed through the air, striking the massive creatures. At the same time, Roman candles, firecrackers, skyrockets, and pinwheels soared through the air. Colorful embers, shimmering sparks, and flaming debris fell upon the Agarthans. Cherry bombs and pointed bottle rockets added to the charred skin and burned flesh, pushing the monsters back.

The water crew then turned the liquid weapons on the gargoyles. Watery streams reached out to the grey fliers, their moist touch turning skin to stone. The gargoyles fell from the sky, stony wings unable to resist gravity's embrace.

The students cheered as the wave of monsters was washed aside, tilting the scales of the battle in their favor.

Suddenly, the landscape took on a strange orange hue.

"Cameron, the Moon!" Elisa shouted, pointing at it with her bow.

The moon reappeared in the sky and turned a soft orange; the Super Blood Moon was here.

Just then, a group of dark, misty creatures flew from the cave entrance, their eyes blazing with vicious hatred. They seemed made from smoke and ash, their forms held together by the flowing gray robes hanging off their bodies. Each wailed a sorrowful scream, as if being tortured, their voices almost hollow, like their hazy bodies.

"Oh no." Rylee darted to my side. "Ghouls, very dangerous. They'll stay high in the air and drop poisonous bits of themselves on the defenseless. A single touch will cause death."

"I'm not letting anyone die today." I rushed to Elisa's side, then paused to catch my breath. "I need you to do something."

"What?"

She gripped her bow tight, but I could tell by her quiver full of arrows that she hadn't fired a shot.

"Close your eyes."

"What are you talking about?" Elisa sounded confused.

"The ghouls are getting closer." Rylee's words came out quickly, on the verge of panic.

I held up a hand, silencing the imp.

"Elisa, just close your eyes." My voice softened and slowed. "I want you to remember the joy of archery. Every time you shoot, I think you worry about not missing as you try to please your coaches,

your teammates, your father . . . but you never try to please yourself."

She opened her eyes and glanced at me, but I pushed her eyelids down with a gentle touch.

"Give up your fear, and just be you. Your Carnelian Chakra stone hanging around your neck can help. Let your awareness drift into the stone and listen to its song. It will help you find your true self. Just relax."

Elisa scrunched her eyes tight, then relaxed her face. Her tense shoulders lowered a bit, then relaxed. She reached for her amulet and wrapped her fingers around the glowing stone.

"Cameron, the ghouls are almost to our battle lines," Rylee whispered in my ear. "When they get over the kids, they'll attack."

I nodded to the little imp, then motioned for the other archers to line up behind Elisa.

"Think about the beauty of a smooth draw," I said. "You sight your target and aim. You can feel your target out there, connected to you. The outcome is already known; you know you'll hit it even before you release the bowstring. In a hushed breath, the arrow is in flight, soaring in a beautiful arc to its goal." I moved right next to her and whispered into her ear, my voice soft, like velvet. "You've forgotten the joy of archery. We need that joy to return."

I pulled an arrow from her quiver and handed it to her. The orange gemstone around Elisa's neck blazed with newfound brilliance, enveloping her in a warm and radiant embrace. A smile of simple joy spread across her face. Elisa fitted it to the bowstring without even thinking, her breathing deep and steady.

"Now raise your bow and aim, but don't aim with your eyes. Relax, and aim with your heart."

She raised her bow and tracked one of the ghouls; it was getting closer.

"Open your eyes and feel the connection between you and the ghoul. Draw back the arrow and feel it striking its target even before you release."

Elisa's shoulders relaxed even more, her bow held rock steady.

"When you know you have it . . . fire." I stepped away with my fingers crossed.

She adjusted her aim, then slowly exhaled and released. The arrow streaked through the air and hit the ghoul, piercing its flowing dark robe. Smoke billowed from the rip in the cloth, causing it to fall to the ground, the monster's life force drifting away on the breeze.

Before I could say anything, Elisa drew another arrow and fired without thinking. The shaft struck a second ghoul. She fired again and again, knocking the terrible creatures from the sky.

"Archers, take out the ghouls." I pointed at the floating nightmares.

The archers drew back their bowstrings and fired on the monsters.

Streams of arrows sliced through the air like a deadly, pointed hailstorm. They tore into the ghouls, ripping them to pieces and clearing the sky. But none of the kids shot as quickly as Elisa. Her arrows pierced ghoul after ghoul as a smile spread over her face, the joy of archery filling her soul.

The archers then turned their bows upon banshees and gnomes, each following Elisa's lead. The arrows hammered into the monsters of Agartha with a vengeance.

Turning, I looked for Karl. He was fighting a group of gremlins, his bat knocking whips from their clawed fingers, then crushing hands and arms.

"Karl . . . phase two!"

Kicking a gremlin backward, Karl turned and ran away from the battle line and toward a four-wheeler. He jumped onto the vehicle and started the engine. I dashed to the ATV and climbed onto the back. Karl hit the gas, and we sped off, weaving between combatants. Swinging the lightning-rope over my head, I flung it at passing monsters, giving them a quick jolt as we shot by.

Karl drove across the battlefield until we reached the edge of the fighting, then kept going. The four-wheeler climbed Oak Hill, named for the two-hundred-year-old Live Oak tree standing vigilant on its peak. Killing the engine, he parked the vehicle behind its thick trunk, then glanced back to see if any monsters followed.

"We're clear." Karl took up his baseball bat. "You ready?"

I nodded. "Let's go."

We ran along the hill, moving from tree to tree, trying to stay hidden from Agarthans' eyes. Oak Hill extended along the edge of the camp grounds, then curved toward the cave. I glanced down the slope. Monsters poured out of the cave, creatures I didn't recognize with long tusks and scaly skin. Glancing between the branches overhead, I checked the moon. Its lunar face still blushed a deep blood-red, the celestial body massive in the sky. Just then, a dark curve spread across the bottom corner of the moon; the eclipse was ending.

"We gotta hurry." I glanced at Karl and pointed at the moon. "If he still has all the Skull Keys when the eclipse ends, the doorway will stay open forever."

"Then let's do this."

We ran across the hill until we reached a point directly over the cave. I dropped onto my stomach and crawled down the incline, Karl holding my feet so I wouldn't fall. I crept through the glistening circle of light, and night transformed into day until I reached the top of the curved stone arch over the cave. Across the battlefield, students fought monsters with tennis rackets, bats, clubs, and shovels clashing with clubs, spears, and clawed fists.

Inching my way down, I reached over the edge of the arch. My fingers brushed against the topmost Skull Key, the only one I could reach . . . the black Skull of Fear. Pulling the Dagger of Stones from my belt, I wrapped my hand around the handle. Light from the seven blazing stones embedded in its handle leaking from between my fingers. I moved forward until my upper body dangled over the edge of the cave. If any monster looked up, they'd see me.

I stopped breathing, the stress too great.

*I hope Karl can hold me, or I'm dead,* I thought, the *what-ifs* trying to invade my mind, but I drove them away by reciting a line from Camp Pontchartrain's Alma mater over and over: *'You taught us that our courage shall shine a golden light and cast away the darkness for fears that we shall smite.'*

I took a breath, letting the oxygen extinguish the burning in my lungs, then reached out and plunged the dagger's tip behind the black skull. It sank into the arch as if carving butter. Tilting the handle, I pried the Skull of Fear out of the stone. The onyx skull came loose and almost fell to the ground, but I caught it with sweaty fingers.

"Pull me up," I moaned.

Instantly, fear and dread wrapped their icy fingers around my mind, but this time, I was ready. Images of Malphas torturing my friends flooded through me, then I saw Camp Pontchartrain in flames, all because of my failures. Everyone turned on me, calling me a failure. The thoughts forced into my brain were beyond terrible, making me want to weep. But when I glanced down at the dark skull in my hands, I remembered one crucial fact. Everything from the Skull of Fear was a lie and wouldn't last forever. I refused to get stuck in a thought-loop, letting the fears make me more and more afraid. Instead, I thought about what it would be like when the fear faded away. I imagined the peace

174

I'd feel when we defeated the Demon Lord. My successes filled my mind instead of the imaginary failures, giving me the courage I needed to keep going.

Karl dragged me backward, pulling me up the hill and to safety. As my body slid across the grass, the dagger's blade dissolved into dust, leaving just the handle, the black stone embedded in the hilt no longer glowing. The circle of light around the cave flickered momentarily, then grew noticeably dimmer. A strange vibration spread across the area.

Malphas instantly turned and stared at the skull keys. "It's gone!" He glanced at the moon, then scanned the battlefield. "Find the Skull of Fear . . . find it NOW!"

We ran back to the four-wheeler, my feet feeling heavy. I could hear the monsters rustling about in the tall weeds, looking for the Skull Key on the ground.

Karl started the four-wheeler and gunned the motor, taking off as fast as possible. I held on with one hand, the other clutching the skull with all my strength as I tried to keep my mind focused on the positive. Fears tore into me, all of them coming from the dark skull, but I let them wash over me, refusing to focus on any of them. Dr. Jen's words echoed through my head, *'The more you focus on your fears, the more power you give them. Let them starve by focusing on the positive instead.'*

I thought about my friends, both old and new, and realized how lucky I felt. The kids at Camp Pontchartrain had seen the real me, with all my faults and strengths, and accepted me. These positive things kept the manufactured fears in place as the war between terror and peace raged within my soul.

"Cameron, the Moon!" Karl pointed to the sky.

I glanced up at the moon. A shadow covered half of the red moon.

"The eclipse is almost over, Karl. If we can keep the Skull of Fear from Malphas, they'll have to return to Agartha."

"Great. Now hang on. We have an army of monsters chasing us."

I glanced to the left and saw every monster on the battlefield converging toward us; we'd been spotted. The Agarthans charged past the students, not even bothering to fight. Instead, every creature ran or flew as fast as possible, each intent on destroying Karl and me. There was no way we could avoid them all.

Escape seemed impossible . . . we were doomed.

# Chapter 26 – Fear-magic

A group of brown-skinned monsters charged at the four-wheeler, curved horns jutting from their heads. Their angry snarls and pointed teeth filled me with terror. Thick, hooved feet tore at the grass, throwing tufts into the air as they closed the distance. I guessed they were minotaurs, and their bulging muscles and sharp teeth shot a wave of panic through me.

"Hurry, Karl. Hurry! They're getting closer."

"We're going as fast as this thing will go."

We drove across the battlefield, weaving to the left and right, trying to keep the minotaurs from grabbing hold of the four-wheeler. The fastest of the monsters surged forward, getting closer.

"It's about six feet behind us," I moaned. "Do something."

I tried the deep breathing exercises, but panic made that impossible. Instead, I took short raspy breaths as if sucking through a straw.

Prickling fear stabbed at my mind, making it difficult to focus. The Skull of Fear somehow sensed this and drove daggers of terror into my soul. Nightmares of what the minotaurs *might* do surged through my mind. I knew these *ANTs* to be lies, but the black skull in my hands made them feel real. My head spun as buzzing hornets attacked me from within, making me almost lose my grip on the four-wheeler. A fall would be fatal.

The minotaur closed in. The monster's hot breath blasted across the back of my neck. It smelled of foul decay, of death. Claws scraped at the back of the four-wheeler, sharp nails gouging the paint.

"Karl . . . please . . . hurry." My weak voice was barely audible over the vicious snarls of the monster.

"Don't worry. I won't let you down." The baseball captain turned sharply just as the minotaur lunged for me. With a growl, the creature stumbled, then bellowed a deep-throated roar and renewed the chase.

Karl headed into the cluster of students. "Cameron . . . on your left . . . NOW!"

I tossed the Skull of Fear to a lacrosse player.

Instantly, the lurking dread and sizzling terror in the back of my mind disappeared.

*I can breathe!*

The girl caught the black skull in the scoop of her lacrosse stick, then threw it to another player. The black skull soared through the air, its polished surface sparkling under the red light of the fading moon. The next lacrosse player, a tall redheaded boy, caught the stone with practiced ease and then ran with it, dodging a group of imps and a cluster of goblins. Two soccer players moved to his side and acted as blockers as they ran across the field, playing keep-away with the monsters of Agartha.

"I want that skull," Malphas screamed. "It's mine!"

The demon extended his nightmare-black wings, took a deep breath, then looked up at the moon and screeched. Silvery sparks formed on his feathered body, then shot outward, engulfing the battlefield, monsters, and students.

Overwhelming panic encompassed my mind, making the Skull of Fear feel like just a bad dream. I fell off the slowing four-wheeler and curled up into a ball, shaking, every other creature and student on the battlefield doing the same. Only the Demon Lord remained standing, his dark form like a shadowy void, consuming all hope. Pain enveloped me, my nightmares attacking me with jagged blades. I gasped for breath as Malphas's fear-magic pressed down on me like an immovable weight.

*Will this ever end?* I thought.

With a great flap of his wings, Malphas rose into the air and glided across the lawn, landing next to the redhead. He picked up the black Skull Key, the demon's body still shimmering with magic, holding the shroud of fear in place.

Somehow, I managed to glance at the Moon. Only a tiny sliver of red still showed across the lunar surface.

*If Malphas gets that skull in place before the Super Blood Moon ends, the doorway will stay open forever.* I clenched my teeth as a feeling, like that moment just before you fall, overwhelmed me. Every nightmare came to life in my mind, crippling fear emerging from my soul as terrible thoughts invaded my senses.

Around me, the other students moaned and wept. None of them were prepared for this kind of terror. But fear was my old friend, and I knew I could stand against it if I had the courage.

I started counting by 9s, then listed state capitals, then made lists of words, but none of the typical distractions worked. With every bit of effort, I forced my chest to move, taking

deep breaths. My head filled with the savage buzzing I'd come to know too well, the Beast claiming its prize . . . me. I struggled against the fear, trying to resist the waves of terror, but it seemed too much. Desperation filled my soul as I struggled in vain against the demon's magic.

Just then, a presence filled my head.

*Don't let Malphas take that Skull Key back to the cave.*

I recognized the voice. It was me, but the words were not my thoughts. They came from another place, or maybe another time.

*You're stronger than you realize,* the other-me said in my mind. *Set aside your fear and be the person you know you can be.* The words became thunder in my head. *Push aside the fear and find a solution, NOW!*

The faintest flicker of courage came to life within me as the other-me in my head disappeared.

An image materialized in my mind. It was the wall in the gym with the camp's Alma Mater written in large, purple letters. And for the first time in my life, I truly understood its meaning.

*"The hallowed shores of Pontchartrain."*

My whispered words drove back the rippling waves of terror a bit.

I climbed to one knee and sang, my voice weak.

*"Will always be our home."*

My words grew louder as I stood. Challenging every terrifying thought, I let the fear pass through me. Imagines of monsters tearing at me with sharp claws tortured my mind. I knew none of it was real; Malphas created the terrible images in my head. They were fake . . . a lie.

*"No matter where our paths may lead,*
*And despite how far we roam."*

Another voice cut through the weeping moans of terror; it was Elisa.

*"Your majesty and history,"*

I took a deep, belly breath, then sang along with her as we struggled to our feet and walked toward each other.

*"Are lessons for lifelong,*
*Alone we strive to face our tasks,*
*But together, we are strong."*

More students rose to their feet and sang their school's song.

"THE FEAR IS A LIE!" I shouted, then raised a fist and brought it down, slamming it into my chest twice. "DON'T GIVE IN . . . EVERYONE SING!"

*"You taught us that our courage,*

*Shall shine a golden light.*
*And cast away the darkness,*
*For fears that we shall smite."*

*Thump—thump,* raise . . . *Thump—thump,* raise.

More kids stood with chins held high, fists pounding chests. The voices of the students became thunder, the sparkling wave of fear shrugged off by distracting lyrics.

*"Camp Pontchartrain*
*our hearts belong to you.*
*Your sons and daughters sing your praise,*
*And to thee remain true."*

I raised my fist in the air again, then brought it down, and the other kids did it with me, *THUMP—THUMP,* raise. *THUMP—THUMP,* raise. The sound grew louder as more kids joined the beat, everyone glaring at Malphas.

"I don't believe it," the demon screeched. "No one can stand against my fear-magic."

"The Order of the Stones can." Mrs. Chakoté moved to my side and pointed at Malphas with her cane, the black stone at the top now dark.

"We'll see." The Demon Lord fumbled with the Skull Key for a moment, then extended its wings.

"No, you don't!" Before I realized it, I was sprinting straight for the monster.

Malphas glanced over his shoulder and sneered, the sharp pointy raven's beak glowing a dull red under the waning Super Blood Moon. He flapped his wings once.

I ran faster, trying to reach him, but I knew he was too far away; I'd never make it.

Malphas flapped them again, then slowly rose into the dark sky.

A tingling sensation formed inside my head. At the same time, everyone around me moved slower, the battle now in slow motion. Malphas's wings beat at the air, at half-speed. Everyone moved as if pushing themselves through thick honey . . . except for me.

I dashed toward Malphas, closing the distance as the demon slowly rose off the ground. Leaping with all my strength, I soared through the air and landed on the demon's back, arms wrapped around the creature's neck as the monster climbed higher and higher.

Time returned back to normal, making me feel dizzy for an instant. The ground fell away as Malphas flew higher. On the ground, the students fell upon the monsters as they started to rise, the Demon Lord's fear-magic slowly fading.

"Drive them back to the cave," Chakoté shouted as she struck at a group of minotaurs with her cane, Leonard by her side.

I gripped Malphas with all my strength. "You aren't taking that skull."

"We'll see, Earther." The Demon Lord laughed. "I'm going to enjoy watching you fall, but first, I think I'll take control of all of your friends and make them my unwilling servants."

Glancing at the ground, I realized most of the students were staring up at us. If Malphas used his glowing eyes, he could put the students under his control.

*I must do something.*

A savage heat started building around the demon's face, a ruby glow covering his scarred beak and feathers.

*He's about to do it, and I can't stop him!* Despair washed over me as he stared down at my friends, their eyes peering straight at us, expecting me to do some kind of miracle and save them all. But all I could do was watch as Malphas prepared to use his demon-magic to take control of their minds and destroy their lives.

# Chapter 27 – Jelly-gun

**S**uddenly, I had an idea. It was a long shot and probably wouldn't work, but it was my only hope.

"Bobby!" I shouted.

The Techie looked up at him.

"Jelly-gun."

"Jelly-gun?" Bobby looked confused.

"Jelly-gun, now!"

"Now?"

I glared at him. "NOW!"

Bobby smiled, then pulled the converted paintball gun off his shoulder and pointed it at the demon.

"Aim for the eyes," I shouted.

Bobby nodded, then opened fire, shouting with joy, "JELLYYYYYY GUNNNNNNN!"

Plastic jelly packets flew through the air, striking the demon's chest first, but slowly the packets climbed up his body as Bobby adjusted his aim. Many of them struck me, but I didn't care. Grabbing Malphas's beak, I yanked it toward the stream of strawberry and grape, the packets splatting against the demon's face and mouth. Finally, an orange marmalade packet hit an eye, the goopy topping covering it completely. Boysenberry and blueberry landed next, completely blotting out the glowing red light.

"Keep it up!" I shouted.

As Bobby fired his jelly-gun, I gripped the monster's neck with one hand. With the other, I pulled a static-shocker from my pocket. Flipping on the power switch, I held the weapon up to my eyes and smiled as sparks danced across the two sharp barbs sticking out of the end.

"Taste my magic, Malphas."

I jammed the prongs into Malphas's back. The sharp points easily passed through layers of feathers and found soft flesh. Sparks danced across the demon like silvery spiders, their electric bite bringing painful convulsions. The electricity stabbed at me as well, but something under my shirt protected me from most of the current.

The Demon Lord's wings faltered momentarily, struggling to keep flapping, then slowly failed. Malphas shuddered and succumbed to gravity's touch; we fell.

With a thud, we hit the ground hard, landing right next to the flickering circle of light surrounding the cave. Malphas's head slammed onto a stone, and he lay there, dazed for a moment. The light trying to leak through the grape and strawberry jelly faded. His eyes closed for a second, and it was long enough for the demon to lose control of his minions.

A gremlin charged straight at us, leaped over me, and ran into the cave entrance. The usual, glowing red eyes looked coal-black, Malphas's enslaving magic now gone, and the demon was too dazed to reestablish his control.

The students fell upon the monster army, hitting and kicking them until they turned and fled, racing back into the cave for safety. It quickly became an all-out retreat, the gremlins, ogres, goblins, banshees, and imps stepping over each other to get back to Agartha, finally free from Malphas's control. None of them wanted to fight their oppressor's war any longer.

I stood, picked up the static-shocker, and stabbed it into the demon again. The last bit of electricity flowed from its battery, then died, the indicator light on the side of the weapon going dark. Pulling my lightning-rope from my belt, I stepped into the glowing circle of light and flung it at the monster, electrocuting the demon again.

Suddenly, Mrs. Chakoté was at my side, pulling me back. "You must stay out of the illuminated circle." She yanked on my arm, but my rage stayed focused on the Demon Lord. I flung the rope at Malphas again and again, the weapon's charge quickly diminishing.

"Cameron." She grabbed my arm and yanked it hard. "Listen to me. If you're in the circle when the doorway collapses, you'll be pulled into the Void, a place of darkness where you'll never age and exist in a terrible nothingness . . . f o r e v e r."

The drawn-out word captured my attention. I glanced at Mrs. Chakoté and then turned my attention to Malphas. The old woman grabbed my arm and pulled me away from the demon, who still writhed in pain.

Malphas slowly crawled toward the cave entrance, trying to escape.

"No. We can't let Malphas go back to Agartha." I glared at Chakoté. "He'll just put them under his control again, and we'll have to face him on the next Super Blood Moon." I stepped forward and dragged the demon away from the cave and toward the edge of the glistening circle. "Help me. Someone help me!"

In a heartbeat, Karl and Leonard stood at my side, but before they could help, Malphas lunged, slashing at my chest with long, dark claws. The talons ripped through my shirt, revealing wide slashes of red underneath. I fell backward, slices of crimson across my chest.

"Cameron . . . no!" Elisa ran to me and knelt at my side. She looked at Mrs. Chakoté. "Help him! The demon cut open his chest. He's gonna die!"

But before anyone could take a step, I sat up and patted my chest, a jingling sound filling the air. "Chainmail . . . painted red with my rubber paint." I gave a short laugh. "It kept me from being electrocuted up there." I pointed to the sky.

Turning to Elisa, I smiled, then stood and bolted toward Malphas. Grabbing the demon again, I pulled on the monster's clawed hand. With all my strength, I dragged the creature back toward the circle's edge. Malphas dug his three-toed bird feet into the weed-covered ground and pushed back, keeping me within the ring of light. Karl put his arms around my waist and pulled. At the same time, Leonard wrapped the lightning-rope around the creature's leg and yanked hard, pulling the claws loose from the soil.

Malphas screamed in rage and wiped the jelly from his eyes, then glared at me, the pitiless orbs starting to glow.

I felt transfixed and couldn't look away. My will to resist crumbled as the Demon Lord's voice echoed in my head, taking control of my mind. I started to release my grip on the monster's arm when—

"JELLYYYYY GUNNNNNN!" Bobby leaped to my side and fired a stream of sticky, sweet packets of grape jelly onto the monster's face, coating the eyes with another thick layer of goo.

The demon tried to wipe it away, but Bobby kept firing, his weapon holding the monster's magic at bay. Together, we dragged Malphas closer to the edge until just his black, clawed hand stuck out of the circle, the rest of the kids safely out of the sparkling illumination.

"The Super Blood Moon," Elisa pointed to the sky.

The last sliver of blood-red craters faded from view as the rest of the Earth's shadow moved across the moon, plunging them into darkness.

The light around the cave flickered as if someone were playing with a light switch. Then, one by one, the Skull Keys fell from the entrance and landed on the ground with a

thud, each growing dark. Finally, the last one, the green Skull of Life, came free and plummeted into the weeds. Instantly, the sparkling field of light contracted like water going down a drain, and with it, Malphas, the Demon Lord of Agartha. The vortex dragged the terrible monster toward the cave as everything grew darker and darker and darker until…

The moon overhead finally slipped past Earth's shadow, showing its silver face once more. The kids cheered and pointed to the lunar body. But when they looked back at the cave, they found the demon gone. Only Malphas's clawed fist remained in my hand, its skin now turned to stone. Slowly, the severed hand shrunk smaller and smaller until it became the size of a small candy bar. I quickly dropped it and checked my own hand, making sure my fingers were still made of flesh.

"We did it!" Bobby shouted. "Jelly-gun to the rescue!"

Other kids shouted with him, "Jelly-gun . . . Jelly-gun . . . Jelly-gun!"

Students from different teams and competing cliques hugged each other. Athletes gave high-fives to Techies, dancers embraced wrestlers; a celebration of joy and equality enveloped them all as the kids of Camp Pontchartrain cheered.

A wrinkled hand settled on my shoulder. I turned and found Mrs. Chakoté smiling down at me. Karl and Leonard approached, as did Elisa, while Bobby was already at my side.

"I knew the five of you could see us past this challenge. The magic in Earth brought all of you together when you were needed the most." Chakoté said. She smiled at each of them. "You've all accomplished great things, but more importantly, you've learned things about yourselves and will never be as you were before."

"Good," Karl said. He put a hand on my shoulder. "It's good to have friends, finally."

I nodded.

"And I'm done pleasing everyone else and doing what *they* want." Leonard removed his football pads and tossed them to the ground. "It's time I followed my passion." He glanced at Mrs. Chakoté. "When school starts in the Fall, I'm gonna do football *and* history; maybe I'll join the History Club." Leonard smiled, his eyes filled with joy, as they should be.

The old woman nodded.

Elisa stepped forward, moved to my side, and hugged me. "You helped me remember something important." She stepped back.

"What's that?"

"I'd forgotten how to enjoy what I do. I was always afraid of missing a shot and disappointing someone or letting my teammates down. I forgot about me." Elisa glanced at the other four members of their party. "We can't forget to enjoy the moment."

"What about you, Bobby?" Mrs. Chakoté asked. "What did you learn?"

"Well, I learned something very important that all of you learned as well." He gave them a mischievous smile as he held his invention over his head. "Jelly-gun is awesome!" Bobby laughed a loud belly laugh, unafraid of embarrassment, as always.

At that moment, I realized Bobby was and had always been totally free and just lived in each moment as if it were his last. I envied my friend.

"Wait, where's Rylee?" Elisa glanced about, looking for the tiny imp.

"He went back to Agartha," Bobby said. "When Malphas lost his power over the monsters, I saw the little imp go back through the gateway. Maybe he'll try to make Agartha a better place. With his newfound courage, I doubt anyone is gonna mess with him." Bobby pulled a bag of Reese's Pieces out of a pocket and looked at them, then put them back. "I'll save those for him in case he comes here again someday."

Elisa nodded. "Rylee was a good friend. He'll be an even better leader."

"Cameron." Mrs. Chakoté tapped her cane on the ground, the stones now dark. "What are you thinking?"

"Well, I'm tired of worrying about what might happen and letting fear rule my life." I shook my head, then ran my fingers through my curly hair. "I know the *ANTs*, the automatic negative thoughts, and the *what-ifs* aren't real. I realize now when the anxiety comes, it won't last forever. It's temporary, and it's all a lie. But I know I'm not cured . . . I doubt I'll ever be cured of anxiety. But I'm starting to understand how to cope with it so it won't rule my life. As long as I have my friends to support me, I can get past the anxiety and hopefully do things any other kids can do." I glanced at my friends and smiled. "I won't worry about failing anymore. Instead, I'm looking for the positive and focusing on success."

"My favorite president said, 'We can complain because rose bushes have thorns, or

rejoice because thorn bushes have roses,'" Leonard said.

I nodded. "Exactly."

"Let me guess, Abraham Lincoln?" Karl raised a curious eyebrow.

Leonard nodded and smiled. "Yep."

Just then, the sound of helicopters filled the air as about a dozen aircraft approached the camp. As they neared, I saw the image of seven circles, each a different color, emblazoned on the side of each chopper.

"Looks like the Order of the Stones finally made it." Elisa put her bow over her shoulder and laughed. "Great timing."

The other kids laughed but grew quiet as Chakoté raised her hands and shook her head. "No, you're wrong."

"What do you mean?" I gazed at the old woman, confused.

She pointed her cane at us five, then turned and pointed it at all the kids on the battlefield, many of them moving closer, listening.

The aircraft landed on the field, and heavily armed soldiers jumped out, each with a Chakra pendant hanging around their neck.

"We didn't need the Order of the Stones and their guns and helicopters because the Order was already here." She slammed the tip of her cane on the ground, the stones giving off a bright flash. "You . . . all of you," she cast her gaze across the students, then settled it on my friends and me. "You're the new Order of the Stones."

"Yeah!" Bobby shouted, the rest of the kids cheering with him.

I raised my fist into the air, then brought it to my chest. *THUMP—THUMP,* raise, *THUMP—THUMP,* raise, *THUMP—THUMP,* raise, the rest of the students joining in. The sound echoed across the school grounds while the soldiers looked about, confused.

As the students celebrated, I listened to the inner recesses of my mind, and for the first time, the faint buzzing that always seemed to be there, waiting, was strangely absent. I was free . . . for now. Bending down, I gathered up Malphas's petrified hand, shoved it into a pocket, and headed toward the shore of Lake Pontchartrain.

"Cameron, where are you going?" Elisa asked.

"There's something I need to do."

"What is it?" Elisa started to follow me, many of the other kids doing the same.

Questions were lobbed at me, but I remained silent as I marched toward the lake. More kids followed, curiosity making them like mice enchanted by the Pied Piper's flute.

I walked up to the ropes course and turned around, facing my fellow campers. "This course has been a source of anxiety and fear for me all summer, but no more."

"You don't have to do this, Cameron," Elisa said.

"Yeah, Cam," Leonard added. "You have nothing to prove to anyone."

"Yes, you do." Karl moved to my side. "To yourself, right?"

I nodded, reached up, and grabbed the rungs of the rope ladder. A buzzing started to form in my head, but I ignored it, the lie unable to still my courage.

"Let's do this thing." And I climbed, the cheers of the kids below wrapping me in a blanket of courage.

"Fear can't stop me. I won't allow it," I shouted as I climbed higher and higher, laughter bubbling up deep from within my soul and exploding outward, filling everyone with joy.

~~~

I hope you enjoyed *Facing the Beast Within.* If you did, it would be a great help to me to tell your friends. The lifeblood of a book is word of mouth and reviews. It would help me a lot if you left an honest review on your bookseller's website so others will know what you thought about the story. Please go to your online bookseller and leave a review. Tell everyone about Cameron's adventure.

Thank you so much for your support.

~~~

**Have an idea for your own story?** Write it out and send it to me. Thousands of young writers have sent their stories, some about Minecraft and some about totally different topics. I've posted them all to my website, here: https://markcheverton.com/fanfic-art/. I'll put your story on my website and send you a link so you can find it but ask your parents first. Parents – this is a kid-safe place where bullying or disrespectful comments will never be tolerated.

**Contact me** – Email me through my website and say hello. I'd love to know what you thought about this story, and I answer EVERY email. If you use your school's

email, it might block my reply, sorry. If you don't receive a reply, maybe use your parents' email, of course, with their permission. Click on **CONTACT** on my website. Don't be surprised if I reply right away.

~~~

The next book in the *Order of the Stones* series is called **Cameron and the Shadow-wraiths**. It should be out near the end of 2024. Time for the monsters of Agartha to get a little payback. I hope you enjoy it.

Here's an excerpt . . . I hope you like it.

# Cameron and the Shadow-wraiths

## Excerpt: Chapter 12 – Alligators

I pulled the quartz pendant out from under my green t-shirt and gripped it with one hand, the other holding my lightning-rope tightly. The chill from Malphas's petrified fist seeped deep into my flesh. It had never done this before, at least not this severely. Reaching under my shirt, I rubbed at the skin, trying to drive away the cold, but it did little good. The stony hand's icy touch penetrated deep, freezing my bones.

*YOUR FAILURE IS IMMINENT.* Malphas whispered, the words amplifying the growing buzz in my head. *SUBMIT TO THE WRAITHS OR WATCH THE DESTRUCTION OF YOUR FRIENDS.* Malphas's words grew louder in my brain. *SPEAK YOUR SURRENDER, AND WE WILL NOT HARM ANYONE.*

The wicked edge of the terrifying words made my skin crawl with disgust as my body shook, fear turning to panic.

*I must stay focused and not let down my friends,* I thought. A malicious laugh echoed through me, making the hairs on the back of my neck stand up straight.

*Get out of my head!* I pleaded.

**188**

More laughter.

Bobby held his flail at the ready, the green aventurine stones giving off an emerald glow. A thin layer of moss formed across the weapon's metallic surface, growing from nothing. The velvety green carpet solidified, forming a hard shell—Bobby's plant-crafting powers at work.

*That's it!*

"Bobby, use your Earth-magic." I pointed to the alligators on one side of the boat. Their noses and eyes glided just above the water's surface, the large, ridged bodies cutting through the swamp like something out of Jurassic Park. "Grab them with grass and weeds."

Bobby glanced at me, then turned to the alligators. He set his flail down and brought his hands together, thumbs and index fingers touching. Closing his eyes, he took a deep breath and extended his arms toward the creatures.

Nothing happened. *What's he doing?* Images of the monsters climbing onto the boat flooded my mind. *He's gotta push them back and—*

Bobby lunged and exhaled. Thin reeds and whip-like blades of grass rose out of the stagnant water, forming a living barrier. Alligators pushed into the green wall, only to be ensnared by the plants. The grass wrapped around the enormous reptiles like emerald serpents. The animals thrashed against the growth, biting at the plants with their powerful jaws. They tore out clumps of grass as they battled against Bobby's magic, slowing their advance . . . for now.

But they weren't giving up.

The alligators stared straight at us as they fought against the obstacle, their eyes solid white with angry black pupils, just like the shadow-wraiths.

"Why aren't they turning around?" Jamis asked. He glanced at me, then focused his gaze on Mr. Wallace.

"A shadow-wraith has possessed them," Rylee said as he unwound his whip and readied for battle.

"Bobby, keep it up," Mr. Wallace said. He pointed to Elisa, then gestured to the alligators on the left side of the boat. "Use your fire-casting power. Push the alligators back."

Elisa held her carnelian pendant and focused her Earth-magic, then brought her fingers together as she'd been taught. Sparks and embers appeared in the air, circling her

thin body as her magic increased. The air in the boat grew dry and hot as Elisa drew in more power from the Earth. The hairs on my arms stood up straight, sweat trickling down my forehead.

Lunging forward, she extended her hands as if stabbing at the swamp. A ball of fire shot out from her hand and fell upon a group of alligators. The burning sphere hit one, then fell into the water. Elisa threw another fireball, followed by another, as she tried to keep the terrifying swamp creatures back. The alligators gave off a deep, guttural growl, like something out of a horror movie. They snapped their massive jaws at the flaming balls, biting at them as if they were annoying insects. The crunching of their teeth sounded like metal against metal.

"Don't let them get close," Mr. Wallace said. "With everyone onboard, the boat is riding low in the water. They can climb in and get us."

That last sentence made me shiver. Panic flooded through me like a tidal wave. The muscles in my body grew tense as my pulse raced.

*What if they get onto the boat? We'll never be able to push them out. What if . . .*

My heart pounded in my chest. I tried distracting myself from all the negative thoughts running through my head. I counted by sevens, then did the breathing exercises Dr. Jen taught me, but nothing helped. My Beast was awake and about to take over. When that happened, I'd no longer be able to think and—

A gust of wind shot across the front of the boat and slammed into the gators. The water frothed up as the wind grew stronger and stronger. I turned and found Leonard standing tall, his eyes closed, and hands extended. His amethyst stone shone brightly around his neck, giving him a purple glow. Taking a deep breath, Leonard punched toward the alligators biting at Elisa's fireballs. A ferocious gust of wind flowed out of him, slamming into the swamp and throwing water, plants, and animals in all directions. Birds flew high in the air, trying to escape the maelstrom while the alligators submerged momentarily.

"Yes!" Leonard pumped a fist, then threw another burst of wind.

The gators came up for air, then dove underwater, their sleek forms moving around the boat. They arose and attacked from a different angle, but Karl was ready for them.

With his sodalite pendant dangling between his outstretched fingers, Karl focused his power on the swamp itself. He gathered his Earth-magic, extended it into the water around the boat, and then pushed. A strong current surged outward from the airboat, shoving everything back. The alligators struggled against the rushing water, their thick tails thrashing to propel their massive bodies closer to us.

Mr. Wallace moved next to me, his green and black malachite stone in his hand. The old man closed his eyes, then held his staff up, the three stones embedded in the wood blazing with magical power.

"Focus your power on my staff. It'll work like an amplifier and make you stronger." Mr. Wallace stepped in front of Karl and held the staff in the air.

Glittering blue-white waves of magic flowed from Karl's hands and wrapped around the staff, then plunged into the water. A violent current surged outward, pushing the alligators back for a moment.

Elisa did the same, focusing her magic on the staff. Balls of super-heated fire spread outward from the enchanted weapon and rained down upon the alligators. Leonard stepped forward and added his wind-casting abilities, as did Bobby. For a moment, it seemed as if their Earth-magic was winning the battle.

I smiled as I watched my friends' heroic efforts, their magic glittering in a kaleidoscope of colors around Mr. Wallace's staff.

*Maybe I could add my magic,* I thought, but my Beast quickly erased the idea. *It'll never work. I can't control my powers because I'm weak and pathetic.* A cold shiver spread down my spine as my pulse raced. I wanted to help but knew I'd fail . . . again.

Something splashed into the water from a small island of dirt and trees.

"Oh no . . . more alligators." I pointed across the swamp.

At least a dozen gators took to the water and swam toward us, their eyes pale white like the other creatures. They charged toward the boat and pushed against the magic, some getting closer.

The largest of the alligators forced its way through Bobby's grass and weeds. Swishing its massive tail, the monster shot toward the boat and slammed against it, almost knocking me off my feet. Rylee used the whip he'd taken off the terrible gremlin last summer. The crystal-tipped end of his whip slashed at the alligator's thick hide, but the creature didn't seem to feel the wounds. I swung my lightning-rope at another beast, the end glancing across the alligator's body. Sparks of electricity danced over the creature's dark skin, but the alligator seemed unfazed.

*Click . . . click . . . click.*

Jamis turned the key, trying to start the boat, but nothing happened. It was as if the battery couldn't provide any electricity.

I turned the power on my lightning-rope to the max and flicked it at the gator. This time, the monster hissed as the electricity bit into its flesh.

*Click . . . click . . .* "It's not working!" Jamis shouted. "Start . . . please start."

*Click.*

I hit the alligator with another blast of electricity, then moved to the back of the boat to check the engine's battery. I set my lightning-rope on the floor and climbed over the storage compartment. Flipping open the engine cover, I peered into the darkness . . . and gasped.

Something had torn through one side of the engine cover, the metal bent outward. Inside, I spotted a red wire dangling loose, the end sliced clean as if intentionally cut.

Something moved in the shadows cast by the moon.

A creature with dark skin, skinny arms, and dark, pointed claws clung to the back of the boat, its harsh, white eyes glaring at me, pupils like two pools of oily hatred. The shadow-wraith pulled its lips back and hissed, a million needle-like teeth filling its mouth.

"Wraith . . . wraith . . . wraith!" I shouted as I stepped back.

I glanced over my shoulder, hoping for someone to help, but the others battled with the alligators.

I was alone.

Two steps behind me, my lightning-rope lay on the ground next to the rope-dart. I shifted my weight, ready to dash for them, but the shadow-wraith hissed and moved toward me. Terror filled my mind as I imagined what *might* happen in the next few seconds. A storm of buzzing hornets blasted through my ears like a hurricane of fear, my heart about to leap out of my chest. I shook for a moment, unsure what to do as the wraith moved closer.

*I need a weapon. I need something.*

Reaching into the storage compartment, I grabbed a handful of whatever I could find. My fingers wrapped around some flashlights. At that moment, the image of that terrible shadow-wraith, Kaz-aTul, popped into my head. When he spoke to us, the wraith leaned out from under the willow but kept one hand within the shadow.

*Maybe they must be touching a shadow . . . let's see what happens if I take that away from this one.*

The hornets grew silent in my head as my mind focused on the plan. I could feel the quartz pendant under my shirt grow warm, offsetting the terrible chill coming from Malphas's fist.

I held six flashlights in two hands and turned them on with my thumbs.

The wraith slammed the lid to the storage container closed, the whites of the monster's eyes shining bright against its dark face.

"Your friendsss will perish here," the wraith said in a hissing voice, sounding like a deflating tire, "then you'll come with me."

"I don't think so." I lifted the flashlights and blasted the monster in the face.

The wraith screamed as it brought a clawed hand up to cover its eyes.

I painted the monster with light, trying to cover every part of its body.

"Hey! I need some help back here," I shouted as I panned the lights across the wraith's flesh.

The monster stumbled backward, steam rising from its body. Reaching back, the wraith found a small pocket of shadow and extended its long fingers, white eyes searching for more darkness.

Bobby appeared at my side; his flail was now covered with thorny vines. "What's wrong back here?" Then he gasped. "That's a shadow-wraith."

"I know. Take some flashlights." I handed him three of the lights. "I think it needs to be touching a shadow to remain here. Get his left side, and I'll get his right."

I split my three flashlights into two hands and aimed them at the monster's body, arm, and leg, Bobby doing the same on the other side. When I erased the patch of shadow to which the monster clung, steam rose from its body.

The creature's eyes darted to the left and right, looking for safety. It extended an arm toward the shade cast by a tree limb. Before it could reach the dark safety, Mr. Wallace grabbed a flashlight from my hand and filled the moon's shadows with a bright light.

Patches of skin started to burn as the shadow-wraith searched for dark refuge but found none.

Rylee appeared at my side, the end of his whip a blur. He struck at the monster, but the crystal-tipped end of the weapon seemed to have little effect.

"They cannot sssave you, boy," the wraith said to me. "You will do asss Kaz-aTul commandsss or watch everyone around you perish."

A spot darker than a moonless midnight formed next to the wraith. It expanded, pushing the world outward as it absorbed the wraith into its shadowy depths. And then the hole collapsed in upon itself, disappearing from sight. With the wraith's absence, the alligators turned and fled back into murky waters.

"Jamis, start the boat . . . NOW!" Mr. Wallace shouted.

"Not yet." I glanced at the old man. "Do you have any tools onboard?"

Mr. Wallace reached into the storage compartment and pulled out a toolbox. I flipped it open and pulled out a set of wire cutters. Quickly, I reconnected the wire and wrapped the repair with electrical tape.

"Now!"

Jamis turned the key, and the motor caught. The fan spun up to speed.

"Hit the throttle, son, and get us out of here." Mr. Wallace pointed to the controls in front of Jamis.

The fan at the back of the boat roared as the craft leaped forward, speeding over clumps of weeds and floating debris. Alligators growled and hissed as we sped by, but none approached.

Fatigue flooded through me as my anxiety ebbed away. My Beast slowly settled itself back into the darkness of my soul, waiting … always waiting. The others sat down as well, arms hanging limp with tired muscles.

None of us spoke as we shot through the swamp. Likely, everyone's thoughts focused on the battle we'd just survived.

*THIS WAS JUST THE BEGINNING.* Malphas's words felt like rusty nails jabbing through my mind, and then they were gone.

But I knew Malphas would be back, as would the shadow-wraiths. I thought about how scared Jessie must feel but felt helpless to do anything about it. Somehow, I must save her, but what if it costs the life of someone I hold dear? Doubt and uncertainty took their familiar place within my soul, pushing aside my useless courage.

I stared across the moonlit swamp, my imagination morphing shadows from trees into terrifying monsters. As we sped across the murky landscape, I felt that evil presence watching me, Malphas's eyes, somehow, on me from the Void. I knew we were heading into his trap, but we had no choice if we hoped to save Jessie before it was too late.

**THE GAMEKNIGHT999 SERIES**
*New York Times* **bestselling series**
**Published in over 30 countries around the world.**

**The world of Minecraft comes to life in this thrilling adventure!**

Gameknnight999 loved Minecraft, and above all else, he loved to grief—to intentionally ruin the gaming experience for other users.

But when one of his father's inventions teleports him into the game, Gameknight is forced to live out a real-life adventure inside the digital world. What will happen if he's killed? Will he respawn? Die in real life? Stuck in the game, Gameknight999 discovers Minecraft's best-kept secret, something not even the game's programmers realize: the creatures within the game are alive! He will have to stay one step ahead of the sharp claws of the zombies and the pointed fangs of spiders, but he'll also have to learn to make friends and work as a team if he has any chance of surviving the Minecraft war his arrival has started.

With deadly endermen, ghasts, and dragons, this action-packed trilogy introduces the heroic Gameknight999 and has proven to be a runaway publishing smash, showing that the Gameknight999 series is the perfect companion for Minecraft fans of all ages.

  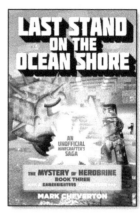

## THE MYSTERY OF HEROBRINE SERIES
### Published worldwide

**Gameknight999 must save his friends from an evil virus intent on destroying all of Minecraft!**

Gameknight999 was sucked into the world of Minecraft when one of his father's inventions went haywire. Trapped inside the game, the former griefer learned the error of his ways, transforming into a heroic warrior and defeating powerful endermen, ghasts, and dragons to save the world of Minecraft and his NPC friends who live in it.

Gameknight swore he'd never go inside Minecraft again. But that was before Herobrine, a malicious virus infected the very fabric of the game, threatened to destroy the entire Overworld and escape into the real world. To outsmart an enemy much more powerful than any he's ever faced before, the User-that-is-not-a-user will need to go back into the game, where real danger lies around every corner. From zombie villages and jungle temples to a secret hidden at the bottom of a deep ocean, the action-packed adventures of Gameknight999 and his friends (and now, family) continue in this thrilling follow-up series for Minecraft fans of all ages.

## HEROBRINE REBORN SERIES
### Published worldwide

**Gameknight999 and his friends and family face Herobrine in the biggest showdown the Overworld has ever seen!**

Gameknight999, a former Minecraft griefer, got a big dose of virtual reality when his father's invention, the Digitizer, teleported him into the game. Living out a dangerous adventure inside a digital world, he discovered that the Minecraft villagers were alive and needed his help to defeat the infamous virus, Herobrine, a diabolical enemy determined to escape into the real world.

Gameknight thought Herobrine had finally been stopped once and for all. But the virus proved to be even craftier than anyone could imagine, and his XP begins inhabiting new bodies in an effort to escape. The User-that-is-a-user will need the help of not only his Minecraft friends, but his own father, Monkeypants271, as well, if he has any hope of destroying the evil Herobrine once and for all.

## HEROBRINE REVENGE SERIES
### Published worldwide

**From beyond the digital grave, Herobrine has crafted some evil, and deadly, games for Gameknight999 to play!**

Gameknight999, a former Minecraft griefer, got a big dose of virtual reality when his father's invention teleported him into the game. Living out a dangerous adventure inside the digital realms, Gameknight trekked all over Minecraft, with the help of some villager friends, to finally defeat the terrible virus, Herobrine, who was trying to escape into the real world.

Gameknight thought that Herobrine was gone for good. But as one last precaution before his death, the heinous villain laid traps for the User-that-is-not-a-user that would threaten all of the Overworld, even if the virus was no longer alive. Now, Gameknight is racing the clock, trying to stop Herobrine from having one last diabolical laugh.

  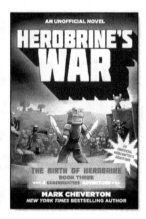

**THE BIRTH OF HEROBRINE SERIES**
**Published worldwide**

**Can Gameknight999 survive a journey one hundred years into Minecraft's past?**

A freak thunderstorm strikes just as Gameknight999 is activating his father's Digitizer to reenter Minecraft. Sparks flash across his vision as he is sucked into the game . . . and when the smoke clears, he's arrived safely. But it doesn't take long to realize that things in the Overworld are different.

The User-that-is-not-a-user realizes he's been accidentally sent a hundred years into the past, back to the time of the Historic Great Zombie Invasion. None of his friends have even been born yet. But that might be the least of Gameknight999's worries because traveling back in time also means that the evil virus, Herobrine, the scourge of Minecraft, is still alive . . .

 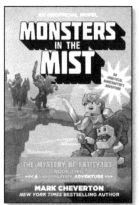 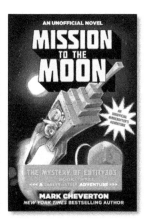

## THE MYSTERY OF ENTITY303 SERIES
### Published worldwide

**Minecraft mods are covering the tracks of a mysterious new villain!**

Gameknight999 reenters Minecraft to find it completely changed, and his old friends acting differently. The changes are not for the better.

Outside of Crafter's village, a strange user named Entity303 is spotted with Weaver, a young NPC Gameknight knows from Minecraft's past. He realizes that Weaver has somehow been kidnapped and returning him to the correct time is the only way to fix things.

What's worse: Entity303 has created a strange and bizarre modded version of Minecraft, full of unusual creatures and biomes. Racing through the Twilight Forest and MystCraft, and finally into the far reaches of outer space, Gameknight will face his toughest challenge yet in Minecraft, both alien and dangerous.

## THE RISE OF THE WARLORDS SERIES

**A brand-new Minecraft fiction series from Mark Cheverton explores the mysterious borders of the Overworld, called the Far Lands.**

The Far Lands is a hidden, mystical area located at the very edge of Minecraft's outer borders, unknown to normal users. There, the life of a young villager named Watcher is suddenly turned upside down when his village is destroyed by a vile zombie-warlord.

That single attack sets off a chain of unexpected events, as Watcher and a handful of his companions vow to save their friends and bring the warlords responsible to justice. But along the way, they'll uncover a terrifying secret about the monsters in the Far Lands, one that could change Minecraft forever.

## THE WITHER WAR SERIES

**Watcher has uncovered an ancient and dangerous secret, and that secret is about to wake up and want vengeance against all the NPCs of Minecraft.**

The Far Lands has been shaped by great wars in its distant past. The echoes of that war still scar the surface of Minecraft, reminding the NPCs how close they came to annihilation. But today, hundreds of years after that terrible conflict, secrets lay hidden, waiting to be unearthed and shown the light of days; but some secrets were never meant to be discovered.

Watcher and his companions uncover one such secret, the Crown of Skulls. The wither, a terrible and violent monster, is a rare thing to find in the Overworld, but that isn't true in the Far Lands. Krael, the Wither King, wants to make the NPCs pay for what was done to his people during that last great war fought centuries ago, and to do that, he needs all three Crowns of Skulls. It falls to Watcher and his friends to hold back the tide of hatred and violence, or see all the Far Lands, and even Minecraft, be destroyed forever.

## THE GAMEKNIGHT999 BOX SET

Get six exciting Minecraft novels in a collectible box. This box set contains:

- *Invasion of the Overworld*
- *Battle for the Nether*
- *Confronting the Dragon*
- *Trouble in Zombie-town*
- *The Jungle Temple Oracle*
- *Last Stand on the Ocean Shore*

## THE GAMEKNIGHT999 vs. HEROBRINE BOX SET

Get six exciting Minecraft novels in a collectible box. This box set contains:

- *Saving Crafter*
- *Destruction of the Overworld*
- *Gameknight999 vs. Herobrine*
- *Phantom Virus*
- *Overworld in Flames*
- *System Overload*

## GAMEKNIGHT999 ADVENTURES
## THROUGH TIME BOX SET

Get six exciting Minecraft novels in a collectible box. This box set contains:

- *Great Zombie Invasion*
- *Attack of the Shadow Crafters*
- *Herobrine's War*
- *Terrors of the Forest*
- *Monsters in the Mist*
- *Mission to the Moon*

## THE WITHERS AND WARLORDS BOX SET

Get six exciting Minecraft novels, featuring the main character, Watcher, in this collectable box. This box set contains:

- *Zombies Attack!*
- *Bones of Doom*
- *Into the Spiders' Lair*
- *The Wither King*
- *Withers Awaken*
- *Wither Invasion*

Kids . . . keep reading and watch out for creepers!

— Mark

Printed in the USA
CPSIA information can be obtained
at www.ICGtesting.com
CBHW071210210124
3648CB00008B/468

9 781735 878164